Praise for the Bow Street Bachelors series

"Pure fun . . . Kate Bateman gives readers just what they're looking for."
—*BookPage*

"Genuine romance that shines through . . . delightful leads and sexy capers."
—*Kirkus Reviews*

"An alluring cat-and-mouse tale between two deserving adversaries. For Regency romance fans wishing for thrills in their to-be-read list." —*Library Journal* on *To Catch an Earl*

"Full of intense emotions and dramatic twists. Intelligent, affable characters make this fast-paced novel shine, especially for fans of clever women and the men who sincerely admire them."
—*Publishers Weekly* (starred review) on *This Earl of Mine*

"Delicious, witty, and ripping good fun! Kate Bateman's writing sparkles."
—*USA Today* bestselling author Laura Lee Guhrke

"Dashing, daring, and deliciously romantic!"
—*USA Today* bestselling author Caroline Linden

"A riveting new voice for Regency readers! Kate Bateman is now on my auto-buy list." —Janna MacGregor, author of *The Good, the Bad, and the Duke*

The Princess and the Rogue

Kate Bateman

St. Martin's Paperbacks

This is a work of fiction. All of the characters, organizations, and events portrayed in this novel are either products of the author's imagination or are used fictitiously.

First published in the United States by St. Martin's Paperbacks, an imprint of St. Martin's Publishing Group.

THE PRINCESS AND THE ROGUE

For information, address St. Martin's Publishing Group, 120 Broadway, New York, NY 10271.

www.stmartins.com

ISBN: 978-1-250-30609-8

Our books may be purchased in bulk for promotional, educational, or business use. Please contact your local bookseller or the Macmillan Corporate and Premium Sales Department at 1-800-221-7945, ext. 5442, or by email at MacmillanSpecialMarkets@macmillan.com.

Printed in the United States of America

St. Martin's Paperbacks edition 2021

10 9 8 7 6 5 4 3 2 1

For Madeleine, who threw *her* diamonds
out of a train window.

Chapter 1.

Princess Anastasia Denisova took careful aim with the hammer.

"Anya, no! Not the tiara!"

Anya sent her best friend a quick glance, then returned her attention to the glittering headpiece in front of her. "We can't hide it like this. We need small, unidentifiable pieces."

Elizaveta groaned, apparently resigned to the inevitable, and Anya quashed a pang of guilt for destroying something so undeniably lovely. Still, a piece of broken jewelry was the least of their troubles. With a silent apology to the artist who'd made such a beautiful thing, she brought the hammer down with a sickening crunch.

The gold setting crumpled and a couple of pea-sized diamonds skittered across the wooden table. Elizaveta made a dive for the nearest one before it shot onto the floor. Anya hit the metal a few more times to loosen the rest of the gems, trying not to wince at the destruction, and scooped the diamonds into a small pile in front of her.

"Now bread."

Elizaveta groaned again in protest. "We've already sewn jewels into our skirts. And your cloak. We don't need to swallow them too."

"You've seen what it's like out there. People are getting desperate. We must take precautions." Anya reached for the baguette on the table, ripped out a piece of the soft center, and pushed one of the smaller diamonds into the lump of bread.

Elizaveta watched her with grim fascination. "But how will we *retrieve* them?"

"By sifting through the contents of our bedpans, I suppose." Anya smiled at her horrified grimace.

Elizaveta drew herself up, her expression stern. "You are a princess of Russia! Second cousin to the tsar. Tenth in line to the throne! You shouldn't be poking around in—"

"Shit?" Anya supplied with a snort.

"Language!"

Anya chuckled. "Is not befitting a princess. I know." She sobered as the grim reality of their situation reasserted itself. "But there are worse things than sifting through bedpans."

Elizaveta reached over and gave her arm a sympathetic squeeze. "Well, when you put it like that—"

"Exactly." Anya tossed the bread ball to the back of her throat, took a mouthful of water from a nearby teacup, and swallowed.

A week ago she'd never have considered destroying the family heirlooms.

A week ago Dmitri hadn't been dead.

Her brother had come to Paris following Napoleon's abdication last year, attached to the Russian envoy, Carl Osipovich Pozzo di Borgo. When Bonaparte had been exiled to the island of Elba, Dmitri had deemed it safe for Anya to join him in the French capital for some shopping and sightseeing, and she'd jumped at the chance.

Paris was everything Anya had dreamed it would be: thrilling, fashionable, exotic. They'd visited galleries and museums, attended salons and balls. The past few months had been a giddy whirl of picnics by the Seine and trips to the modiste.

Napoleon's audacious escape from his island prison had smashed that pleasant idyll. Dmitri had been away, assisting at the Congress in Vienna, and Anya had been naively certain that Bonaparte would be stopped long before he reached Paris. When Marshal Ney defected, and turned a large part of the "Royalist" French army over to his former commander, it had come as a nasty shock.

Then the troops stationed outside the city walls had defected, and King Louis had abandoned the city. Elizaveta had urged Anya to do the same, but Anya hadn't wanted to leave for St. Petersburg without Dmitri. His last letter, dated ten days ago, had said he was accompanying di Borgo to Belgium to liaise with the British commander, Wellington.

And then news had come of the battle, near the Belgian town of Waterloo. The allied British and Prussian troops had defeated Napoleon, but at a terrible human cost.

Anya told herself there was no need to worry about Dmitri. He was a diplomat, not a soldier. He wouldn't have been anywhere near the battlefield. He was just too busy to write, that was all. She considered travelling to Brussels herself, but there wasn't a carriage to be had—almost every wheeled conveyance was being used by panicked citizens to leave the capital. And how could she hope to find him in all the confusion? No, she would stay in Paris and wait for him to come to her.

Anya stared down at the glittering stones on the table.

She barely recalled the visit from General di Borgo. All she remembered was the blood leeching from her face when he'd told her of Dmitri's death. The sick dread that had clutched her heart, Elizaveta's arms around her as her grief escaped in noisy, gasping sobs.

Now, two days later, her tears had dried. A hollow, aching sadness remained.

She'd told Elizaveta they would return to St. Petersburg, but in truth it held little appeal. What was left for her there? A series of beautiful, empty palaces filled with the ghosts of happier times. Her parents had died five years ago, both carried off by the same fever. Now that Dmitri was gone, her closest male relative was some distant cousin in Moscow, who'd hound her to marry the first fortune-hunting fool who came her way.

Her father had refused plenty of suitors over the years. Men like the scheming Vasili Petrov, who hadn't wanted *her*, merely the cachet that marriage to a Russian princess would bring. Anya was adamant that her union— like that of her own parents—would be based on mutual respect and appreciation, and not financial inducement. She'd seen far too many unhappy arranged marriages at court to consider settling for one herself.

After her father's death, Dmitri had done the refusing. Now he was gone too.

Pain and grief balled inside her, but Anya pushed them away. She had to be practical, for Elizaveta's sake. She pinched off another piece of bread, inserted another diamond, and swallowed it down.

Concealing a selection of gemstones inside their clothes was an expedient thing to do, considering the volatile situation outside. It was a long way from Paris to St. Petersburg. Two women alone would be an easy target for would-be thieves. If Anya's baggage was stolen, they'd have the jewels sewn into the hem of her cloak. And if her cloak was stolen too—well, then the diamonds she'd just swallowed would be a last resort.

With bleak humor, she wondered how long it would take for the gems to work their way through her body. A few days, probably. How horrified her former tutors would be to know she'd been called on to make such an obscene calculation.

Elizaveta finished stitching a small pearl choker into the lining of a walking dress and picked up the mangled baguette. "That's quite enough. You'll make yourself sick if you have any more." She scooped the remaining loose jewels into a reticule and folded the newly weighted garments over her arm. "I'll go make us some tea."

Tea, in Elizaveta's opinion, was the answer to everything.

After she left, Anya sat listening to the heartbreakingly normal sounds of the street outside. Carts rattled, birds sang. Tradesmen haggled. How could the world carry on as if nothing had happened? How was it possible to feel so alone amongst hundreds of thousands of people? The ache in her chest intensified. Thank God for Elizaveta. Without her dear friend, she'd be truly alone in this world.

Footsteps echoed on the stairs, too heavy to be Elizaveta returning with a tea tray. Anya frowned. Another visit from General Di Borgo? She stood and started for the door, but it opened after only the briefest of knocks. Her skirts swirled around her ankles as she came to an abrupt stop.

"Count Petrov!" she managed. "This is . . . unexpected."

It definitely wasn't "a pleasure."

Back in Russia they said: *In a foreign country you are glad to see even the crow from your own land.* But that wasn't true. She wasn't glad to see Vasili Petrov, at all. If she'd had her wish, she'd never have set eyes on him again.

Back in St. Petersburg, they called him handsome, with his pale blond hair and cool blue eyes, but Anya had known him since childhood. He was sly and vindictive, always jockeying for position. A preening peacock who bragged of his female conquests and his luck at the gaming tables with equal pride. She narrowed her eyes. He was neat as a pin, pure military perfection in his powder-blue uniform edged with gold braid. Unlike General di Borgo, whose head had still been bandaged beneath his battered hat, Vasili didn't look as if he'd been anywhere near a battlefield.

"Have you just arrived in Paris?" she asked. "Were you at the battle in Belgium?"

Vasili removed his pristine white gloves, tugging at the tip of each finger before folding them carefully in his palm. "Alas, no. We arrived a few hours after the French retreat. It was all over by then."

A wave of indignant fury welled up inside her. Why should a bastard like Vasili be spared, and good, brave men like Dmitri die?

Vasili slapped his gloves against his thigh and his pale gaze roved over her as if he were inspecting her for flaws. "I heard about the death of your brother. You have my condolences, Princess."

His stiff, emotionless tone was an insult. How *dare* he? Dmitri was a hero who'd died serving his country, whereas Vasili—

He took a step toward her. Anya swallowed a gasp of astonishment as he dropped to one knee and caught her hand in his. She tried to pull away, but he had a firm grip on her fingers.

"Princess Anastasia—Anya—" he murmured. "With

Dmitri gone, you need a protector. A husband. Please, do me the honor of—"

Anya shook her head in horrified disbelief. "Don't be ridiculous! I'm going back to St. Petersburg. On my own. I don't need anyone's protection."

Vasili's fingers tightened painfully on her knuckles. "No, Princess. You're going to marry me."

Chapter 2.

Anya quelled a spurt of incredulous anger. "I most certainly will not. My father denied your suit three years ago. As did my brother, when you persisted. You want my dowry, Vasili. You have no regard for *me* at all."

A cynical smile curved the corners of his mouth beneath his blond mustache. She'd always disliked men with mustaches.

"I don't deny it," he said coolly. "Why should I apologize for being ambitious? We'll make a good team, you and I. You're intelligent, for a woman. You know how to run a household, order servants. You'll make an excellent hostess." His gaze swept her features and a greedy, lecherous look kindled in his expression which made her skin crawl.

"You know full well you're beautiful. Admit it, you loved having all the boys panting after you at court, didn't you? And this ice princess facade? I'll melt it. Bedding you will be no hardship at all."

Anya snatched her hand away from his. Her expression must have shown her disdain because he raised an amused brow.

"What's the matter? I'll make you like it."

She sent a panicked glance at the door. Where was Elizaveta?

Vasili was watching her closely. In a sudden move, he stood, pulled her to her feet, and yanked her hard against his chest. Anya cried out and tried to pull away, but he caught her wrists in his fists, like manacles.

"You don't have any choice in the matter, Princess," he hissed. "We will be wed. As soon as I can find a priest."

"Release me at once."

An ugly, belligerent glint lit his eyes. "You'll wed me if I ruin you."

Her blood ran cold. "Don't touch me!"

"Who's going to stop me?"

Anya fought a wave of revulsion as his mouth crashed down on hers. His lips were hard and punishing. She shook her head, struggling violently, but he was bigger, stronger. His tongue probed her lips, seeking entrance. She let out a shocked cry and managed to free one wrist, then slapped him on the side of the head. Hard. He stumbled back with a muffled curse.

She wiped the back of her hand across her mouth and sent him her most imperious glare. "I will *never* marry you, Vasili Petrov. You're a traitor!"

Anya felt a stab of triumph before the magnitude of what she'd just admitted dawned on her. She could have bitten off her tongue.

Dmitri had told her in confidence that Vasili, or someone close to him, was suspected of passing information to the French. He'd hinted that he would be investigating the matter as soon as he returned from Vienna.

Vasili's eyes narrowed into slits. "So. We can do away with the pretense, can we? That's good. It makes everything so much easier."

He smoothed back his ruffled hair. Anya returned his hostile glare with one of her own.

"Your brother spoke to you about me." It was a statement, not a question. "Of course he did. The two of you were always close. He thought I was helping the French."

"Were you?"

"As a matter of fact, yes. They pay extremely well."

Anya gasped at the casual way he admitted to treason. Good God, the information he'd traded had led to the death of thousands of men. It had led to Dmitri's death.

"Bastard!" she breathed, incensed. "You traitorous *whoreson*!"

Vasili chuckled. "Tsk. Such language, Princess."

Anya fought the urge to slap the smug look off his face.

"Dmitri intercepted a letter of mine," Vasili continued. "He sent it to you."

She didn't have to feign her look of confusion. "No, he didn't."

"Don't lie to me! Where is it?"

"I never received any letter. I swear."

Vasili's face settled into a cold, murderous mask. Before Anya knew what he was about, he lifted his hand and dealt her a backhanded blow across the face. Blinding pain was quickly followed by astonishment and outrage. No one had ever hit her before. She cradled her stinging cheek and glared up at him through watering eyes.

He gave a sickly smile. "It doesn't matter. Whatever evidence you have, or don't have, your brother is dead. And a wife can't give evidence against her husband."

Anya sucked in a breath at his horrifyingly simple

plan. He would marry her to ensure her silence. She would be trapped in marriage to this brutal, sneering thug.

Vasili backed toward the door. "You will stay here until I return. And don't think to run. There's nowhere I won't find you. If I have to come after you, I will be most displeased." He flicked a glance at her burning cheek and smirked. "Your brother always allowed you too much leeway. But you'll learn to respect your husband."

Anya glared up at him and smiled. "Never."

Vasili sensed Elizaveta's presence behind him a fraction too late. He swung around, but she brought the Chinese vase down on his head with all her strength; it shattered as it made contact with his skull. His eyes slid closed and his big body collapsed onto the rug with a satisfying thump.

"Excellent timing," Anya gasped. "Thank you!"

Elizaveta glanced down at Vasili's prone form with a grimace of distaste. A patch of blood was seeping through the blond hair on the back of his head. Anya battled a wave of nausea.

"Is he dead?"

"I don't know, and I don't care," Elizaveta said briskly. "He deserved it, threatening you like that." She poked Vasili with the toe of her boot and gave a disappointed sigh. "No, he's just out cold."

Anya's hands were shaking. Vasili had hit upon an uncomfortable truth: without a male protector, she *was* dangerously vulnerable. If he'd truly tried to molest her, she doubted she'd have had the strength to stop him. What if Elizaveta hadn't come? It didn't bear thinking about.

They hurried out into the hallway. Anya locked the door and dropped the key into the flower vase—now conspicuously lacking its twin—which flanked the door.

"We can't stay here. Not now that he's found us."

"Should we go to the authorities?" Elizaveta asked.
"Or to General Di Borgo?"

"I doubt either could help. The whole city's in tur-
moil. There's too much going on." Anya shook her head,
her thoughts in a whirl. "Although, this chaos might
work to our advantage. If we disappear now, we'll be
harder to trace."

She didn't doubt Vasili's threat to follow her. His
pride was fierce, and he hated to be thwarted. She hurried toward her bedchamber with Elizaveta hard on her
heels. Vasili would expect her to head back to Russia.
Even if they managed to evade him on the journey, he
would catch up with them in St. Petersburg and attempt
to enact his absurd plan there. They needed another des-
tination. And to throw him off the scent.

"What if I pretend to kill myself?"

Elizaveta frowned. "What?"

"As a diversion. I'll leave a note. I'll say I can't bear
to live without Dmitri and would rather die than marry
Vasili." Anya's voice cracked at the mention of her
brother, but there was no time to grieve him now. She
had to think. To act.

"You think he'll believe it?"

"It's worth a try. At the very least it will give us some
time before he starts looking for us."

Anya glanced around her comfortable bedroom. She
had a wardrobe full of clothes, silver-backed brushes and
mirrors, a host of expensive luxuries she'd always taken
for granted. She pushed down a brief pang of regret.
"We'll have to leave all of this behind."

Elizaveta nodded decisively. She selected a small
bag and thrust a few choice articles inside, then picked
up Anya's travelling cape and the reticule of diamonds.
"Thank goodness we didn't leave these in there with him."

Anya pulled her leather jewelry box from the back of the wardrobe. "I have some coins. And we can take a few more jewels. Vasili won't know what's missing." She grabbed the satchel she used for watercolor paints and thrust her favorite pair of leather ankle boots inside, along with a shawl and a few clean chemises. "Hurry! Heaven knows how long we have before he wakes up."

She rushed to the writing desk in the corner, snatched up a pen and paper, and dashed off a short note proclaiming her intention to throw herself into the Seine. That done, she joined Elizaveta at the front door to the apartment. A thousand contradictory thoughts crowded her brain.

Good God. How had it come to this? Thrust from a life of peaceful contentment into one of terrifying uncertainty, all in the space of a few days. If they ran, they would be just like every other citizen out there; they'd have to make their own way in the world without the cushion of rank or fortune to ease the way.

The thought was oddly beguiling. Anya might never have experienced the hardship of living without family, or wealth, or social status, but she'd developed a certain amount of cunning while learning to survive the scandals and machinations of the Russian court. Neither she nor Elizaveta were fools. They were determined and resourceful. They would rise to this challenge. And really, could whatever awaited them out there be worse than the fate Petrov had planned for her?

She doubted it.

Anya took a fortifying breath. This might be an ending, but it was also a beginning. A chance to experience all that life had to offer. Her whole life she'd been seen as little more than a means of enrichment or a political pawn; it was time to see what she could achieve on her own.

She grasped Elizaveta's hand. "Are you sure you want

to come with me? I can give you enough money to get back to St. Petersburg, if you want."

Elizaveta returned the squeeze. "I wouldn't dream of leaving you, my love. What's the plan?"

"All right. We'll find a carriage heading north, toward Belgium. There will be plenty of wounded soldiers returning home. We'll attach ourselves to them and say we're widows, or looking for our husbands. We'll go to England. Vasili won't think to look for us there." Anya gave a decisive nod. "Think of an English surname."

Elizaveta wrinkled her nose. "Smith? Brown? What was the name of the family in that English book we read last year? Bennett?"

"Perfect. You can be Elizabeth—no, Lizzie—Bennett. Or Smith, if you prefer. And I shall be Anna. Anna Brown. From this moment, Princess Anastasia Denisova is dead."

Chapter 3.

One year later. September 1816.

Sebastien Wolff, Earl of Mowbray, frowned down at the dead man at his feet and sighed in irritation.

He wasn't dressed to investigate a murder. He'd been about to leave for the opera and a visit to the infamous Mrs. Haye's brothel in Covent Garden, when his two best friends, Benedict Wylde and Alex Harland, had arrived at the Tricorn Club, commandeered his carriage, and effectively kidnapped him.

Alex had let out a slow sarcastic whistle when he'd seen Seb's immaculate evening clothes. "Look at you, pretty boy," he teased.

"Oh, sod off," Seb said amiably. "You're just jealous. Your coats never fit this well. What's going on?"

"Conant's got a new job for us," Ben said, referring to their superior, the head of Bow Street and de facto head of police in London, Sir Nathaniel Conant. "Murder. Behind a tavern, down at the East India docks."

"That's hardly a reason for us to investigate," Seb said crossly. "People are killed down there every night of the week. Bar brawls, robberies gone wrong. It's not our territory. What's so different about this one?"

"Sounds like the deceased was a visitor to our shores. The innkeeper saw him drinking with another man and overheard them speaking Russian or Prussian—something foreign, at any rate. They seemed to be on friendly terms, but not fifteen minutes later, our man was found in the side alley with his throat slit."

"I still don't see what it has to do with us," Seb groused. "Two foreigners had a disagreement and one of them ended up dead. It was probably over a woman. Or cards. Let the local magistrate deal with it."

Alex shook his head. "The mention of Russia is what interests Conant. Castlereagh and the Foreign Office have been looking for a spy who passed information to the French about Russian troop movements before Waterloo. They think someone warned Napoleon the Russians were on their way."

"Bastard," Ben muttered savagely.

Seb nodded. All three of them had been left scarred by their years in the Rifles that had culminated in the bloody carnage at Waterloo. That the three of them had survived was nothing short of a miracle.

"Information's still getting out. A Russian delegation arrived last week for trade talks, and Conant wants us to keep our ears open for anything that might identify the leak. So we're investigating anything that involves Russians. Dead or alive."

Seb snorted. "Keep our ears open? Ha. Only one of my ears *works*, thanks to Bonaparte."

"I'll keep my eyes peeled," Alex added dryly, and Benedict chuckled at their gallows humor. A canon blast at Waterloo had permanently damaged the hearing on Seb's left side. Alex had lost a portion of his peripheral vision in the same explosion.

The carriage lurched to a stop at the end of a dark alley. The three of them got out, eliciting a slew of bawdy comments from a couple of whores on the corner.

"Ooh! Come 'ere, gents. Sally'll show you a good time."

Ben ignored them and headed for the front door of the tavern. "I'll talk to the landlord."

Seb nodded to the man posted at the alley entrance to protect the crime scene and slipped between the overhanging buildings, followed by Alex.

Here, in the stinking slums that clustered round the Thames docks, murder was commonplace. Human life was cheap. Seb wrinkled his nose against the rank smell of piss and stale beer that mixed with the fetid odor of the nearby river to create a nauseating miasma. The creak of ships moored at the water's edge could be heard above the rattle of carts and the occasional angry shout. A rat scurried behind a pile of refuse.

Blood and death didn't bother him. He'd seen so much of it during his years in the Rifles, he'd become immune. Sometimes the fact that it *didn't* affect him worried him a little. His emotions, good and bad, seemed distant, unimportant. Had he lost the ability to be horrified or surprised by anything anymore?

Seb dismissed the thought and crouched down, careful to avoid the black pool of blood that glistened on the filthy cobbles. No point ruining a good pair of boots. The dead man wore plain clothes, nothing flash that would have attracted the attention of a thief. He lay sprawled like a marionette whose strings had been cut. Seb searched the man's pockets and withdrew a leather money purse. "This wasn't a robbery."

Alex pointed at the man's hand. "He's still wearing a ring on his little finger too. Someone wanted him dead, but not for gold."

Seb tugged the ring from the corpse and squinted at it in the dim light. It was too dark to see the markings on it, so he slipped it into his waistcoat pocket. "I'll take this home and look at it there."

Alex bent to examine the man's neck. "It's a clean wound, almost professional. Someone knows their way around a blade. There's not much evidence of a struggle. The poor bastard probably never suspected a thing."

Seb straightened, imagining the scene. "He did it from behind. Put an arm across his neck and cut, then dropped the body. No sound. Very efficient. Sneaky bastard." He flicked a glance at the dead man's face and experienced a fleeting stab of pity. He was young, barely thirty, maybe the same age as himself. Too young to die. Especially like this, so far from home.

Benedict appeared at the far end of the alley.

"Do we have a description of the suspect?" Alex asked.

"The innkeeper says he was wearing a hat pulled low over his face and a heavy overcoat. Said he was big, maybe six feet, with pale hair."

Seb rolled his eyes. "A big blond Russian. Well, that certainly narrows it down."

Alex grinned at his sarcasm. "There are Russian immigrants all over the city. It could be someone with military experience, a former soldier maybe, considering the precision of the wound."

"He might not even *be* Russian," Seb said irritably. "The innkeeper could have been mistaken. They could've been speaking Cornish or Welsh. We're wasting our time."

Ben shrugged. "Well, I doubt there's any more to learn here, at any rate. Let's go. The locals can take it from here."

Back in the carriage, Seb said, "So, Conant wants us to listen out for Russian gossip, does he? At the Tricorn?"

The Tricorn, the gambling club the three of them had opened following their return from Waterloo, had become one of the most popular gaming houses in London. Seb, Alex, and Benedict had lived there together until Alex and Ben had both found themselves wives and moved out a few months ago.

Seb would never have admitted it aloud, but he missed them. Despite the constant noise and excitement of the club itself, the private apartments were depressingly quiet. He never brought women back there; he enjoyed the privacy of his personal domain, but it was rather dull, with just him and the servants rattling around.

Not that he was lonely. Of course not. But maybe he should take in a lodger? There must be hundreds of chaps who'd jump at the chance of living in a gambling hell—

"Yes, but quietly," Alex said, and Seb realized with a jolt that he'd been woolgathering. "We don't want the delegation to know we suspect one of their countrymen."

"I haven't seen any Russians at the club yet," Seb said, "And even if they do come, I doubt they'll be discussing sensitive information in such a crowded place."

"They might, if they're speaking Russian and don't think anyone else can understand what they're saying," Alex said reasonably. "Or if they're very drunk. *In vino veritas*, as they say."

"What good is it to us even if they do talk?" Seb grumbled. "Can you speak Russian? Because I bloody well can't."

"I can say a few curse words." Benedict chuckled. "And ask for a drink. But that's about it."

"Maybe we should find ourselves a native speaker?" Alex said. "Employ them to loiter about on the gaming floor listen in to conversations? I'll make some inquiries."

Seb reached into his waistcoat and withdrew his

pocket watch. "Bugger. I've missed the first half of the opera. I might as well go straight to Covent Garden."

"You're never going to find a decent woman in a brothel," Ben said with a slight frown.

Seb sent him a smile sure to irritate. "That's precisely why I'm going. It's the *in*decent ones I'm after."

Alex leaned forward, his hands dangling loose between his knees. "Since Ben and I moved out, you've been playing and working too hard."

Seb snorted. "That's bollocks. I don't gamble. I rarely drink to excess. Women are my only vice. What is it about you married people? You get yourselves legshackled, and then nothing will do but to try and snare everyone *else* in the parson's mousetrap. You're like two fussy old women. I'm not ready to settle down just yet. I'm having far too much fun being a reprobate."

"Marriage really isn't that bad." Alex laughed.

Seb rolled his eyes. "Haven't you got better things to do than nag me about my love life? Or maybe, being married men, it's your own lack of action between the sheets that has you so interested? Trying to live vicariously, boys?"

Alex snorted at the insult. "Not me. Emmy's at a charity gala tonight, but rest assured when she gets home, she'll show me just how much she's missed me." His lips curved in a contented smile and Seb grimaced in disgust.

"I'm not lacking in that department either, thank you very much," Ben added smugly. "Marriage does not equate to celibacy, Seb."

"I never said it did. I just didn't think you'd both be so content to get it from the *one source* for the rest of your days." Seb shook his head in mock horror. "Seems a damn shame. When you think of all the available women out there, crying out for the love of a good man—"

Alex shook his head. "You haven't attended many *ton* functions recently."

"Because I'm sick of fending off scheming debutantes and bored housewives. No woman's worth facing an irate husband or an angry father over pistols at dawn." Seb leaned back into the comfortable squabs of the carriage. "Tarts are honest and uncomplicated. They don't expect anything more than a tumble in the sheets for the price agreed. There's no hurt feelings, no clinging when it's time to end things. No delusions of marriage."

He glanced between his two friends. "The fact that you've both found one woman you want to spend your life with is amazing—but it's never going to happen to me."

He frowned. The conversation was steering nauseatingly close to the kind of self-indulgent, romantic sap usually reserved for women over a cup of tea. Seb had always been a cynic, but having witnessed the transformation of his two closest friends from rakish jokers to happily married men, his unshaking belief that romantic love was as fictitious as a virgin in a whorehouse had been undermined.

"Both of you were attracted to your wives as soon as you saw them, correct?" he said.

Alex and Ben nodded.

"But you were attracted to other women before you met them, so clearly physical attraction isn't enough. There must have been something more. Some spark that set them apart from all the rest."

"I thought it was irritation at first," Alex said with a reminiscent smile.

"I wanted to throttle her." Benedict chuckled.

"Well, then." Seb crossed his arms. "I'm still waiting to find that gorgeous someone who irritates me enough to want to strangle her. Until then, I plan to enjoy my bachelor status to the hilt."

Alex sighed. "I thought we could come for supper. I miss Lagrasse. I've been dreaming of his puddings for weeks."

"Then I'm afraid you're doomed to disappointment." Seb grinned. "I've given him the night off." He glanced out of the carriage window. "We're nearly at Covent Garden. I'm off to Haye's to see what all the fuss is about. Harwood says she has the finest girls in London. You can set me down here."

Chapter 4.

"Sweet violets! Penny a bunch!"

Anya crossed the bustling square of Covent Garden, nodding a friendly greeting to several of the stallholders who plied their wares in the haphazard chaos of London's largest outdoor market. She dodged a costermonger's barrow boy, staggering under the weight of a wheelbarrow dangerously overloaded with turnips, and smiled at the eel pie vendor on the corner. She'd never been brave enough to actually try an eel pie, but the smell that emanated from beneath the cloth-covered baskets was surprisingly inviting.

She and Elizaveta had been in London for almost a year, but she never tired of the myriad sights and sounds. It was still so strange and foreign, such a contrast to the gilded, glittering palaces she'd known in St. Petersburg, or the cultured order of Paris. London was beauty and ugliness pressed close together. Foul gutters and vibrant flowers, filthy death and pulsing life, danger and excitement, all rolled into one fascinating metropolis.

Anya ascended the steps that led to the small apartment she shared with Elizaveta. Covent Garden certainly wasn't the most genteel of neighborhoods, but that suited her purpose very well. She had no desire to mingle with the elevated members of society who resided a few streets to the west in Mayfair.

Not that their finances would allow such a luxury. She'd had to sell most of her precious diamonds to afford the rent on even this tiny apartment, and her wages, though generous, only just enabled them to live within their means. Lodgings in Covent Garden were always in high demand due to its proximity to both the theatre district and the fashionable enclave of St. James's.

Elizaveta glanced up from her sewing when Anya let herself into their small front room. "How was the dowager duchess?"

"In fine fettle, as ever." Anya carefully removed her hat.

"Who's incurred her displeasure this week?"

"Lady Jersey. Apparently the wine she served at her soiree was 'an insult to vintners everywhere.'"

Elizaveta chuckled. They both enjoyed the elderly dowager's acerbic insights into the workings of the *haute ton*. It was better than reading the scandal sheets.

When they'd first arrived in London, Anya had been dismayed to realize how completely unprepared she was for any form of meaningful employment. She'd visited an employment agency, naively confident that her ability to speak English, French, and Russian, and her extensive knowledge of literature, history, and geography, would qualify her for the position of governess or tutor. Not so.

The pinch-faced woman behind the desk had given a wheezy, cynical chuckle. "Have you looked in a mirror, child? No wife will want you within a hundred leagues of her husband or her sons, believe me. Women want tutors who are stout and ugly, preferably with whiskers and warts, so they don't pose any temptation."

Anya had stifled a sinking feeling. "I can teach manners and etiquette to girls."

"I have no openings for that, I'm afraid."

"Perhaps I can become a translator for a bookseller, then?"

The woman gave a dismissive sniff. "There's not much work to be had for anyone right now, what with all the soldiers back from the war. Everyone's looking for work. And very few men want to employ a woman, unless it's for pleasure."

"I don't want to do that," Anya said firmly.

The woman sent her a speculative glance. "Are you sure? You're a good-looking girl. I could recommend you to some of the better establishments."

"Thank you, but no."

The woman shrugged. Anya's spirits dropped even further, but she pasted an enthusiastic smile on her face. Elizaveta was depending on her. "Perhaps I could learn a trade of some sort? I'm not afraid of hard work. I could be an apprentice."

"You're a bit old for that," the woman said bluntly. "How old are you? Twenty?"

"Twenty-two."

"Hmmm. Seamstresses like young girls, to train up. So do milliners." Seeing Anya's crestfallen expression, the woman smiled. "Buck up, girl. I do have one position open. It's companion to the Dowager Duchess of Winwick. I warn you, the woman's a harridan. Eighty if she's a day, and as eccentric as they come. She don't suffer fools—she's dismissed four secretaries this year already. But the salary is generous. If you can stay long enough to earn it."

Anya tried not to wince. "It sounds perfect. What would I have to do?"

"The duchess requires you to visit her four days a week, to read to her, help her with correspondence, and generally do anything else she requires."

"I'll do it."

In the end, it had been a perfect fit. Anya had liked the dowager duchess immediately. She was as sharp as a pin and keenly observant, with strong opinions—which were usually correct—and a love of scandal and gossip. Her scathing commentary on almost everyone in the *ton* was extremely amusing, and a friendship had developed between the two of them, despite the fifty-year age difference. Anya thought of the older woman as an additional grandmother.

On several occasions, the dowager had tried to coax her to move into the huge Grosvenor Square townhouse she inhabited, but Anya had refused, citing Elizaveta, and her need for independence. Recent events, however, had caused her to reconsider that option. Her roommate had gained a beau; a handsome, charmingly disorganized barrister by the name of Oliver Reynolds.

Elizaveta had found work as a seamstress for Ede and Ravenscroft, a tailor in Chancery Lane specializing in ceremonial robes; black cloaks for judges in court, gowns for university dons, and the ermine-trimmed capes worn by peers for the state opening of Parliament. They'd met when Oliver had come—in a great hurry—to buy a new set of court robes for an appearance at the Old Bailey. He'd set fire to his previous set by leaving them too close to the stove. Elizaveta had assisted him, and by the end of the encounter, they had both been equally smitten.

Elizaveta snipped off the end of her thread, smoothed her hand over the fur-edged cloak she'd been trimming, and glanced at the mantel clock Anya had purchased from the pawn shop down the road. Unlike the beautiful, hard-paste porcelain produced by the Russian factories, this was a cheap, soft-paste English piece that resembled a lump of cake icing that had melted in the sun. The gaudily painted, lopsided couple supporting the clock-face looked permanently intoxicated. Anya loved it.

"I should go and get ready," Elizaveta said.

"You're meeting Oliver tonight?"

"Yes. He's taking me to see Edmund Keane play Sir Giles Overreach at Drury Lane again."

"I heard his first performance was so powerful that Mrs. Glover actually fainted on stage."

Elizaveta giggled. "Oh yes, he's quite terrifying. Which gives me the perfect excuse to clutch Oliver and for him to put his arm around me!"

Anya laughed approvingly. "You're shameless."

The sound of someone tripping on the stairs, and a muffled oath, interrupted them, and Elizaveta rolled her eyes fondly. "That will be him now."

Anya shook her head. Oliver was tall and thin, with the air of a man who'd grown to adulthood without ever becoming accustomed to the additional size of his own body. He was always bumping into things and sporting interesting bruises on his person. If there was a runaway donkey, a pot of ink to spill, or a set of steps to trip up, Oliver would find them.

Luckily, his physical ineptness masked a mind as in-cisive as a razor. He was a formidable barrister, fiercely intelligent, though prone to going off on obscure tangents if distracted. Elizaveta, with her practical, organized na-ture, was the perfect complement to his haphazard style. Anya had no doubt the two of them would be blissfully happy together.

The looming possibility of their engagement, however, had forced her to question her own future. She loved her job with the dowager duchess, but it didn't give her much opportunity to mingle with many men her own age.

Unlike Elizaveta, who was firmly entrenched in the working classes, Anya had found herself in a strange subset of society reserved for governesses and penniless-yet-genteel poor relations. She featured somewhere above servants and tradeswomen, but below the landed gentry and aristocracy, who lived off the income from tenants, property, and investments.

She had all of those things back in Russia, of course. And despite her disappearance, she had no fear that her property would have been dispersed among the remaining members of her family. A few weeks after they'd arrived in London, she'd written to her trusted man of business in St. Petersburg, informing him that she was taking an extended tour of Eastern Europe. She'd been sure to request that should anyone—especially one Vasili Petrov—inquire about her, that Mr. Lermontov feign complete ignorance of her whereabouts. Since Lermontov's family had served as financial advisors to the Denisovs for well over a hundred years, Anya was confident of his discretion.

Oliver's arrival interrupted her recollections.

"Good evening, Miss Anna," he said, removing his cap to reveal a thatch of mussed, sandy hair. His smile widened as his gaze found Elizaveta. "And good evening, Lizzie. Sorry I'm late. There was a rat on the steps of my office, but when I went to chase it away, it turned out to be a kitten. The poor little mite was soaking. Some cruel bugger had tried to drown it, I think."

His brows drew together in a disapproving line. "Of course, I couldn't just leave it there to die. I had to get it some milk and find someone to look after it, and"—he extended his arms to the sides in a hapless gesture—"well, the end result is that I'm late. Are you ready? We'll have to hurry if you want to catch the opening act."

Elizaveta shot Anya a laughing look at her beloved's habitual tardiness and sent him a dazzling smile. "You're a good man, Oliver Reynolds. Not everyone would have been as kind as you."

Oliver's neck reddened at her praise.

"Let me just get my hat and my gloves, and we can be on our way."

Elizaveta took the few steps needed to cross the room and enter her bedchamber and reappeared moments later, tying the laces of her cloak. "There. All ready. Are you sure you'll be all right on your own?" Her last comment was addressed to Anya.

Anya nodded, amused by her friend's concern. She refrained from saying that if anyone accosted her, she'd be sure to hit them over the head with a vase. Elizaveta still didn't like to joke about their near miss with Petrov.

"I won't be here for long," Anya said. "I'm going next door. I promised Charlotte I'd continue the girls' lessons. You two have a wonderful evening."

Chapter 5.

Half an hour later, Anya slipped through the back door of London's most exclusive brothel and smiled at the owner, her friend and neighbor, Charlotte Haye. The infamous madam was dressed in the height of fashion, her naturally blond hair arranged in an elaborate style, her voluptuous figure displayed to its best advantage in a gown of lavender silk.

Anya divested herself of her gloves and bonnet. "Are the girls ready?"

"They are indeed. Tess is looking forward to reading a whole chapter on her own. And Jenny's been practicing her penmanship all week. Amy's with a customer, but she'll be down as soon as she's free."

Anya's smile dimmed a little. When she'd first realized that the house next to the modest apartment she and Elizaveta had rented in Covent Garden was a brothel, she'd been dismayed. But a chance encounter with Charlotte on the front steps had led to an invitation to tea, and

Anya had discovered that the notorious Mrs. Haye was one of the kindest, wittiest women she'd ever met.

The interior of the brothel was as tastefully appointed as an ambassador's residence. Charlotte had spared no expense to make her rooms as luxurious and appealing as possible, and the strategy had clearly worked, because the place was frequented by only the wealthiest and most aristocratic of clients.

Despite her stunning good looks, Charlotte herself did not entertain clients, although she received no shortage of offers. Anya had never asked how she'd ended up as one of London's greatest procuresses, but from a few things Charlotte had let slip, she'd deduced that an unfortunate incident with a duplicitous fiancé had set her on the path to what most people would regard as ruination. There was, and never had been, a Mr. Haye.

Charlotte, in turn, had never pried into Anya's past, although Anya had no doubt that she was burning with curiosity. Anya had introduced herself as "Anna Brown," and Charlotte had never questioned it.

Anya's feelings on the world's oldest profession were mixed. There was no doubt that the young women who lived with Charlotte were well cared for. Charlotte protected them like a mother hen, scooping them off the streets and settling them in the house whenever she had a vacancy. She provided them with their own room, food, and clothing, not to mention contraception and regular visits from the doctor. She personally vetted any gentleman who wished to visit "her girls," and encouraged the women to only accept the "jobs" they fancied, and refuse the rest. Being selective only added to their appeal.

Anya had never heard any of the women complain about their life—indeed, most seemed grateful that Charlotte had saved them from destitution, violence, and starvation on the streets—but Anya was sure many of them would prefer an alternative means of earning a living if it were offered to them. One afternoon, over tea and cakes with Charlotte, Anya had suggested that the girls might benefit from learning skills that would aid them in leaving a life of prostitution if they wished. Charlotte had agreed, and that was how, on the evenings Anya wasn't with the dowager duchess, she'd begun to teach them to read, write, and solve basic arithmetic.

"You'll have to use the front parlor this evening." Charlotte's distinctive, throaty voice was entirely unfeigned. "I'm having the study repapered. I'll tell Winslow to direct any visitors to the red salon. You shouldn't be disturbed."

Anya nodded and made her way to the front of the house to find her charges. She stepped into the room in time to hear Tess say, "Well, that's a right load of old bollocks, Jen."

"It is more polite to say, 'I'm afraid I disagree with your assessment, Jenny,'" Anya said dryly.

Tess's sweet, freckled face turned pink in embarrassment, and the two girls dropped into hasty curtseys, talking all the while. "Oh, Miss Anna, I'm so sorry. I 'ad no idea you was there."

"It's quite all right, Tess. I've heard far worse. But still, do consider modifying your language. As a milliner's assistant, you'll need to be polite to the customers."

Anya had to hide a smile at the irony of chiding *anyone* on their vocabulary. Elizaveta still frowned at her in private for "profanities unbecoming a princess." Her English had certainly expanded to include an impressive number of curse words during their months in Covent Garden.

Jenny went over to the desk in one corner, and Anya gestured to Tess to open the book of fairy tales from which she'd been learning to read. "Tess, you read, and Jenny, you write down what she says."

Both girls nodded obediently.

"Little . . . Red . . . Ri—ding . . . Hood," Tess said slowly, her finger following the words as she went along. Anya sent her an encouraging smile.

"Excellent, Tess! Keep going."

"Once . . . up—on . . . a . . . time—"

The door opened. Anya glanced up, expecting to see Charlotte with a tea tray, but instead, a man she'd never seen before appeared in the doorway, and for one ridiculous moment, she thought Tess had summoned the wolf from the storybook.

He was tall and lean, with a lithe vitality that made the very air vibrate. His skin was tanned, his hair a black windblown mass around his face. His dark eyes swept the room and settled on Anya, and for the first time in her entire life, she lost her train of thought on account of a man.

He stilled, his hand resting on the doorknob, and his mouth curved into a smile that made her flash hot and cold at once.

"Good evening, ladies. I'm sorry to interrupt. I was looking for Mrs. Haye."

Something odd fluttered in Anya's stomach. His voice was like sandpaper and velvet.

Jenny and Tess jumped to their feet, rushed forward, and stopped a few inches away from him, both of them talking at once.

"Mrs. 'Aye is in the back parlor, my lord," Jenny said breathlessly.

Tess sent him a shamelessly provocative glance. "It's a pleasure to see you 'ere, my lord. Is there something I can 'elp you with?"

Jenny batted her eyelashes. "Or me?"

But the man's gaze was still fixed on Anya. Heat rose in her cheeks at his boldly appraising scrutiny. She pressed her lips into a disapproving line.

His features had a Mediterranean look, all dark so-
phistication, a corsair masquerading as a gentleman. She'd
never seen anyone so uncompromisingly handsome. What
was a man like *this* doing in a brothel? Surely he could get
any woman he wanted with the crook of his finger?

A nervous sensation coiled in her belly. The thought
of him doing things—the kind of things a man did with
a woman in a brothel—made her feel quite hot and bothered. Still, she *certainly* wasn't going to be the one who
provided whatever service he'd come here for. No matter
how ridiculously good looking he was.

She cleared her throat, intending to excuse herself, but
the gentleman spoke first, sending a charming smile that
somehow conveyed sincere regret to the two women in
front of him.

"Would you two ladies mind going to fetch her for me?"

Tess and Jenny both sagged in disappointment at the
subtle dismissal. Tess shot a wide-eyed glance over her
shoulder at Anya. "We'll all go," she said, clearly trying
to save Anya from being left alone with the visitor.

The gentleman shook his head. "That won't be necessary." He stepped aside and held the door wide for Tess
and Jenny to leave.

With no other option, they scurried out, and Anya's
heart thumped in her chest as the man closed the door
behind them with a click. Half the room still separated
them, but a fizzle of something—not quite fear, more
like awareness—prickled under her skin.

Anya held her ground as he prowled toward her. His
gaze travelled down her body and back up in a slow, simmering appraisal, lingering for a long moment on her lips,
and he let out a short, almost surprised laugh of disbelief.

"Well. I must admit I was skeptical when I heard men
swear that Mrs. Haye offered the finest girls in London.
But now I see it was nothing short of the truth."

He took another step closer, and Anya caught a hint of a subtle, masculine scent that made her stomach do another little flip.

His dark eyes met hers. "I'm not a man who wavers over a decision. And considering where we are, I know you don't need pretty words or meaningless platitudes. Name your price."

Chapter 6.

Anya was momentarily rendered speechless. She drew herself up, noting that this man was a good head and shoulders taller than herself. Her eyes were level with the diamond pin that sparkled in the folds of his cravat.

"I'm afraid you are mistaken, sir. There's no amount of money that would induce me to entertain you."

A flash of something that could have been annoyance, or merely amusement, flared in his eyes. "Oh, come now. There's no need for games. Just tell me how much. I'll pay Mrs. Haye, and we'll both go upstairs."

Anya could scarcely believe her ears. The part of her that wasn't rooted to the spot with amazement and irritation was, paradoxically, rather flattered that he seemed so determined to engage her services. A wicked, impish impulse compelled her to say, "And what if I said a night with me would cost you five hundred pounds?"

"Then I would pay it."

She jerked her shocked gaze to his—and realized he was entirely serious.

Who *was* this man? Jenny had called him "my lord." He must be both as rich as Croesus, and *out of his senses*, to squander such an exorbitant sum on one night with a stranger.

This close, she could see the sensual fullness of his lips, the faint hint of dark stubble on his jaw. Her pulse pounded in her throat.

The corner of his mouth quirked up as he leaned closer, as if to impart some choice piece of gossip. "I feel compelled to point out that I don't actually require your company for the whole night." His gaze flicked over her features like a caress. "A couple of rather intense hours should accomplish everything I have in mind."

Anya's corset seemed inordinately tight. Even the most forward of rakes in the Russian court hadn't been so direct.

"I'm sure we'll find ourselves compatible," he murmured. "But perhaps we should check?"

He stepped closer. It was a matter of pride that she didn't step back. Soon, barely an inch separated them and the air seemed to thicken, to hum. His dark gaze held hers in challenge as he lifted his hand and stroked his fingers lightly across her cheek.

He'd removed his gloves. Hot and cold prickled where he touched, like snow crystals landing on her skin.

He spread his fingers and slid them along her jaw, his thumb tilting her chin a little higher, and Anya had no doubt she was being seduced by an expert. Her breath was coming in shallow pants, and she didn't have an ounce of willpower to resist.

Not that she wanted to. Excitement made her stomach swoop as his warm breath sloughed across her cheek. This was too good an opportunity to miss. The man was clearly a rogue, but why deny herself the adventure of allowing him to kiss her? She was both curious and intrigued.

His lips touched hers, neither tentative nor impatient, just the perfect weight, and Anya closed her eyes. He kissed her again, a little firmer this time, and she parted her lips instinctively. His low murmur of approval sent a shiver down her spine.

When he slid his tongue against her lips, her knees almost gave out. Men had tried to kiss her this way before, but she'd always pulled back, repelled. But this, this was *glorious*. He wasn't conscious of rank, afraid to offend. He was simply a man, showing a woman his desire.

His teeth caught the fullness of her lower lip in a playful tug and the delicious sensation sent jolts of heat spearing through her body. Anya rose up on tiptoe, caught the lapels of his jacket, and pulled him down, returning the swirl of his tongue with artless enthusiasm. He tasted like brandy. Like sin. She wanted to keep on doing this forever.

The click of the door barely registered in her mind, but his reflexes were clearly better than hers. He dropped his hand and stepped away with a cool rush of air. By the time Charlotte swept into the room like a lilac-clad angel, a perfectly acceptable distance separated them.

He turned with an ease that belied the throbbing tension in the room. Anya took a flustered step back and sucked in a steadying breath. *Good God! What was she doing?*

"Lord Mowbray!" Charlotte's smile was radiant as she held out her hand in greeting. He bowed low over it. "Welcome. We've not had the honor of your company here before. But I'm confident we'll be able to cater to your every need. I see you've met my good friend, Miss Brown?"

The man turned back to Anya and his lips twitched in amusement. "We hadn't got as far as introductions."

"Oh, well, in that case, Miss Anna Brown, the Earl of Mowbray."

He bowed, and Anya made a stiff curtsey, silently laughing at observing the formalities when he'd been kissing her witless moments before.

"Sebastien," he said. "I feel sure you should call me Sebastien."

"My lord," she said, just to annoy him, and felt a jolt of dark pleasure at the irritated twitch of his brows. As a member of the aristocracy—presumably a wealthy one—he doubtless had everyone he met obeying his commands. A little insubordination would do him a world of good.

"My girls are most anxious to meet you," Charlotte said.

"I don't need to meet any of your other girls. I've made my choice. I would like to engage the services of Miss Brown."

Charlotte sent Anya a quick, questioning glance and gave a soft laugh. "Oh, I'm afraid that's out of the question. Miss Brown is not one of my girls."

Anya picked up the book of fairy tales Tess had abandoned and clasped it to her chest like some kind of medieval shield. She was still shaky and breathless. "Indeed, I am not. Lord Mowbray, enjoy your evening."

She started for the door, but he sidestepped to block her escape and sent a dark glare at Charlotte. "Mrs. Haye. If this is some paltry attempt to try to secure a higher sum from me, it is quite unnecessary. You know of me?"

Charlotte nodded.

"Then you will also know that I have more than enough funds to afford whatever exorbitant fees you care to charge."

He strode over to the inkpot Jenny had abandoned on the desk, dipped a pen into it, and began to write on a blank sheet of paper. "I, Sebastien Wolff," he said aloud as he wrote, "promise to pay Mrs. Haye of Covent

Garden the sum of five hundred pounds." He signed his name at the bottom with a flourish, thrust the paper at Charlotte, and raised his brows impatiently.

Charlotte sent Anya a comically incredulous look.

"It's no scheme, my lord," she assured him hastily. "As much as I would *love* to take your money, Miss Brown is not for sale. For any price."

Anya was barely listening. All she could hear was the ringing in her ears as she finally made the connection that had been eluding her ever since she'd heard the name Sebastien Wolff.

This man was her employer's great-nephew.

She'd never met any of the dowager duchess's relatives in person. She'd seen a few portraits, of course, dotted about the house, but the shockingly masculine specimen in front of her bore little resemblance to the dark-haired young man in those paintings.

The duchess was inordinately fond of her youngest nephew. He regularly came to visit her at the Grosvenor Street mansion, but Anya had never been present; she'd always made sure to slip away whenever the duchess was expecting company. The fewer people in the aristocracy who saw her, the better.

The chance of anyone recognizing her, either from Paris or from her life in St. Petersburg was slim, but until she had absolute confirmation of either Vasili Petrov's death, or his marriage to some other unfortunate female, she refused to take any unnecessary risks.

Wolff sent her a molten look. "Are you sure I can't change your mind, Miss Brown?"

Anya stifled a near-hysterical snort. The man was temptation incarnate.

His surname was certainly apt. She'd seen a real wolf once, back in Russia. She and Dmitri had been out riding and a lone male had followed them for several miles, running parallel within the tree line. She'd caught flashes of its silver-grey fur, heard the tireless crunch of its paws in the snow as it ate up the miles, easily keeping pace with the horses.

This man had the same unblinking stare and sinuous grace. He exuded the same subtle threat of danger. Anya shivered. Sebastien Wolff might appear civilized, in his perfectly cut jacket and snowy-white cravat, but every instinct told her to beware.

She'd thought Vasili's clumsy assault in Paris had given her a permanent distaste for men, but she was horribly tempted to take Wolff's outstretched hand and allow him to draw her upstairs. To let him show her the pleasure he seemed arrogantly confident of providing.

The thought was enough to shock her into action. "Good night, my lord."

With a regal tilt of her chin, she hurried from the room and heard Charlotte's husky laughter as she moved forward to intercept him. Anya rushed back to the kitchens, desperate to leave, and found a cluster of girls chattering like a bunch of excited magpies.

"Is it true?" Amy asked, catching Anya's sleeve. "The big bad Wolff? 'E's never been 'ere before."

"It *is* 'im," Jenny insisted. "My friend Kitty's seen 'im 'undreds of times at the theatre."

"The last of the Unholy Trinity," Amy sighed reverently.

"Unholy Trinity?" Anya echoed.

"That's what everyone used to call 'em. Lords Mowbray, Melton, and Ware. Before the war, before they were earls, they were the most shocking rogues you can imagine. But Melton and Ware are married now. Mowbray's the only one left."

Long Meg, a ravishing natural redhead, chuckled. "Wonder what 'e likes? I bet 'e's a right handful, big man like that. Think 'e wants a five fingered handshake?" She made a crude gesture with her hand, fingers meeting thumb as if encircling a pipe.

Jenny gave a theatrical shiver. "'Ave you seen the size of 'is 'ands? I tell you, girls, I'd do 'im for free."

Anya snatched up her bonnet and gloves and made for the door. She truly didn't want to hear any more of the conversation, but she couldn't help looking back as Charlotte came in.

"What does he want, Charlotte?" Jenny asked.

"Let *me* take care of 'im!" Amy pleaded.

"I'll do whatever 'e asks," Long Meg declared.

Charlotte looked unusually harried. Two small lines had appeared between her brows. "Not the main course," she said briskly, sending Anya a speculative look that Anya couldn't begin to decipher. "Just something to take the edge off."

The girls let out a collective sigh of disappointment, but Anya's stomach tumbled in dismay. For all his protestations of wanting only her, it seemed Lord Mowbray was prepared to accept the ministrations of any female after all. She told herself she wasn't disappointed.

Charlotte turned to the brunette on her right. The girl had the most captivating mouth Anya had ever seen, with pouting lips and a fetching beauty mark on one cheek.

"Nan, you're best with your hands. You go."

The rest of the girls started to protest, but Nan looked like she'd been handed the keys to paradise. Anya quashed a sudden twinge of—jealousy? Surely not. She had no desire to do *that* to a man. The whole thing had sounded quite disgusting when the girls had first described it to her in the spirit of "broadening her education."

But the question of what Sebastien Wolff might look

like, naked, *aroused*, intruded upon her brain and refused to leave. What might have happened if she'd said yes?

Impatient with herself, she waved her gloves at Charlotte over the heads of the fluttering horde. "I'll see you tomorrow, Charlotte!"

She heaved a sigh of relief as she trotted up the back stairs to her own apartment. Her lips were still tingling, her blood pounding in her ears.

So. She'd met Sebastien Wolff. *Kissed* Sebastien Wolff. It had been wonderful. Extraordinary. But one thing was very clear: she must never encounter him again.

Chapter 7.

A week after her unsettling encounter with Wolff, Anya slipped into the library of his great-aunt, the Dowager Duchess of Winwick.

"Oh, there you are, Anya," the duchess said, glancing up from her seat at a handsome rosewood writing desk. "I have a present for you." She indicated a large, leather-bound book in front of her. "It's a collection of Russian fairy tales. Just look at these marvelous illustrations!"

Anya crossed to the desk. A lump of emotion balled in her chest at the bittersweet pleasure of seeing her native language. Cyrillic was such a beautiful alphabet. She stroked her finger over a gilt-enhanced picture of a golden prince in a garden with a flame-colored bird perched in an apple tree. It was as richly decorated as a medieval manuscript.

"Thank you," she stammered. "I don't know what to say. It's wonderful."

"The whole thing's in Russian," the dowager said, with

a glint of challenge in her eye. "I got it from a rare book dealer on Publisher's Row. I thought you could translate it into English, and I'll have it printed and bound. I like the idea of being a literary patron. We'll make a special edition and I'll give copies to all my friends."

"I think that's a wonderful idea."

The dowager nodded. "I thought of it last week, at the Russian ambassador's reception." She gave a dismissive sniff. "Much as I hate to disparage your fellow countrymen, the food was rather inferior. And Dorothea Lieven is the most dreadful gossip alive. She wants to know everything about everyone. You should have seen the way she was clinging to Lord Castlereagh. Like a vine over a trellis."

Anya hid a smile. The newspapers and caricaturists often lampooned the ambassador for having a wife far more skilled at maintaining diplomatic relations than himself.

"A whole bunch of your countrymen were there, in fact," the duchess said. "Tsar Alexander's sent some kind of trade delegation. I'd be surprised if you didn't know some of them."

She sent Anya a quizzical look that was supposed to be innocent, but fooled Anya not a bit. The dowager was fishing for any hint of scandal.

"One chap was particularly popular with the ladies," the duchess said with studied casualness. "A war hero, so they say. Count Petrov, his name was."

Anya felt the blood drain from her face. "What?"

The duchess was watching her closely, a shrewd gleam in her eye. "He's been telling a fantastical story. Says he's searching for his missing fiancée who disappeared just after he proposed. No ransom note was ever received, but he firmly believes she was kidnapped and brought here, to England. He's been looking for her for months.

He's never given up hope that she'll be found alive. Isn't that romantic?"

"No!" Anya practically shouted.

The dowager gave a self-satisfied nod, as if her suspicions had been confirmed, and Anya cursed inwardly. She might have known she wouldn't be able to keep the story from the duchess indefinitely.

"He says he doesn't care if she's been ruined by her captors," the duchess said mildly. "His love for her will forgive any slight. He'll marry her even if she's ruined."

Anya couldn't keep silent. Blood was pounding in her temples. She grasped the surge of anger, since it was preferable to the icy shards of fear that had pieced her on hearing Vasili was here, in London.

"*He* will forgive any slight? It's not *his* honor that's in question! It's the woman's right to forgive—or not to forgive—as she sees fit." She thumped her palm on the leather tabletop. "This is what I hate about 'polite society.' If a woman is taken against her will, she's ruined. If she gives herself to a man *willingly*, before marriage, she's ruined. Yet no one expects a *man* to go to his marriage bed untouched. It's such a double standard!"

"Bravo!" The dowager chuckled. "And I quite agree. Society's full of such inequalities and ridiculous expectations. If Count Petrov's fiancée disappeared, I'm sure there's a far more reasonable explanation than kidnapping. Perhaps she didn't really want to marry him?" She studied Anya's burning cheeks. "In fact, I think that's *exactly* what happened."

Anya met her gaze and felt resistance bleeding out of her.

"We've become friends over the past months, have we not?" the duchess said softly.

"Yes, ma'am. And I have been extremely grateful for your kindness toward me."

The dowager snorted. "Oh, pish. It's hardly kindness to enjoy the company of an intelligent young woman. Most girls in the *ton* are vapid, well-bred twits. I get far more from you than you get from me. And you can trust me to keep your secrets, child. You *are* Petrov's missing fiancée, are you not? The Princess Denisova?"

Anya sighed. "I am the princess, or, at least, I *was,* but I am *not* Petrov's fiancée. He wanted to marry me, and I refused. On several occasions. He did not take the rejection well."

"Men rarely do." The dowager's expression darkened. "Did he hurt you, child?"

"He would have done, if Elizaveta hadn't hit him with a vase. I tried to make it look as though I'd killed myself. We escaped Paris and came here. I hoped he'd forget all about me."

"Apparently not," the duchess said grimly. "What a tangle. I take it he's the reason you never wanted to attend any society gatherings with me?"

"Yes."

"Well, he's here now, whether by luck or design." A mischievous twinkle appeared in her dark eyes. "Do you know, I've grown quite tired of the *ton* lately. So exhausting. I need a little time in the country, to rusticate. You can keep me company." She closed the book of fairy tales with a decisive thump. "Bring this along. It's much quieter at Everleigh. You'll be better able to concentrate."

Anya reached down and gave the dowager an impulsive hug.

The older woman stiffened in surprise, then returned the gesture with an affectionate chuckle. "There, there. It will be all right. Do you recall my youngest nephew, Sebastien?"

Anya straightened in alarm. *Recall him?* She hadn't stopped thinking about him for the past week. That kiss had been the stuff of epic fantasy and fevered, confusing dreams.

She'd finally asked Charlotte what had happened after she'd left the brothel. To her surprise, instead of taking Nan upstairs, Lord Mowbray had made his excuses and left.

She shouldn't have felt relief. The man was a stranger. A healthy, single male, fully within his rights to sate his physical needs wherever he chose. She shouldn't care who or what he did.

But part of her was glad.

"I don't believe you've ever met him," the duchess said, oblivious to Anya's inattention. "Nor his older brother, Geoffrey. He's heir to the dukedom, of course, but a bit of a stick in the mud. Sebastien's my favorite. He's an utter rogue, but always willing to help. I'll ask him to accompany us to Everleigh as an outrider, for extra protection."

"Oh, I'm sure that won't be necessary!" Anya said quickly. "I'm sure he's very busy. Didn't you tell me he owns a gambling club?"

"He does, indeed." The dowager nodded, a hint of pride in her expression. "And he's made a damn fine go of it too. I expect you're right, however. He *is* very busy. Perhaps he can suggest a couple of burly young men instead? It doesn't hurt to be sensible."

Anya's shoulders sank in relief. The thought seeing Sebastien Wolff again was . . . unsettling.

"How long do you need to get packed?"

"An hour or so. And I would like to say goodbye to Elizaveta. She finishes work at four."

"She's welcome to come too. Everleigh has twenty-two bedrooms."

Anya shook her head. "She wouldn't want to leave her

employment. Or her beau. I think she'll be glad of the space."

The dowager nodded in understanding.

A weary sense of déjà-vu gnawed at Anya as she walked back toward Covent Garden. Going to the country was a sensible precaution, but she hated the thought of running away. It felt like cowardice. The fact that she needed to hide from Petrov *yet again* made her blood boil with impotent frustration.

She kicked a flurry of leaves with her boot, startling a nearby pigeon. If she were a man, she'd have faced Petrov long ago on a dueling field. She'd have made him pay for his treatment of her, and for his treachery. Justice would have been served.

As a woman, she had no such recourse, nor did she have a male champion to stand on her behalf. How many more times would she have to disrupt her life to escape men like Vasili Petrov?

Chapter 8.

Benedict poured two generous tumblers of brandy and held them out. Alex nodded his thanks, but Seb barely roused from his gloomy contemplation of the fire.

"Alex, do you have any idea why our friend is frowning at my fireplace as if he wants to tear it apart?" Benedict poured himself a glass of amber liquid. "Did someone disparage the cut of his coat? Malign his cravat?"

Alex snorted in amusement. "It's even worse than that, I'm afraid. The end of days is upon us. Seb's finally met a woman who could resist him."

"You don't say?" Benedict slid sideways into his own leather wingback and hooked one knee over the armrest. "Tell me more."

Seb shot them a disgruntled glare. They sat like two hefty, irritatingly good-looking bookends on either side of him. "Oh, bugger off."

"That's what *she* said, I gather." Benedict snickered. "Only rather more politely. Where did he meet this miracle?"

"At Haye's," Alex supplied. "Last week. Seb tried to engage her 'services,' but it turns out the woman was only a visitor, and not one of Haye's infamous girls. Neither the prospect of five hundred pounds nor Seb's devastating good looks could sway her."

Ben opened his eyes wide in feigned astonishment. "But who could resist all that manly glowering? And the brooding. No one does dark and brooding like our Seb. Not even Byron." He pursed his lips as he tried not to laugh. "She must have been blind as well as simple, Seb. You had a lucky escape."

Seb sent him a poisonous glare. "Will you shut up, before I throw you out the window?"

"You can't." Ben chuckled. "This is my house. It would be unforgivably rude. And Georgie would kill you. She's very much against defenestration. Especially when it involves her husband."

"She'd forgive me. Eventually," Seb said darkly.

Benedict laughed, uncowed. "Does this mystery lady have a name?"

"Anna Brown. Although if that's her real name, I'm the fat Prince of Wales. She had a foreign accent, French mixed with something else. She certainly wasn't English."

The name Anna Brown was all wrong for her, Seb thought crossly. It conjured images of a dull, dried-up spinster, not a luscious blue-eyed beauty whose every gaze was a challenge and whose body called to his in the most sinful of ways.

"He's been looking for her all week," Alex continued, clearly relishing Seb's discomfort. "And as you can tell from his expression, he's had no luck."

"It's as if she's disappeared into thin air," Seb grumbled. "I asked the girls at the brothel, but none of them would tell me anything."

No amount of bribery had worked, and in truth, he'd been astonished by their loyalty. He'd offered life-changing sums, but none of them had talked and they'd earned his grudging respect. In his experience, most people had a price at which they'd conveniently discard their morals and their so-called allies. But the whores had protected Miss Brown with silence.

She'd clearly earned their trust and affection. From his years in the army, he knew that inspiring such devotion was no small accomplishment.

It was difficult to find someone in a city with over a million inhabitants, but not impossible. When asking at Haye's had failed, he'd enlisted his Bow Street resources and his contacts in London's criminal underworld, confident they would succeed in unearthing "Miss Brown's" true identity and location in no time.

They'd failed.

"We're supposed to be the finest bloody investigators in England," Seb growled to nobody in particular. "Our network of informants stretches from Land's End to John o' Groats. How can one small, extremely distinctive woman evade us? It beggars belief."

Benedict took a slow sip of his brandy. "Why are you still looking for her, if she refused you? There are plenty more fish in the sea."

Seb took a gulp from his own tumbler and tried to find words that wouldn't make him sound like a raving lunatic. He could barely explain it to himself.

"There was just . . . something about her. I don't know. She's a mystery. An enigma. I want to know why she turned me down. I hate it when a case remains unsolved."

Alex and Ben shared a knowing look that immediately raised his hackles. He finished his drink and crossed to the sideboard for a refill.

When he'd first seen Anna Brown at Haye's, he'd almost lost the power of speech. He'd seen hundreds of beautiful women, had slept with plenty of them over the years, but none of them had made the world stand still, as she'd done that evening. He'd felt a gut punch of recognition, of connection. Which was clearly impossible, because they'd never met before. And yet his every sense had reached out, seeking her, wanting her. Byron, or Shelley, or another of those overly dramatic poets would have said his soul called out to hers, or something equally nauseating. Still, it had been the strongest reaction he'd felt for anything or anyone in a very long time, and he wanted to explore it further.

"Maybe she just didn't like the look of you?" Benedict gave a wicked chuckle.

Seb eyed the window longingly. He'd pay Georgie for the repairs. "She was interested," he growled.

He knew how to read women. He'd seen the answering spark of interest, of fascination in her eyes. Her enthusiastic reaction to his kiss hadn't been feigned either. He was sure that if they hadn't been interrupted, he could have kissed away her reservations, taken her upstairs, and enjoyed several delightful hours making love to her. Both of them would have left the encounter sated and content. He knew how to please his partners. It was a matter of personal pride. Now things were left unfinished between them and it . . . bothered him.

"Maybe she's happily married?" Alex said.

Seb shook his head. "She wasn't wearing a wedding band. And she didn't know how to kiss."

He'd found her artless enthusiasm utterly delightful.

Ben and Alex shared another raised-eyebrow look at the revelation that he'd kissed her.

"A widow, then?"

"Wouldn't have been introduced as *Miss* Brown," Seb finished.

They all sat in contemplative silence for a moment.

"I should have offered more," Seb muttered.

Alex let out a sigh. "There you go, thinking money can solve every problem."

"It usually does. Admit it. Life's a great deal easier now that the three of us have it."

"So cynical," Alex tutted.

"She's not the *only* woman who ever turned him down," Benedict said suddenly. "Don't you remember, Alex? There was that girl, years ago, when we'd just come down from university? What was her name? The silly one with black hair. From Norfolk."

"Julia Cowes," Seb supplied wearily.

Trust Benedict to drag up that sorry farce. He'd been all of nineteen, young and relatively innocent, intoxicated by his first taste of London and foolishly convinced he was in love. He'd quickly learned his lesson.

Alex snapped his fingers. "That was it! The fair Julia. At one point I thought you were on the verge of asking for her hand."

"Her hand wasn't the only thing she wanted to give me," Seb said dryly. "It was also her father's crippling mortgages and her brother's impressive gambling debts. As soon as she found out I was only a second son, untitled, and penniless to boot, she dropped me like a hot brick. I thank her for showing me just how mercenary the ladies of the *ton* can be."

"A salutary lesson," Alex murmured.

"She came to see me last month, actually," Seb said. "She married old Skeffington while we were away in Portugal."

Benedict frowned. "Isn't he at least sixty?"

"He is. But as rich as Midas, which made him an attractive prospect, at least financially. Julia thought I'd be interested in an affair, seeing as her husband was so often away from home."

Benedict rolled his eyes. "Please tell me you refused."

"Of course. No married women, ever."

"I'd never cheat on Emmy," Alex said fervently.

"And I wouldn't cheat on Georgie," Benedict added. "And not only because she'd have me shipped off to the Arctic if I were unfaithful. I don't *want* to sleep with anyone but her."

Sebastien shook his head, pretending to be disgusted by their post-marriage monogamy.

In truth, Ben and Alex's marriages were two of the few happy ones he'd ever encountered. They'd both been fortunate enough to make a love match. They not only desired their partners in a physical sense, but they'd also found an inner compatibility that bound them together, one of shared humor and values.

Seb's own family was the antithesis of that, a sordid tangle of infidelity and scandal. It was the worst kept secret in the *ton* that his father hadn't been married to his mother at the time of his conception. The duke's first wife, Lady Sarah, had died giving birth to his older half-brother Geoffrey. Seb was the result of an affair the duke had had with a volatile Italian Contessa, Maria Wolff, herself already a young widow.

When Lady Sarah had died, the duke had promptly married the already pregnant Maria to legitimize his son and ensure he had a "spare," in case Geoffrey proved as sickly as his mother.

The marriage had not proved a happy one. Seb's mother had been far too spirited to be content to stay in the country seat and play duchess. She'd returned to

London and taken a series of lovers, and the duke had remained in the country and continued his rakish ways with a steady succession of ever-younger actresses and courtesans.

Seb's mother had died of smallpox when he was eight, and his father had vowed never to remarry. Women, he declared, just weren't worth the bother. In a perverse show of solidarity for his spirited mother—and a desire to distance himself from his domineering father—Seb had adopted the surname Wolff at school and used it ever since.

It was no wonder his views on the subject of marriage were jaundiced.

"I suppose it's not surprising that you thought Miss Brown would take your five hundred pounds," Alex mused, almost as if he'd followed the direction of Seb's thoughts. "Julia would have jumped at the chance. So would most women, in fact."

"Which makes me wonder why Miss Brown said no." Seb frowned. "She didn't look particularly well-off. Her dress was decent quality, but several seasons old. And she wasn't wearing any jewelry."

"There's only one explanation," Benedict said. "If she's not already married or a widow, she must be a virgin, holding out for a respectable offer."

Seb's stomach twisted. Surely fate wouldn't be *that* cruel.

"What was she doing in a brothel, then?" he demanded. "No respectable single woman would be on friendly terms with an infamous madam and a gaggle full of lightskirts. It doesn't make any sense."

The mystery of the whole situation plagued him. Not only why the elusive Miss Brown had refused him, but why he, in turn, had refused the undeniably lovely alternative Mrs. Haye had offered him that evening. He'd lost all interest in other women.

It was damned irritating. Where the hell had she gone?

"Enough about Seb's love life, or lack of one," Alex said. "Any news on the Russians and our potential spy?"

Benedict shook his head. "Georgie and I attended the Lievens' reception the other night and met most of the Russian delegation, including Prince Trubetskoi. I invited him to the Tricorn for a few rounds of cards, so we'll see if he takes me up on the offer."

Seb shrugged. "And I haven't had any luck finding out what crest was inscribed on that ring we took from the dead man at the docks. I'll keep trying."

"The Dread Dowager Duchess was at the Lievens'," Ben added with a smile. "She said you hadn't visited her in an age."

Seb grunted. "That's not true! I had supper with her only last week. And besides, she mentioned something about going to Everleigh for a week or two." He clapped his hand to his forehead in sudden recollection. "Oh, hell! She asked me to lend her a couple of men to escort her down to Oxfordshire. I completely forgot." He glanced over at the clock.

"When?" Ben asked.

"Today."

"Oh dear." Alex chuckled. "Someone's going to get a dressing down."

Seb stood and tossed back the remnants of his brandy. "Bugger. It's too late to ask anyone else. I'll have to go myself."

The *ton* called his great-aunt the Dread Dowager Duchess with good reason, but the old battle-ax was one of his few family members he actually *liked*. He'd feel dreadful if anything happened to her. And a promise was a promise, after all. He might be all kinds of scoundrel, but he always kept his word.

Ben peered out of the window. "It looks like rain," he said with an infuriating smile. "Have fun."

Seb sent him an obscene hand gesture that had endured since the Battle of Agincourt and cursed his own sense of familial duty in three different languages.

Chapter 9.

Anya slipped through the bustling flower market, still brooding. It was sheer luck that she glanced up and saw the tall figure descending the front steps of Haye's. Male callers were commonplace at any time of the day or night, but there was something about the flash of pale hair and the size of the man that sent a prickle of warning down her spine.

She ducked behind a flower seller's stand. The overpowering scent of rotting flower water and overblown hyacinths filled her nose as she peered around a bucket of tulips.

Another glimpse confirmed her worst fears; Vasili Petrov paused on the pavement, his forehead furrowed in an expression of frustration. As she watched, he replaced his hat, wrinkled his nose in distaste at a ragged posy seller on the corner, and set off toward St. James's with long, purposeful strides.

Anya took a deep, calming breath and willed her hands to stop shaking. She felt vaguely sick. Good God!

If she'd walked a little faster, if she hadn't paused to admire that bonnet in the window on Bond Street, she'd have run right into him.

What was he doing in Covent Garden? Was it mere coincidence that had brought him almost to her doorstep? Or something more sinister?

Thoroughly rattled, she knocked on Charlotte's door.

"That man," she said without preamble. "The blond one who just left."

Charlotte's rosebud mouth pursed in anger. "Count Petrov? One of your countrymen, I believe. He'll not be allowed back, I assure you."

Anya's stomach gave a somersault of dread. "Why? What did he do?"

"He asked if I had any Russian girls, but I told him no. He settled on Tess, but after only a few minutes, she came running back downstairs saying he'd slapped her. He said she wanted it rough, and he got carried away, but Tess says she never agreed to that. I told him to leave." Charlotte frowned. "Do you know him?"

"I know he had a bad reputation with women back in St. Petersburg," Anya said with perfect truth, deftly dodging the direct question. "I'm glad you told him he wasn't welcome."

She forced a breezy smile to her lips and pretended to dismiss the subject of her boorish countryman—as if he wasn't the very reason she was being forced to leave.

"I came to tell you I'm going to spend some time in the country with the dowager duchess. A few weeks, I expect. Will you keep an eye on Elizaveta for me? I don't like the thought of her staying in the apartment alone."

Charlotte's face softened into a smile. "Of course I will. Don't worry about her. And I doubt she'll be spending too much time alone, with that lawyer of hers to keep her company." Charlotte's arch smile indicated she approved of that particular liaison.

"Thank you," Anna breathed. "Now, I must go and pack. The dowager wants to leave right away. Tell Tess to keep practicing her reading!"

As she mounted the stairs to her own apartment, Anya's stomach still churned at the uncomfortably close call. The fact that Petrov was in Covent Garden and looking for Russian girls didn't bode well. Had he somehow picked up her scent?

She packed a small travelling bag, noting with detached amusement that she could now fit everything she needed into one small receptacle. When she'd travelled from St. Petersburg to Paris, she'd had at least fifteen trunks of various clothes, shoes, and other accessories. Sometimes she missed having such a frivolous, expensive wardrobe, but she was also proud of the way she'd learned to economize since coming to London. She'd become adept at haggling with the market traders for the best price, at wearing her dresses for more than one paltry season.

When Elizaveta finally returned, she told her about Petrov's unexpected appearance.

"What a dreadful coincidence!" Elizaveta murmured, aghast. "Imagine if he'd seen you."

Anya nodded. "Far too close for comfort. Which is why I'm going with the dowager to Oxfordshire. No chance of accidentally running into him there."

"Do you want me to come? I'm sure I could ask work if—"

"No need. I doubt Petrov would recognize you, even if he saw you. And I know how much you're enjoying Oliver's company." Anya laughed at Elizaveta's furious blush and gave her a fond hug. "It'll be deadly dull, I promise. No plays, no noisy operas. You'll have much more fun here." She leaned back and fixed her friend with a serious stare. "But please, be careful. We both know what he's capable of."

Elizaveta nodded. "You too, my love."

Anya kept a sharp lookout for Vasili, or anyone else, following her, as she walked the half mile back to Grosvenor Square, but detected nothing out of the ordinary. She found the dowager ready to leave.

"You look worried, child. Whatever is the matter?" The dowager's eyes were as shrewd and as inquiring as a raven's.

"Count Petrov was in Covent Garden. He was asking questions of my neighbor, Mrs. Haye. I'm worried that he's somehow discovered where I live."

The dowager rose to her feet with the aid of her favorite silver-topped walking cane. "I can't see how he would have managed that, my dear. But I say it's a good thing we're headed into the country, hmm? Better safe than sorry."

Anya nodded. "Are you sure you still want to go? I don't want to put you in any danger."

The dowager snorted. "Oh, pish. A bit of danger would add a welcome dash of excitement to my life, let me tell you." She nodded to Mellors, her stone-faced majordomo, as he opened the door and helped her into the waiting carriage. "Thank you, Mellors. Now come along, Miss Brown."

English carriages were not at all like Russian troikas. For one thing, they were completely enclosed. Anya climbed up into the luxuriously appointed interior and smiled in delight. Her luggage, what little of it there was, had been stowed in the exterior box by the duchess's burly coachman, John.

The sky promised snow, or at the very least rain. The duchess drew a fur-lined travel rug across her lap and leaned back against the velvet seat. Anya placed her feet on the warm brick on the floor and tugged the edges of her favorite Russian travelling cloak around her. It was the one she'd bought in Paris, hemmed with diamonds; pale blue wool edged with white ermine and embellished with silver thread. Elizaveta always joked that it made her look like the fictional Russian Snow Princess, Snegurochka, the daughter of Winter himself.

"Ready, yer ladyship?" John the coachman called down.

"One moment!" Anya replied.

The dowager raised her brows in inquiry, and Anya sent her an apologetic smile. "It is a Russian superstition. We must observe a moment of silence to ensure a safe trip."

The dowager chuckled. "What wonderfully strange customs you have, my dear. What good does a minute of silence do? I suppose it might offer the chance to remember all the things we've forgotten to pack."

Anya laughed. "I'm not sure, but everyone does it."

"Very well, let us have our minute of silence. Heaven forbid we get stuck in a thunderstorm."

The bustle of Grosvenor Square continued outside as the two of them sat quietly for a brief moment.

"There. That should suffice." The duchess frowned. "No sign of any outriders. I did mention it to Sebastien, but the wretch must have forgotten. Never mind. John has a blunderbuss under his seat." She rapped smartly on the carriage roof with her walking cane. "Onward!"

They lumbered out of the mews and into Grosvenor Square, with its well-tended central garden lined with smart black-painted railings. Each resident of the stately houses which faced the square had a key to unlock the private gate and gain access to the garden.

The carriage soon turned onto Park Lane, then headed

west toward the Knightsbridge turnpike. Buildings gave way to fields and trees and a chill wind blew through the cracks between the door and window.

The dowager's country estate lay several hours' drive to the west of London. Anya watched the changing landscape with interest. When she and Elizaveta had crossed from Belgium and made their way to London last year, they'd been too tired and worried to take note of the scenery. And since arriving, they hadn't had enough money to venture from the capital.

A flock of sheep clustered together to shelter from the wind. Perhaps winter was coming early this year? Charlotte had said that England didn't experience such impressive snowfall as Russia, but Anya liked being warm, so that didn't bother her at all.

The idea that she might never return to her native land elicited a brief, wistful pang of homesickness. She quashed it. She'd made the right decision. However difficult life was here, however reduced their circumstances, she and Elizaveta were safe.

Or at least, they had been. Was Vasili's presence in London merely coincidental? Or had he received some clue that she was hiding here? Anya shivered at the possibility. She was glad to be leaving London.

They passed Hammersmith, then a public house called the Dog and Duck and rumbled onto the vast, lonely stretch of moorland known as Hounslow Heath. The sky had grown steadily darker, bringing a gloom to the landscape that matched Anya's brooding thoughts.

She sent a fond glance over at the dowager, who had fallen asleep, her head propped against the corner of the padded seat, her mouth slightly open in repose.

It began to rain, and Anya cursed quietly. Russians believed that rain on the day of your trip was good luck, but muddy roads would make the journey even slower.

The clouds seemed to have come down almost to the ground; they formed a mist that made it difficult to see.

A cry of alarm sounded from above. A crack like thunder rent the air, and the carriage gave a sharp jolt. The horses reared in the traces, whinnying in distress, and the dowager jerked awake with a start. Anya grabbed the leather strap by the window to steady herself as the carriage lurched and rocked on its springs.

She squinted through the rain-spattered window and saw three men on horseback burst from the trees and thunder down the hill toward them. Her heart seized in fright. All three of them were wearing hats pulled down low, with scarves tied over their faces to disguise their identity. Each one carried a firearm.

John's blunderbuss discharged above them with a deafening roar.

"What on earth is going on?" the dowager demanded.

"Footpads, ma'am," shouted the coachman. Metal clicked as he struggled to reload. "Three o' the devils, coming down fast." Another shot rang out, this time from the brigands, and a sound like gravel flung against the carriage panels made Anya duck instinctively. John cursed. "Hit, b'gad!"

"Good heavens!" the dowager cried. "John, are you shot?"

"Aye, ma'am! But 'tis only me arm. I'm—"

The three assailants were upon them before he could say more.

"Stand and deliver!" the nearest one bellowed, wheeling his horse. His two companions positioned themselves on the opposite side of the coach, their weapons at the ready.

The dowager stiffened in outrage. "Well, *really!*"

Anya's heart was thundering, but she almost smiled at the older woman's disgruntled tone. The dowager gave an irritated sigh, as if being held up on the King's Highway was a regular inconvenience. She reached down between the cushions and pulled out a small drawstring purse. "So much for your minute of silence, my girl. Highwaymen! Don't worry. I keep a small amount of silver for just such an eventuality. Pull down the window."

An icy blast of rain splattered Anya's face as she slid down the glass. The dowager tossed the purse out of the window, where it landed with a dull chink in front of the hooves of the leader's mount.

"There," she called out crossly. "There was no reason to injure my coachman, you brute."

While the other two robbers kept their weapons trained on the coach, the leader dismounted and scooped up the purse. He weighed it in his hand, silently assessing its value, then slipped it into the folds of his dirty brown jacket.

The dowager spoke again. "Now, I'm sure you fine gentlemen have homes to go to, and I very much dislike being kept out here in the cold. Move aside."

Anya held her breath, hoping the ordeal was over, but the leader shook his head.

"No. Out of the coach."

Anya frowned. The man's voice was thick, his vowels slurred. Was he drunk? A cold shiver of fear slid down her spine. Get out? That wasn't usual, was it? Surely robbery was *all* these ruffians had in mind and nothing worse?

"Get down? We'll do no such thing!" the dowager said imperiously. "It's raining."

Anya gasped as the door was wrenched open.

"I said, get out!" The man reached in and grabbed her by the arm. She reared back, struggling.

"Unhand her!" The duchess took a swing at the man

with her cane, but it was no use; Anya was pulled clear from the carriage. She half fell onto the road and gave a gasp of pain as her ankle twisted beneath her. Her foot slipped in an icy puddle.

"This her?" the leader rasped, glancing over at the other two riders as if for confirmation. He caught the hood of her cape and tugged it back to expose her face and hair. Confused, Anya glanced up at the nearest man, but all she could see was a pair of pale eyes between hat brim and scarf. The eyes narrowed on her face, and he nodded briefly.

"Da. Is her. We go."

Anya's stomach plummeted as she placed the man's accent. Russian. These weren't footpads. They were *kidnappers*. How in God's name had Vasili known where to find her?

"Come on, then! Take her."

The leader tugged Anya to her feet and thrust her toward the second man. She began to fight in earnest. She swung her fist and made contact with her captor's jaw. He cursed and stumbled back, and she pressed the advantage, clawing at his face. His scarf fell away, revealing a swarthy, ugly face she'd never seen before.

He gave her a shake that made her teeth rattle in her skull. "Stop, woman!"

The mounted Russian reached down to pull her up onto his horse, but they were interrupted by the third man's warning growl.

"Quick! Someone comes. A rider!"

The relentless beat of hooves reached Anya's ears and a thrill of hope tightened her chest. She squinted back down the road.

A black horse came thundering around the bend, its mane and tail flying. The rider was a dark shape hunched low over the horse's neck. His greatcoat streamed behind him like wings, like some hell-sent rider of the apocalypse. Anya's breath caught in her throat.

The rider straightened in the saddle; he had a rifle in is hand. Surely he wasn't going to try to shoot from a moving horse? No sooner had the thought formed than Anya saw him take aim—straight toward her—and her heart lurched to a stop.

The man next to her cursed. She heard a crack and saw a puff of smoke rise from the rider's weapon. The hold on her arm slackened, and she turned to find her captor sprawled on the ground at her feet, his eyes wide and staring. A red trickle of blood seeped from the hole in his chest into the muddy puddle next to him.

One of the mounted brigands fired his weapon, and the leader's loose horse bolted away down the road. The approaching rider ducked and fired again, from a second gun, and the Russian slumped dead in the saddle. His mount reared, confused by the suddenly unresponsive weight on its back, and the body slipped sideways. The terrified horse raced for the trees, but the corpse's foot was still caught in the stirrup; it bounced along, caught by the leg, as it went.

Anya could barely comprehend what she was seeing. She glanced up at the third and final footpad. His scarf had fallen from his face, and she got a good look at his features. With a harsh shout, he kicked his heels to his horse's sides and thundered off up the hill after his fallen brethren.

Anya turned—and suppressed a scream as her savior's enormous horse clattered to a stop directly in front of her. It reared, pawing the air, almost threatening to trample her, but the rider kept his seat with consummate skill, and she felt a surge of admiration. As a horsewoman herself, she knew the strength it took to control such a gigantic beast.

She peered up at the rider, her heart pounding, trying to see the man who'd come to her rescue, but he was silhouetted against the grey sky and rain obscured her vision. Then, the dry voice of the dowager came echoing from the interior of the coach.

"Well, Sebastien. That was *quite* the entrance. Still, better late than never."

Chapter 10.

Seb's heart thundered against his ribs as he brought his lathered mount under control.

What the bloody hell had his great-aunt got herself into now?

He'd spurred Eclipse into the fray without a thought. After so many years in the Rifles, it had been second nature to ride toward the enemy when shots had been fired, and he'd dealt with the footpads swiftly and efficiently. He was only sorry he hadn't been able to reload his Baker quickly enough to finish off the third man.

He glanced up at his aunt's coachman, who was in the process of tying a handkerchief around his bleeding forearm.

"You were hit, John? How badly are you hurt?"

"Nothing too bad, milor'. Just a few pebbles o' shot. Good thing them rascals had fowling pieces and not rifles like yersel'. They ain't half so accurate." He sent Seb a wide grin of admiration. "That were some fine shootin', sir, from a movin' horse."

Seb sent him an answering smile. "Well, I should hope so. I spent three years in His Majesty's Rifles. Never thought I'd need the skill in England, though."

Reassured that the coachman wasn't seriously injured, he turned his attention downward. Dorothea was peering out of the carriage with a faintly amused expression, but it was the woman standing beside the carriage, the one in the pale blue cloak, who caught Seb's attention. Recognition, swift and hot, speared through him.

It was *her*! The woman from the brothel. What in God's name was *she* doing sharing a carriage with his great-aunt?

"You!" He wrenched his gaze from her shocked face and glared at Dorothea. "What the hell is going on?"

The dowager sent him a congratulatory smile. "I'm so glad you arrived, Sebastien. That was impeccable timing. It was a shame you had to kill them, however."

He glanced at the corpse on the roadside. "They were footpads. They would have hung anyway. This way was quicker."

The dowager's brows twitched. "True, but we can't question dead men."

"Why would you want to?"

"They weren't merely thieves. They were kidnappers."

Seb frowned. "Why would anyone want to kidnap you?"

"I'll have you know, I'm an extremely desirable target," the dowager said with mock offence. "But it wasn't me they were after." She glanced over at the woman in the road. "It was her."

Seb turned back to the beauty in front of him.

"I don't think you two have met," the dowager said. "Anna, this is my great-nephew, Sebastien. He's the Earl of Mowbray. Bastien, this is Anna Brown. My companion."

"Anna Brown?" Seb repeated scornfully.

"That's right," the girl said stiffly. There was a hint of something in her eyes, a flash of challenge that made his pulse pound in response.

"And Miss Brown is your companion, you say?"

The dowager glared at him. "Yes. Haven't I just said so? She's been with me for almost a year. What of it?"

"You're being gulled." He narrowed his eyes and subjected the girl to a slow, deliberate inspection from head to toe.

She straightened her spine and sent him a haughty look, despite the fact that she was spattered with mud and her hair was in wild disarray. She was several inches shorter than himself—and he was still astride Eclipse—yet she somehow still managed to look down her nose at him.

God, she was as striking as he remembered.

Thanks to her, he'd endured a week of self-imposed celibacy and a succession of ridiculously erotic dreams. Several times he'd actually awoken in the throes of a climax—something he hadn't done since he was a randy, under-sexed youth. Now, against all logic, the object of his heated fantasies was here. Standing in front of him in the middle of Hounslow Heath, looking shocked, bedraggled, and still—impossibly—gorgeous.

Seb pinned her with a hard stare.

Her blue eyes were framed by lashes a few shades darker than her honey-colored hair. The thick coils were askew from her struggle, falling down around her face, and her skin was pale except for a slight flush on her cheekbones, pink roses against snow.

His cock twitched, but her beauty only served to annoy him. She was clearly not what she seemed.

"She's not a companion," he said bluntly. "She's a—" He paused, unsure of the phrase he sought. "An impostor," he finished. "Have you checked your jewelry box recently? I wouldn't be at all surprised to find she's been robbing you blind."

No wonder she hadn't wanted his money back at Haye's. She was probably pilfering things from his great-aunt.

The beauty gasped in outrage. "How dare you? I would *never*—"

The duchess burst out laughing. "Oh no! Sebastien, you're quite mistaken. Anna would never steal from me. Come, why are you being so disagreeable?"

"It's obvious. She's trying to wheedle her way into your good graces, to gain your trust."

"That's absolute codswallop," the duchess said in a tone that brooked no argument. She glanced over at the girl and her expression sobered. "She's a young woman in very grave danger."

Seb glared the girl. "Why? Why would anyone want *you*?"

She flinched at his scathing tone, and the two women exchanged a telling, complicit glance. His anger increased. They were hiding something, both of them.

"What's your *real* name?"

The girl gave a resigned huff. "Anya."

"Anya," he echoed, rolling the word around his mouth experimentally. "Excellent. Progress. You're Russian?" That would explain the accent he'd detected back at Haye's. Russian mixed with a hint of French. Intriguing.

"Yes."

"Anya what?"

"My family name's not important."

He raised his brows. "Considering those men were apparently trying to kidnap you, I'd say it was of rather vital importance, wouldn't you?"

She scowled at his sarcasm. "Anya—Ivanov."

He didn't miss her minute hesitation. Ivanov was one

of the most common family names in Russia, the equivalent of Smith or Brown in England. She was *still* lying to him, the little charlatan.

"Who would want to kidnap you? Do you owe someone money?"

"It's nothing like that." The dowager sighed. "Anya used to be personal maid to the Princess Denisova. The princess took her own life in Paris last year, but there are those in St. Petersburg who refuse to believe she's dead. Since poor Anya was a witness to her mistress's final hours, they wish to question her about it."

"So why don't they just call on her?"

"Anya refuses to speak of it, and I fully understand her reluctance to reopen such painful wounds. The Princess Denisova is gone. There's no more to say." The dowager nodded decisively. "I was taking her to Everleigh to escape those who would bedevil and distress her. But it appears they were more determined than we anticipated."

A thoughtful look came into his aunt's face, which gave Seb pause. He'd witnessed that same calculating expression before. It usually preceded Dorothea giving someone a scathing set down or making a startling pronouncement sure to offend.

"Hmm. The more I think about it, the more it makes perfect sense."

"What does?" he asked warily.

"Well, clearly Anya needs more protection than a feeble old woman and a handful of servants can provide at Everleigh. She needs someone used to dealing with rogues and scoundrels. You must protect her, Sebastien. Take her back to the Tricorn with you."

"What? No!" Seb said, at precisely the same moment the girl said, "Absolutely not!"

"I can't let you carry on to Everleigh unescorted," Seb protested.

The dowager waved her hand. "Oh, pish. I can't imagine I'll be held up *twice* in one evening. John is barely hurt, and I have lots of servants to coddle me when I get there." She turned to the girl. "You'll be vulnerable in the country, now they know you're with me. Sebastien is the best there is. You can stay with him, under his protection, until those seeking you give up and go home."

"Now wait just a minute—" Seb said.

The dowager sent him a wide smile, the faux-innocence of which fooled him not a bit. Dorothea was meddling, curse her, and he could only guess at her motives.

She wasn't matchmaking, that was for certain. She wouldn't foist someone of the lower classes at him as a potential wife, however beautiful she might be. Even before he'd been made an earl, he'd been expected to choose some talentless twit from the *ton* if he ever wanted to marry. Which he most assuredly did not.

Did she mean the girl for his mistress? He doubted it. Dorothea seemed genuinely fond of her. He couldn't believe she'd willingly offer her up for ruination. Seb frowned, completely confused.

"You've been on your own at the Tricorn since Alex and Benedict found themselves wives," the duchess continued reasonably. She turned to Anya. "He was only saying the other week how boring it was. You can host her in one of their old suites, Sebastien. You'll barely notice she's there." Her rheumy eyes sparkled with devilry.

"A gentleman's club is no place for a lady."

Since when had he ever been concerned with propriety? Talk about the devil quoting scripture.

"She's not a lady. She's a lady's *companion*. And really, is now the time to be quibbling over social niceties? Our lives were in mortal danger tonight."

Dorothea set her jaw and a militant light came into her eyes. "You wouldn't deny me this one request, Sebastien, would you?"

Ugh. Seb felt himself caught, pinned like an insect on a naturalist's board. He cast around for another argument, but the girl spoke up.

"The men are dead or gone, ma'am. There's no reason for us to change our plans."

"Do you really believe whoever sent them won't try again?" the duchess asked.

The girl shot a panicked glance over at Seb. "But it wouldn't be seemly for us to live under the same roof."

"Who will know? It's not as if you'll be going out together in the *ton*. Indulge me, child. I won't rest easy until the threat to you is gone."

The edge of desperation in the girl's tone made Seb feel a lot better. Indeed, the more he thought about it, the more he realized this was the perfect opportunity to install the defiant chit under his own roof and discover exactly who she was and what she was about. Why was he even arguing?

"On second thoughts, I believe your plan has considerable merit, Dorothea."

The girl looked at him in dawning horror. Seb suppressed a smile.

"I can protect her far better at the Tricorn than at Everleigh."

"No!" She shot a desperate, pleading glance at the duchess. "Who will read the papers to you?"

"Oh, I'll get one of the other servants to do it. And I have plenty of friends to visit in Oxfordshire. I won't be bored."

She beckoned Anya closer to the carriage, and Seb strained to hear their hushed conversation.

"I couldn't live with myself if anything happened to you, my dear. You're the granddaughter I never had."

A suspicious sheen gathered in the dowager's eyes, and Seb blinked in shock because Dorothea rarely allowed herself to exhibit anything as unseemly as emotions.

The girl sighed, then nodded. "As you wish."

She shot a glance of pure dislike at him, as if this were somehow all *his* fault, and his body throbbed in response. Anticipation poured through his veins at the forthcoming challenge. Oh, this was going to be fun.

He maneuvered Eclipse forward. "You'll have to ride with me. Put your foot on mine and give me your hand."

With a huff, she did as he instructed, and he hauled her up to sit sideways in front of him, her legs draped over his thigh. The feel of her slim body in his lap made his head spin. Eclipse sidled sideways in protest at the additional weight, but Seb controlled him easily with a squeeze of his knees.

The fur trim of her cloak tickled his throat as he put his arms around her waist. Her hair whipped across his cheek and the scent of her filled his nose. She smelled delicious, like jasmine and rain, and he suddenly felt like laughing aloud. He felt positively barbaric, like a Viking raider returning home with his prize.

He wheeled them in a wide circle as Dorothea sent them a cheery wave. "Do be careful, my dears. Send word as soon as you can!"

Seb kicked his heels to Eclipse's flanks. The horse started forward and triumph surged through him. Anna Brown, Anya Ivanov—whatever she wanted to call herself—was at his mercy. She was lying to him. And he wouldn't stop until he'd uncovered every secret she was guarding.

Chapter 11.

Anya's head was spinning. How had she ended up galloping back toward London in the arms of this handsome, arrogant stranger? A man who'd dispatched two of his fellows with apparent ease and even less remorse.

She couldn't shake the feeling that she'd been saved from one set of kidnappers only to be snatched away by another. Out of the frying pan and into the fire. And the dowager duchess, her dear friend, had sanctioned it.

No, that was unfair. The dowager hadn't betrayed her secret, not even to her own kin. And there was logic behind the decision to ask Wolff to guard her. The man was a literal hero. He'd received numerous medals for his service during the wars against Napoleon, and his recent ennoblement had, according to the dowager, been awarded for some invaluable service he'd provided for the Prince of Wales.

He certainly knew how to handle a rifle. The skill it must have taken to shoot the man who'd been holding her was astonishing. A wave of nausea rose up as she recalled the blood in the mud. She'd never seen a dead man before.

She was intensely aware of her captor. The wind was bitter, but his arms were strong and his warmth pressed against her side. For a brief moment, she allowed herself to absorb the sensation of simply being held. She hugged women—Elizaveta and Charlotte—all the time, but they were small and soft and sweetly perfumed. Being held in this man's embrace was an entirely different experience. One that was, paradoxically, both comforting and nerve-wracking.

To distract herself from his proximity, she said, "You took a terrible risk shooting that man from horseback. What if I'd moved? You could have killed me, instead."

That would have put an end to Vasili's scheming.

He gave an arrogant snort. "Unlikely. Thanks to Bonaparte, I've had plenty of practice in shooting from that distance. It was a calculated risk."

Anya raised her brows at his supreme confidence, even as a twinge of envy assaulted her. If only she possessed such a deadly talent. Vasili would think twice about threatening her if she could shoot the tassel from his boots at fifty paces. Unfortunately, rifle shooting hadn't been part of her extensive education. She'd never even fired a pistol.

She readjusted her position. It was uncomfortable on his lap, both physically and emotionally. The hood of her cloak had come down; her face was cold, but she could feel the heat of Wolff's breath against her neck. She shivered with an unsettling awareness. Sidesaddle was no way to travel any great distance.

"Stop," she demanded. "This hurts my—it's too uncomfortable."

Wolff reined the horse to a halt. "Giving orders, Miss Brown?" he said dryly. "You've certainly learned to emulate the imperious tones of your employer."

Anya bit back the scathing retort that sprang to her lips. She was supposed to be a servant; she really should try to be more reverential. Even if it pained her.

"I was merely going to suggest that I ride behind you, my lord," she murmured, trying to appear properly chastised.

"You mean astride?" His disdain was clear; *ladies* didn't do that. They didn't raise their skirts above the knee for modesty's sake. Well, damn that. Let him think she came from peasant stock. They could ride much faster if she were behind him, and it would be far more comfortable for the horse.

She lifted her chin. "Yes."

Anya restrained herself from telling him she could probably ride better than he could, skirts or no skirts. She and Dmitri had been taught by a pair of Cossack brothers who were masters of the skill and had once been part of a famous circus act. She'd learned tricks that would put an equestrienne at Astley's Amphitheatre to shame.

With an indifferent shrug, Wolff let her slide to the ground, then swung her up behind him. Her face heated as she hitched her skirts above her knees and settled herself with him between her open thighs. It was an utterly indecent position. Thank God she was wearing thick woolen stockings and that her cloak was long enough to cover most of the exposed leg.

She tugged her hood up to protect her from the rain and with great reluctance looped her arms around his waist. The position drew her front against his back. Not an inch of space separated them. The sensation of his hard muscle against her breasts and stomach made her catch her breath. He was so *big*. So wide and so unmistakably male. There wasn't a soft place on him anywhere.

He tensed at the sudden contact, then caught her hands and repositioned them higher up on the flat plane of his stomach. "Hold on," he said gruffly.

Anya turned her head sideways and rested her cheek against his shoulder. She could feel the play of muscle beneath his clothes as he rocked gently with the horse's gait, could smell the leather of the saddle and a faint masculine cologne rising from his wet greatcoat.

Her stomach gave a little twist. She'd never experienced such immediate attraction to another person in her life. It was highly disconcerting.

They couldn't travel quickly, not with both of them on one horse, and she fell into a kind of dull stupor. The rain didn't so much fall as envelop them in a grey mist. Wolff's body was the only point of warmth in an otherwise frigid world, and she clung to him as to a lifeboat in a tempest.

At long last they left the lonely desolation of the heath and made their way back to civilization. Hamlets gave way to the outskirts of the city, then more populated streets, and eventually she spied the familiar green expanse of Hyde Park.

The Tricorn Club was situated in St. James's Square, only a stone's throw from Anya's tiny apartment in Covent Garden. Anya heard a clock strike midnight as they finally arrived, but the lights and laughter emanating from the front of the club indicated that for the patrons within, the night was still young.

Wolff guided the horse around the back of the building to the private mews where they were greeted by a yawning stable boy. Anya slid easily off the horse without waiting for assistance, keen to put some distance between herself and her "host." His nearness during the journey had been most disturbing. She wasn't sure whether to think of him as a captor or as her savior.

Wolff hardly spared her a glance. She followed him up a set of steps, through a shiny black door, and into what she assumed was the private part of the club.

The faint hum of conversation filtered through the walls, and Anya looked around with interest. She'd never been inside a gentleman's lodgings before. It didn't seem all that mysterious. A tall tiled entranceway gave onto several rooms, but before she could peer inside them, a door at the end of the corridor opened and a giant of a man lumbered into view. He was as broad as a Cossack, with a square jaw and a nose that had clearly been broken more than once.

"Ah, Mickey," Wolff said, greeting the giant with a smile that softened his face and made Anya's heart catch in her throat. "We have a visitor. This is Miss Brown. She's to be our guest for the next—" He glanced at her uncertainly, as if trying to decide on a suitable timeframe. "Few days? Weeks? For an indeterminate stretch of time, let us say."

Anya didn't like that. It sounded like a prison sentence being passed down by a judge.

The giant sent her a friendly nod. "Ma'am."

"She'll be staying in Benedict's old rooms." Wolff shrugged out of his greatcoat. "I trust they're made up?"

"Yes, sir. May I take your cloak, ma'am?"

Anya nodded and allowed the manservant to take it from her.

She was wearing one of the three gowns she owned, the plainest of the ones she'd brought from Paris. After a year of almost constant wear, it was sadly out of style and had faded from the original cheerful lavender to a dreary dishwater-grey. The damp skirts clung to her, and she shivered despite the warmth of the hallway.

"Does the lady have any luggage to bring in?"

Wolff chuckled. "She does not. Miss Brown is that rarest of creatures—a woman who travels without a mountain of luggage." He shot her a laughing glance, and Anya glared at him. She didn't even have a dry change of clothes, curse him.

He seemed impervious to her disapproval. He strode forward and she followed him, peering into the various rooms as they passed. They all appeared to be tastefully and expensively furnished, although with a decidedly masculine flavor. No pastel ruffles or Meissen shepherdesses here. She followed him up a wide, curved staircase and along another corridor. He opened a door into a suite of rooms that contained a desk and chair and a pair of comfortable-looking armchairs grouped in front of an unlit fire. He gestured to an inner doorway. "Bedroom's through there."

Anya was so tired, she barely managed to nod. She had no energy to fight. The warmth of the house seemed to be leeching the strength out of her. She wanted to crawl into bed and sleep for a week.

He stepped back from the door. "If you need anything, I'll be in the rooms next door. We'll talk in the morning. I shall expect you in my study at ten o'clock. Good night."

Anya frowned as she heard the key turn in the lock, then snorted in amusement. He clearly trusted her as little as she trusted him. No matter. For now, she rather appreciated the extra security. Where did he think she would go, anyway? She couldn't risk endangering Elizaveta by returning to Covent Garden.

She made quick work of stripping off her damp gown; she'd learned to undress herself without Elizaveta's assistance months ago. Shivering a little, she tugged the pins from her hair and slipped between the welcoming sheets on the large four-poster bed.

It galled her that she needed to accept Wolff's protection. She didn't like to be beholden to anyone, but it would only be for a short time. She would hide here for a week or two until Vasili returned to Russia, and then she'd return to her normal life.

Would Wolff expect payment for his hospitality? Anya frowned into the darkness. She could sell one of her few remaining diamonds if absolutely necessary. But as he'd said at the brothel, he already had plenty of money. He didn't need more.

Would he exact payment for his protection in some other form? A curl of something that wasn't exactly fear twisted in her stomach. The way he'd looked at her, as if he wanted to gobble her up, made her shiver. His opinion of her was ridiculously low. He thought she was a whore, a woman who would stoop to swindling an old woman. And yet, back at the brothel, he'd made no secret of the fact that he desired her.

No doubt she would discover his terms in the morning.

Chapter 12.

Anya awoke to an unfamiliar room. The previous occupant—Benedict, Wolff had called him—had left no personal belongings. Only a faint tang of some masculine scent remained. She donned the dirty lavender-grey dress with a grimace of distaste and for one wistful moment, allowed herself to remember what it had been like to go shopping in Paris, able to buy whatever she wanted without considering the cost.

She'd had dresses in every shade of the rainbow and for every possible occasion, from velvet pelisses to sheer-as-a-whisper evening gowns designed to bring a man to his knees. She'd rarely worn a single dress more than once, let alone for six months straight.

She shook her head. She'd been a spoiled child, with no concept of hard work nor the value of money. Now, she knew the cost of a loaf of bread to the nearest penny.

Her new bedroom was certainly more luxurious than her sparse lodgings in Covent Garden. She'd had to sell one of her precious diamonds to pay for six months' rent upfront, and although the rooms had been furnished, the pieces were practical rather than attractive.

The giant footman, Mickey, brought a tray of breakfast and a reminder that "his lordship" would see her in his study at ten. She sent him a sunny smile and watched his thick neck flush in embarrassment. Clearly the man was less confident with women than his master.

She found Wolff downstairs, seated behind an imposing leather-topped desk in a book-lined library. Her heartrate increased in anticipation of a confrontation, and she tried not to notice how the charcoal grey of his jacket and the white of his shirt were the perfect foils for his tanned skin and dark eyes.

He did not stand when she entered the room, as a gentleman would for someone he considered a lady, and Anya smiled inwardly at the subtle snub. He waved her to the seat opposite him, and she braced herself for an interrogation.

"Miss Brown—"

"Ivanov."

He narrowed his eyes. "I don't believe your name is Ivanov any more than it is Brown. I don't know why you feel the need for continued secrecy, but you'll tell me eventually. Until then, I'm going to call you Miss Brown because it's easier to say."

He raised his brows, challenging her to object, or to confess, but she kept her lips firmly closed. He shrugged.

"When did you start to work for the dowager duchess, Miss Brown, and why have I never seen you at her house?"

"I entered her employ in September last year, Mr. Wolff," she countered, echoing his tone. "And I can only assume your visits never happened to coincide with mine."

A muscle ticked in his jaw at her pert answer, but she refused to be the one to break eye contact. She would not be cowed.

"It's 'my lord,'" he said silkily. "I'm an earl."

At the brothel, he'd told her to call him Sebastien. Clearly that privilege had been withdrawn. She opened her mouth to reply, but he forestalled her.

"There are very few people whose welfare I care about, Miss Brown, but my great-aunt happens to be one of them. I don't appreciate you putting her at risk, even by association. You have endangered her by your refusal to talk to the people who want to investigate Princess Denisova's death. Which is a perfectly reasonable request, especially if she died in suspicious circumstances."

"They weren't suspicious. She'd just received news that her brother had been killed at Waterloo. She was distraught. So much so that she jumped off a bridge into the Seine."

His eyes narrowed. "You sound more angry than upset."

"Of course I'm angry. I loved her like a sister." Anya bit her lip and took a calming breath. "I do not wish to discuss it further. With anyone."

"Very well. But if I'm to protect you, even for a few days, I need to know who you're trying to avoid."

She saw no reason not to tell him. "His name is Count Vasili Petrov. He's a guest of the Russian Ambassador, Count Lieven."

"I've met Petrov."

Anya's heart gave an irregular beat. "Here, at the club?"

"No. He's never come here, to my knowledge."

She let out a silent sigh of relief.

"I met him at a reception last week. He's the one looking for his missing fiancée. Does he mean Princess Denisova?"

"Yes. But they were never truly engaged. He asked for her hand on several occasions, but the princess had no desire to marry him. Her family refused on her behalf."

"He refuses to accept she's dead?"

Anya raised her brows and sent him an arch look. "He's the kind of man who thinks so highly of himself that he cannot believe a woman would leave him. Or refuse him."

She injected just enough scorn into her tone that he caught the inference; she believed *him* guilty of the same sin.

His brows drew together, but he didn't rise to the bait. "Why did you come to England after the death of your mistress? Why not return home?"

"I'd been the princess's companion my whole life. She was my dearest friend. With her gone, there was nothing left for me in Russia. My parents are dead. I had no fiancé or husband waiting for me. The princess gave me some of her jewels before she died, so I decided to make a new start somewhere fresh. I sold them to pay for my passage and applied for a post as secretary-companion to your great-aunt."

He watched her silently for a moment, absorbing this, and she fought not to fidget.

"All right. The duchess clearly likes you"—he paused, and Anya just knew he was mentally adding *although God knows why*—"so I'll humor her. For now. I assume Petrov's diplomatic duties will only keep him here for a short time. He may have discovered your connection to the dowager, but nobody knows you're here with me now. You'll be safe as long as you stay put."

"One man might know—the one who escaped last night. He could have recognized you as the dowager's nephew."

"That's true, although unlikely. I doubt he got a good look at me from that distance. Did you see his face?"

"Yes."

"Would you recognize him if you saw him again?"

"I think so. Your servants won't talk?"

He sent her an affronted look. "Of course not. They're loyal to me."

He raked a hand through his hair, which only served to rumple it attractively. She chided herself for noticing.

"This situation has been thrust upon both of us. God knows, I have no desire to play nursemaid to you, or to anyone, but I've never been one to shirk my duty. We must simply make the best of it."

Anya nodded. His dark gaze brought a tingle to her skin as he sent her an odd, speculative look. She could almost hear him thinking.

"Since your presence here is unavoidable, you might as well make yourself useful. Pay for your keep, as it were."

Her stomach fluttered in alarm.

"I happen to be working on a case for Bow Street that requires the translation of a number of Russian documents. You can decipher them."

Her tension eased a fraction, accompanied by the very faintest sense of disappointment. She'd thought he meant to proposition her again. "Very well. I can do that."

"Good." He leaned back in his chair, tugged open a drawer in his desk, and withdrew a large stack of papers. "You can start straight away."

Anya frowned as he deposited the mountainous pile on the desk in front of her. His lips twitched as he noted her obvious displeasure.

"Unless you have any objection of course?"

She ground her teeth. So, he was going to demand his pound of flesh, was he? "None at all," she said sweetly. "Would you like me to work in here?"

She prayed he would say yes. She would snoop through every one of his drawers as soon as he left her alone. She would know more about this man who was holding her under polite house arrest.

"No. I have work of my own to do. There's a desk in your suite you can use."

"So, I'm to spend all my time indoors?"

"That would be the most sensible option, yes." He sent her a dry look. "I'm sure you have a lively social calendar, Miss Brown, but you'll have to curtail your regular amusements if you wish to remain undiscovered."

She narrowed her eyes at his withering sarcasm. He probably thought her "regular amusements" included spending her evenings at Haye's brothel on her back or on her knees.

"You want my protection?" he continued softly. "You'll follow my rules. Of course, you're more than welcome to leave at any time, although I suspect Petrov will catch up with you fairly quickly if you do. He might already have discerned your home address."

Anya clutched her hands together and fought a pang of guilt and worry for Elizaveta. Would Vasili's men dismiss her as just a roommate? Or would they hear her accent and realize she shared a closer connection with Anya? Would they threaten her?

She bit her lip, plagued by indecision. What a choice. Was she safer staying close to the wolf, residing in his den? Or trying to navigate the flock alone? Unfortunately the answer was obvious. Accepting temporary defeat, she drew the topmost couple of documents toward her and began to skim through them then glanced up in shock. "These are confidential military communications. How did you get these?"

Wolff gave a disarming smile. "We have our ways."

"You mean spies?"

"Agents. Sources of information. Yes."

She studied the letters again. Some were almost a year old, dated a few weeks before Waterloo. June the eighteenth; it was a date etched into her memory, the day she'd lost Dmitri.

"So you want these translated? What do you wish to know?"

"I want a list of every person mentioned in these dispatches. Even if they seem inconsequential. It will be extremely tedious, but it's important work."

"Why? Who are you looking for?"

"A Russian who was passing information to the French. The bastard's treachery cost countless lives. I lost good friends at Waterloo. Men I'd fought with for years. Men I'd come to love like brothers. If the traitor's not already dead, I want him brought to justice."

His voice had deepened with passion, and Anya fought to keep her expression neutral, even as her heart thudded against her ribs. *Vasili.* Surely he was talking about Vasili? There couldn't be that many Russian traitors out there, could there?

"That's a noble goal," she managed evenly. "Do you have any suspicion who it might be?"

"Someone close to the tsar, or to one of his advisors. Unfortunately, the French spy who was his contact is dead, so we can't get any more details from him. All we know is that the French called him 'The Cossack.'"

He rubbed his fingers over his jaw and Anya fought an internal debate. Should she tell him that Dmitri suspected Vasili? If Vasili was indeed the traitor, he deserved to be caught and punished. But she was supposed to be the princess's servant. How would she have been be privy to such information?

"I believe I know who your traitor is."

Wolff's bows rose to his hairline.

"The man you seek is Count Petrov."

He didn't bother to hide his disbelief. "The very man

you wish to avoid? That's rather convenient, isn't it? What proof do you have?"

"Nothing concrete," she said. "But I believe it's one of the reasons the princess refused to marry him."

He tilted his head silent question.

Anya tried to adopt a properly contrite demeanor. "I'm ashamed to admit it, but I happened to overhear a private conversation between the princess and her brother, Prince Dmitri, a few weeks before he died."

"What was it about?"

"Dmitri told the princess he suspected Petrov of spying for France. He said he would be investigating the matter as soon as he returned from Vienna."

"Did he find any proof?"

"I don't believe so. He went straight from Vienna to Waterloo, where he was killed."

"Hmm."

Anya bit her lip. Wolff didn't look convinced. "However," she said, and he glanced up again. "I also know that Petrov came to see the princess after Waterloo, convinced that Dmitri had found some evidence and sent it to her for safekeeping."

His dark eyes glittered with interest. "And had he?"

"The princess denied it. But Petrov admitted to her that he was the spy."

There was a beat of silence as he digested that. "You heard this admission?" His eyes bored into hers as if he could burn the answer from her brain by willpower alone.

"Yes. I was standing just outside the room."

"Did Petrov know you heard him?"

"It's possible."

He let out a low exhale. "Well, no wonder he's looking for you. He doesn't want to know how the princess died; he wants to know how much you heard, and whether he needs to buy your silence." His expression darkened. "Or *ensure* your silence. Those men probably weren't sent to question you, Miss Brown. They were probably sent to kill you."

A cold wash pebbled her skin. The same possibility had presented itself to her too, but to hear it spoken out loud, so baldly, made it somehow far more frightening. More real. She didn't think Vasili would have ordered her killed—at least, not until he'd married her, but as soon as he had full control of her land and estates, she wouldn't be at all surprised if she met with a tragic "accident."

Wolff was watching her, his dark eyes intense. "You called him Dmitri," he said softly.

Anya stilled. Damn. The man noticed every tiny, betraying detail.

"And there's a softness in your face when you speak of him. Was he your lover?"

Was that a flash of jealousy in his tone?

"No!" She wrinkled her nose in instinctive recoil at the thought of kissing her own brother, and her expression must have been believable because Wolff chuckled. The odd tension in him evaporated as quickly as it had come.

"I take it from that reaction that he was not."

"Prince Denisov was my friend," she said reproachfully. "He was a good man. I loved him like a brother."

Wolff leaned back in his chair, his long, lithe body seeming to take up an inordinate amount of space. "If you're telling the truth, then we share a common enemy."

Anya bristled at the inference that she might be lying, but he ignored her silent offence.

"We need proof. I can't just go and accuse him of being a traitor. Petrov has powerful friends. Depending on his role, he might even have diplomatic immunity. Bow

Street will need concrete evidence before it can act." He nodded at the pile of papers in front of her. "Let's hope we find something in there."

He tilted his head, still thinking, and Anya tried not to notice the intimidating breadth of his shoulders and the blunt, masculine beauty of his hands. Even relaxed, in his own domain, he exuded competence, an aura of quiet power.

"If Petrov *is* the spy, then he's dangerous. He might even be a murderer. Another Russian, probably an informant, was killed last week, down at the docks." He tapped his fingers on the leather desk. "The suspect was a tall, light-haired man. It could have been Petrov."

Anya swallowed a lump of fear. That Vasili was capable of such a violent act was no surprise. He was a brute who used his size to intimidate. If only Dmitri *had* sent her whatever proof he'd found. She could have given it to Wolff, he could have arrested Vasili, and her problems would have been over.

She would have been free to leave here, instead of being forced into close proximity with Wolff—a terrifyingly handsome, enigmatic man.

He was without a doubt the most attractive man she'd ever met. Not some golden prince from a fairy tale, more like his dark-haired, cynical stepbrother. The scapegrace of the family who'd left home to seek his fortune and become a dark sorcerer. His features were saved from being pretty by a masculine jaw and the upward slant of his eyebrows, which gave him a faintly diabolical air. His self-confidence bordered on arrogance, but she couldn't deny the allure of the glint in his eyes. The man was a walking promise.

His nearness made her aware of him as a man and herself as a woman in a way she'd never before considered. They were unchaperoned, completely alone, save for some distant servants belowstairs. And yet she trusted him. Rogue he might be, but there was honor at his core, beneath the cynicism. He was clearly no stranger to violence, but unlike Vasili, she doubted he'd ever use force with a woman. He was so charming, so beguiling. He could probably tease out desires a woman never even suspected she possessed.

Anya gave herself a mental shake.

She would not be another one of his conquests.

Chapter 13.

Anya spent the rest of the day reading through the pile of correspondence Wolff had given her, noting down the various names.

She also scrawled a brief note to Elizaveta, and another to Charlotte, telling them not to worry, but that she was being personally protected by the dowager duchess's great-nephew, and would be staying at the Tricorn Club for an indefinite period.

She smiled as she imagined their different reactions to reading *that*. Elizaveta would be scandalized at the impropriety and worried for both her safety and her morals. Charlotte was far more likely to crack one of her saucy, speculative smiles and pour a drink in her honor.

Anya folded both sheets together and directed them to Haye's. Vasili had somehow managed to learn that she worked for the dowager duchess. It wasn't impossible that he might also discover her home address and set someone to intercept the mail. Since Haye's received a great number of missives every day, from gentlemen making

"arrangements," one more note would hopefully not attract any undue attention.

At lunchtime, Mickey brought in a tray of stew and
crusty bread and agreed to have the stable lad deliver
the letters for her. The baguette was as good as the ones
Anya had eaten every morning on the Rue de Passy in
Paris; Wolff clearly had a talented chef.

It was a pleasure to enjoy even simple soup when it
was made with gristle-free steak and more than one veg-
etable. Elizaveta was a competent cook, but their strait-
ened circumstances meant they'd rarely bought the best
cuts of meat or the freshest produce. Desserts had become a distant memory.

She went back to the translations. They were frustratingly difficult to decipher, thanks to some truly appalling
handwriting, and all were exceedingly dull, concerned
mainly with rations and supplies, troop movements and
ammunition requests.

By dinnertime, she was thoroughly bored and no
closer to discovering anything useful than she had been
that morning. She pushed back from the desk and tried
to ease the aching muscles in her neck. As if on cue,
Mickey appeared, hunching his giant shoulders in what
she assumed was his way of trying to appear less intimidating.

"'Is lordship thought you'd like a bath." He gestured
to a door just across the hallway. "There's one of 'em
new-fangled bathing rooms in there. Linens too."

Anya almost did a little dance of delight when she discovered the large copper tub filled with water. It was big
enough to immerse her whole body in, double the size of
the miserable tin hip-bath she and Elizaveta shared back
at their lodgings.

She stripped with unseemly haste, piled her hair in a
haphazard coil on the top of her head, and sank into the

steaming water with a sigh of bliss. Tension leeched out of her as she luxuriated in the warmth. She let down her hair and washed it thoroughly, noting that the soap was a feminine jasmine scent. She raised a brow. Did Wolff have such a regular supply of women who bathed here that his household kept a supply of floral soap? Or had he somehow guessed it was her favorite? Probably the former.

When the water finally cooled enough to be unpleasant, and her fingers and toes resembled wizened prunes, she dried herself off and ducked across the corridor to her own rooms. The idea of putting her dirty dress back on was depressing, but she stopped short on the threshold of the bedroom when she saw what lay across the bed—a dress, one that certainly didn't belong to her.

She stepped closer, reaching out to touch it before she even realized what she was doing. It was exquisite, something Charlotte would wear, a gorgeous midnight-blue watered silk gown with little puff sleeves and a draped bodice.

A note lay on the fabric, the white card stark against the shimmering blue.

Your lavender gown offends me, as it would anyone with a modicum of taste. Wear this.

The sloping copperplate undoubtedly belonged to Wolff, despite the absence of a signature. Anya didn't know whether to be amused or annoyed by his high-handedness. Did he think she wore the grey dress because she *liked* it?

The new gown fit like a dream. Wolff was doubtless well-versed in calculating a woman's measurements. Anya shivered in guilty pleasure as the silk chemise that had also been provided slid against her skin. She'd become so used to rough cotton, it felt as sensual as a caress. Every nerve ending quivered in happiness. *Temptation, thy name is satin.*

Her well-washed stockings had been replaced by a pair of embroidered silk ones, her practical, mud-covered boots replaced by a pair of highly impractical slippers. She put them on without a moment's hesitation.

The only omission had been a corset. Anya wondered if it was deliberate, or whether Wolff had truly forgotten that women needed such things. Perhaps the women with whom he consorted didn't bother to wear them.

The girl who stared back at her from the mirror was a foreign creature, someone she hadn't seen for over a year. With a jolt, she felt like herself again, like Princess Denisova, poised and carefree. Able to go anywhere, do anything. It was a lie, of course. She was Anya Ivanov now, trapped in this cage of her own making. What good did it do to pine for what was gone?

Mickey rapped on the outer door. "There's dinner downstairs, miss."

"Will his lordship be eating with me?"

"Not tonight. He's dining out."

Anya quashed a feeling of pique. She shouldn't want to see Wolff's reaction to her in these clothes.

She followed the giant down the curved staircase and into a room with a gleaming mahogany sideboard and matching table. A single place setting had been arranged at one end, and she ate in solitary splendor.

The lack of company was made up for by the exquisite food: salmon, beef, almond syllabub. Mickey offered her wine, and Anya took two glasses of a wonderful French burgundy.

There was still no sign of Wolff, so she placed her napkin on the table and went exploring. He hadn't expressly forbidden her to do so, after all.

She discovered a salon and a billiard room, and the stairs down to the kitchens, but her steps drew her down a long picture-hung corridor with a door at the far end. The murmur of conversation on the other side of the mahogany indicated this was a way into the club, but she had no desire to open it. Instead, she followed a narrow staircase up, up, and found herself on a kind of minstrel's gallery overlooking the main gaming floor.

The air was warm up here, near the roof. A carved fretwork screen shielded her from sight while giving an excellent view of the comings and goings in the room below. The tsar had something similar in all the royal palaces; spy holes, places to see, but not be seen. Dark corners perfect for clandestine assignations.

The club was a riot of color and noise. Green baize-topped gaming tables, cream playing cards, the spinning red-and-black of the roulette wheels. Most of the men were clad in dark colors, but the women flitting between them were like exotic birds, some more gaudy than others. Most of them had chosen to preserve their anonymity by wearing masks.

The excited hum of conversation, broken by the occasional cheer or groan, filled the place with a lively energy that made Anya's nerves tingle.

A movement behind her had her heart leaping to her throat, and she knew without looking that it was Wolff. She kept her face to the front as he stepped close behind her, felt the disturbance of the air as his legs brushed her skirts. The subtle scent of his cologne made her suck in an unsteady breath.

"Who gave you permission to be up here?"

"No one. But then, no one forbade me either."

He rested his hand on the rail next to her hip and leaned forward to look at the scene below. Anya sneaked a glance at him from the corner of her eye. The glow from the lamps lit his features while the fretwork screen cast a pattern of shapes across his face. He looked like a jungle cat, speckled by foliage, watching his prey from the shadows.

He was so tall, so evidently physical beneath those elegant clothes, but she didn't find his size intimidating. Instead, she found it rather thrilling. He turned, resting his hip against the rail, and focused his attention on her. His gaze burned the side of her face.

"That dress is a definite improvement."

"Thank you. I appreciate it. Although you must know that it will take me some time to repay you."

He flicked his fingers in a dismissive gesture. "I don't expect you to. It's a gift."

She opened her mouth to argue, but he placed his index finger over her lips and she was momentarily shocked into silence. He wasn't wearing gloves. The sensation of skin on skin sent a shimmer of bright energy through her.

"Not a gift for you," he said, and there was laughter in his voice. "For me. As someone who likes his guests to maintain a certain level of sartorial elegance."

He dropped his hand, but her lips still tingled.

"So, tell me, what you were doing at Haye's if you weren't supplementing your income as one of her girls? I'm curious."

Anya stiffened at the unexpected change of topic. So, they were back to that, were they? She should have known he wouldn't let it go. He was a man who liked answers.

Would he believe her reasons for being there were entirely innocent? A perverse part of her wanted to see how he'd treat her if he thought she was a fallen woman, fair game. Would he try to proposition her again? Did she want him to?

She certainly wanted to be kissed again. The memory of it made her whole body thrum.

"I had some business there," she murmured vaguely.

He reached out and touched the side of her neck, the faintest brush across her skin. Instant flames bloomed beneath his fingers.

"Business. Hmm." His tone was dubious. It was clear he didn't know what to believe. "Are you promised to another? A husband? A lover?"

Anya closed her eyes. Her body's reaction to him was so unexpected. So strong. Princess Anastasia would never have had the chance to dally with such a charming rogue. But she was Anna Brown. Anya Ivanov. Unfettered by the restrictions of polite society. Why shouldn't she seize the chance to experience a little passion?

"I'm promised to no one." Her voice was almost a croak.

Some of the tension in his body relaxed, as if he was relieved by her answer.

"Then why did you say no?"

His thumb pressed lightly over the pulse in her throat, then trailed up to her jaw. He tucked a stray tendril of hair behind her ear, the gesture as casual as if he'd done it a thousand times before. "Even if you didn't want my money, we could have had such fun."

"I—" Words failed her. "I . . . don't have much experience . . . with that sort of thing."

"Look at me."

Anya opened her eyes and was instantly caught in his gaze. He was so close, so tempting. She couldn't recall the last time she'd been in such close proximity with anyone. She could see the black ring around his brown irises, the sinful curl of his lashes. A room full of people stood not fifty feet away, but for all intents and purposes, they were alone.

The corners of his mouth quirked upward. "That certainly explains something that was bothering me, Miss Brown."

"It does? What?"

"Your kiss."

"What about it?"

A teasing smile hovered at the edges of his mouth. "How can I put this? Although enthusiastic, it lacked . . . polish. Technique."

Her mouth fell open, and he chuckled softly. "Now, don't get offended, but when it comes to kissing, I'm afraid you could do with a little practice."

What conceit! Did he critique *all* his partners in such a way? Anya couldn't decide whether to be insulted or entertained. She settled for sarcasm. "And I suppose you're an expert on the matter?"

"I've had some experience, yes." His gaze dropped to her lips and a hot flush swept over her skin.

"Are you offering to be my tutor?" She'd meant to sound dry and cynical, but to her dismay, it came out breathless instead.

His gaze flashed back to hers, and she found herself drowning in the abyss of his eyes.

"Yes," he said, utterly serious. "I am."

Anya threw caution to the wind. She lifted her chin in haughty, regal challenge. "All right then, Mr. Wolff. Show me."

A flare of triumph flickered across his face. He lifted his hand to cradle her nape, his eyes never leaving hers, and a shiver skittered down her spine. He used the pad of his thumb to tilt her chin up, and Anya parted her lips in anticipation as he leaned closer. The sandpaper-roughness of his jaw as it brushed against her cheek was both alien and thrilling.

His lips found hers. When he skimmed the sensitive

flesh of her lower lip with his teeth, Anya almost groaned. She felt him smile against her mouth. He kissed her again, softly to ease the sting, and his tongue slid out to taste.

Her heart gave an irregular jolt. She opened to his silent demand, granting him access to her mouth, and his fingers tightened on the back of her head in silent approval. Her eyelids fluttered closed.

He kissed her slowly, languidly, as if they had all the time in the world. His tongue tangled with hers, a glorious advance and retreat, a voluptuous slip and slide of breath and skin that made her feel like she'd had one too many glasses of champagne. In the small, still-functioning part of her brain, Anya dizzily acknowledged that Sebastien Wolff wasn't just a good kisser; he was an expert, a virtuoso.

She surrendered to the red-hot darkness with delight. Excitement coiled low in her belly, stoked by his wicked, talented mouth. Who'd have thought his lips would be so soft, so delicious? She slid her arms around his neck and pressed closer, greedy for more. Her breasts squashed against the hard plane of his chest as she tangled her fingers in his thick hair.

With a groan that reverberated through her body, he dropped his hands to her upper arms and pulled away. He rested his forehead against hers.

"That, Miss Brown, is a definite improvement."

His breath was as unsteady as her own, and Anya felt a little spurt of feminine triumph. The attraction wasn't all one-sided, then.

"Come to my room." His voice was an octave lower than usual, all gravel and smoke. It made her toes curl in her slippers. "Let me show you the rest."

The pop of a champagne cork and a raucous cheer

from below pulled her back from the brink of insanity. Anya took a step back, amazed and rather appalled by the fever he'd ignited so effortlessly.

"No! I can't. I'm . . . Good night, my lord." She turned and fled down the stairs.

To her relief, he let her go.

Back in her room, she cooled her burning cheeks with her palms. She'd been so close to saying yes. True, they were practically strangers, but there was no denying the attraction between them.

Anya fell onto the bed, utterly confused. Her whole life she'd cherished the romantic dream that she would save herself for a husband, for the man she'd choose as a lifelong partner. She wanted someone she could respect and love. Someone who would share the responsibilities of running the family estates, and who'd make her laugh during the mind-numbing ceremonial functions she was expected to attend at court.

Her pickiness in choosing a husband had been acceptable—even expected—of a wealthy Russian princess. But she wasn't that princess anymore. She was an ordinary citizen, an exile. A twenty-two-year-old secretary-companion with little money and even fewer marriage prospects.

Sebastien Wolff could never be associated with permanence, but if she wanted an *affaire*, he was the perfect solution. He wasn't pretending to have any deeper feelings for her other than a healthy physical magnetism. He was making no promises except to provide her with an unparalleled sexual experience.

Why had she refused him? She should have taken what he was offering and satisfied her curiosity to know the pleasure Charlotte's girls insisted could be had between a man and a woman.

Anya expelled a long, frustrated breath and tried to calm her racing heart.

What was Wolff thinking now? Was he cursing her name? Would he go off to somewhere like Haye's and slake his lust with a more willing partner?

She told herself she didn't want to know.

Chapter 14.

Seb took a deep, calming breath and willed his iron-hard erection to subside.

"Anya Ivanov" was a walking contradiction. Prim and proper one minute, melting passion in his arms the next. Who *was* she? The inquisitive part of his nature, the one that fitted so well with his role of Bow Street investigator, demanded he find out. Knowledge was power, and he wanted every one of her secrets.

She was clearly well educated. No mere peasant would end up as maid to a princess, and her mannerisms and speech all told of an inbred familiarity with the *haute monde*. Maybe she came from an old but impoverished Russian family? She could be like Benedict, descended from a proud and ancient lineage, but hampered by a perpetual lack of funds. There were plenty like that in the *ton*. Estates were mismanaged. Fathers developed a fatal propensity for gambling. Anya struck him as someone who'd fallen on hard times.

Yet she was resilient. Instead of bemoaning her reduced

circumstances, as so many other women of his acquaintance might have done, she'd realized that her mental faculties were a valuable asset and found work with his great-aunt.

Seb frowned. His aunt was no miser. Surely she was paid enough to afford a relatively decent lifestyle without the need to engage in whatever "business" had her visiting Haye's late at night?

Did she yearn for the luxuries she'd once enjoyed with her former employer, the princess? Rich clothes, jewels, expensive perfumes? No. That didn't fit. That well-worn travel dress of hers was evidence of a frugal nature. The only hint of luxury he'd seen was that fur-lined cape she'd been wearing—the one that made her look like a wintry fairy princess. But she could have been given that by her mistress. Or simply taken it when she realized the woman was dead.

Seb rested his hands on the railing and stared sightlessly at the gaming room below. Women had physical needs, sexual urges, just as men did. She was unmarried. She had no husband or permanent lover. Perhaps she'd been at Haye's for precisely the same reason *he'd* been there? To scratch an itch. He hadn't heard that Charlotte Haye provided for women as well as for men, but it was possible.

But if she *had* been there for pleasure, why hadn't she chosen him? Not only wouldn't she have had to pay, but he'd offered her the eye-watering sum of five hundred pounds for the pleasure.

Seb shook his head. No, that scenario didn't fit either.

Perhaps she'd been there to gain some experience in a relatively safe environment? His heart gave a thump as a jolt of desire shot straight to his groin. God, he'd have been only too happy to have provided her with that service. The chemistry between them was extraordinary.

He'd never felt anything quite like it. Why was she so reluctant to follow it to its natural conclusion?

He couldn't remember the last time he'd been so obsessed with a woman. His dark good looks, courtesy of his Italian mother, meant he'd never had to work too hard for female company. Perhaps it was the mystery, the irresistible challenge of Anya Ivanov, that called to him?

With a slow exhale, he turned his attention to the gaming room below. The scene was familiar, and it filled him with the usual deep sense of accomplishment. He, Alex, and Benedict had made this, created it from nothing and made it a success.

He needed to get down on the floor and show his face. Usually mingling with the guests was no hardship. He was naturally sociable; his charisma and easy wit gave patrons a sense of stability, and his genial hospitality convinced them to play deeper, stay longer, laugh louder. It was good for business.

After the brutal hardship of his years in the Rifles, it was good to be somewhere that catered for the enjoyment of life. To celebrate the simple human pleasures of decent food, excellent wine, diverting entertainment, and convivial company. He was profoundly grateful to have survived. It seemed like he owed it to himself, and to those who hadn't been so fortunate, to enjoy life to the fullest.

Yet as he watched the assembled crowd, he was seized by a niggling sense of dissatisfaction. Before the war, he'd been just like all those other men down there, chasing an elusive high from a win at the tables or a night of heavy drinking. He'd been single-minded in his pursuit of pleasure.

It seemed like vacuous frippery now. There was more to life than whoring and cards, and thankfully he'd found an outlet for his energies in his work for Bow Street. He derived a great deal of satisfaction from working to prevent crime, or from catching those responsible.

His older brother, Geoffrey, might have inherited the responsibility of running their late father's estates, but Seb could live his own life of integrity and worth by helping make the streets of London a safer place. He'd been blessed with a strong body and a keen brain; it only seemed reasonable that he use both in the service of those less fortunate than himself.

But still, professional satisfaction wasn't the same as personal satisfaction. He'd witnessed the changes in his two friends, Alex and Ben, since they'd both married. There was a steady contentment about them both now, a sense of having found a true purpose in life. They lived to make their wives happy.

Was *that* what he was lacking? The reason for his strange dissatisfaction, despite his wealth and outward success? A partner with whom to share it? Seb shook his head. He lacked nothing, except physical release. He was just frustrated, that was all. As soon as the mysterious "Miss Brown" came to her senses—and into his bed—that frustration would be dealt with in the most pleasurable way.

Chapter 15.

Wolff entered her suite without knocking. Anya glanced up from the desk and then swiftly back down, determined to pretend the incendiary encounter on the balcony the previous night had never happened.

It was easier said than done. The knowledge was a humming awareness between them, tugging like an invisible thread. She cleared her throat and willed the heat in her face to subside.

"I've been through all these letters. There's no mention of Petrov or anyone named the Cossack."

She'd found a mention of her brother, though, a single casual reference in a list of those near Wellington at Waterloo, and her heart had felt like a stone, heavy in her chest.

Wolff shrugged, the movement emphasizing the muscled breadth of his chest beneath his shirt. "It was a long shot, anyway. I have a better plan." He leaned one shoulder casually against the doorframe. "I've been looking

at the club's members' list and very few of your countrymen are on it. I want to lure them here so I can watch and
listen to them."

"I thought the plan was for me to avoid my countrymen? Can't you observe them at a *ton* party?"

"I want a relaxed setting. A man behaves very differently in a gaming club among his friends than he does at
a public ball where ladies are present."

"There were ladies on the gaming floor last night."

"There were *women*. None of them were ladies."

Ah. He meant demimondaines, mistresses. Actresses
and whores.

"You won't be in any danger," he said. "You'll stay
here, out of sight. Can you suggest some ways to attract
them?"

"Perhaps you're not providing the entertainment they
want."

His lips thinned at the suggestion that his beloved
Tricorn was anything less than perfect, and Anya suppressed a smile. He really was arrogantly conceited
when it came to his business. When it came to most
things, actually.

"And what is that?" he said testily. "We have cards,
dice, roulette. The best French chef in London. An in-
comparable wine cellar."

"You can get those anywhere." Anya paused, enjoying
the way he seemed to be hanging on her every word. "If
you really want to attract Russians, you need vodka."

His disgusted expression almost made her laugh out
loud. "What's wrong with brandy and port?"

"Nothing, but Russians prefer vodka. Believe me,
nothing gets a Russian drunk enough to spill his secrets
like vodka."

He frowned, apparently considering this revelation.
"All right, I'll try it. It can be a novelty. Something that

sets the Tricorn apart from clubs like Crockford's and Brooks's."

"You could host a whole Russian evening," Anya suggested, warming to the idea. "Have your chef make all kinds of Russian foods in honor of the delegation. That will bring them in for a taste of their homeland."

A frown marred his perfect forehead. "There may be a slight problem with that. Monsieur Lagrasse is not only the best French chef in London, he's also the most temperamental. There's a strong chance he'll refuse to cook such foreign monstrosities."

"Let me talk to him."

With a shrug and a sigh that indicated she was wasting her time, Wolff led her down the curving main staircase and to the top of the steps leading down to the kitchens. The clatter of pans and a stream of French curses echoed up from below.

"I warn you, he won't thank us for invading his kitchens. He's a despot worse than Bonaparte. This is his own personal fiefdom."

Anya sent him a droll glance. "I'm sure we'll get along famously."

"Can you cook?"

"Not at all. My housemate Elizaveta is the one who saves us from eating bread and jam every night."

Wolff shook his head. "This is going to be a disaster."

They reached the bottom of the stairs and entered a large, airy kitchen. The room was set half-belowground—the high windows revealed a set of steps leading up to the cobbled mews at the back of the club. An impressive assortment of shiny copper pans and bunches of dried herbs hung from hooks on the ceiling, and a huge cooking range emitted a sweltering heat. Two maids were in the process of chopping vegetables, and a short, rotund gentleman wearing a black apron was elbow-deep in a large copper bowl. This, Anya surmised, was the great Lagrasse.

As they watched, he withdrew a ball of bread dough, threw it down on the tabletop, and proceeded to slap and pummel it with his fists as though he wanted to ensure the thing was completely dead.

He glanced up with a fearsome frown, not at all subservient at the appearance of his lordly employer, and his thin black mustache quivered in irritation.

"My lord. Zis is a most inconvenient time. I am at a crucial stage wiz my dough. If you wish to 'ave food for two 'undred zis evening, I would appreciate no interruptions."

Anya suppressed a smile.

"Monsieur Lagrasse," Wolff said evenly. "This is my guest, Miss Brown. She has some suggestions for you."

The chef glared, clearly astonished that anyone should be questioning the perfect composition of his menu. Anya stepped forward, keen to forestall any objections, and spoke rapidly in French.

"It is an honor to meet you, sir. I hail from St. Petersburg, and believe me when I say that tales of your culinary genius have spread even as far as there."

The Frenchman broke out into a delighted grin. "Why, but you speak the mother tongue like a native, my girl!"

Anya smiled. "Please, call me Anya. And of course. We Russians love everything French. I spent a wonderful year in Paris before I came here."

She held out her hand and the little man bowed over her fingers in formal greeting.

"What are these suggestions of yours?"

From the corner of her eye, she saw Wolff raise his brows in shock, although whether it was at her flawless French or the fact that she'd managed not to infuriate his volatile employee, was unclear.

"Lord Mowbray has assured me that you're the finest chef in London, and from the food I tasted last night, I'm inclined to agree with him."

The little man puffed up like a rooster, and Anya threw out her lure. She'd dealt with temperamental artists like this before, both in Russia and in Paris. She knew just how to handle him. Men like Lagrasse needed to be constantly challenged or they lost their spark.

"However—"

Lagrasse sent her a steely look. "Madame?"

"I've also heard of a rival of yours, a man named Eustache Ude."

From behind her, she heard Wolff let out a low groan of disbelief.

Lagrasse's face reddened. "Ude? Bah! He used to be in the service of Napoleon's mother, but he works at Crockford's now. Crockford pays him two thousand pounds a year! And for what? The man's *pièce de résistance* is nothing more than mackerel baked in clarified butter."

Anya adopted a serious expression. "And I am quite certain you're the better chef. But still, people talk. Wouldn't you like the chance to prove it, once and for all?"

Lagrasse's mustache twitched and his eyes took on a steely glint. She had him.

"What do you suggest?"

"Well, clearly you're both exceptionally skilled when it comes to preparing French cuisine. But isn't the ultimate test whether you can master food from a different country? To prepare it so well that even natives of that country pronounce it the best they've ever had?"

She paused to let the idea marinate. "Lord Mowbray would like the Tricorn to serve some Russian delicacies in honor of the tsar's delegation. I've bet him you can produce food so authentic that even *I* won't be able to tell it was prepared by a Frenchman."

Anya held her breath. The gauntlet had been thrown down. She prayed the chef would rise to the challenge.

He did not disappoint. He drew himself up to his maximum height of five foot two. "Madame, there is nothing you can ask of me, no recipe so complex that I, René Lagrasse, cannot master."

"That's precisely what I told Lord Mowbray. I shall be your official food tester. I will judge each dish before we serve it to the club's patrons."

"Which foods do you suggest?"

"Let me think. The first that comes to mind, of course, is blini. They're tiny little Russian pancakes. Similar to your crêpes, only made with a yeasted dough, which makes them lighter. You can serve them with any number of things, sweet or savory. I personally like them with smoked salmon, sour cream, and caviar. Or with honey."

Lagrasse nodded. "Very well. But pancakes are not very complicated."

"That is true. You could try *medovik*. It's a layered honey cake which takes a great deal of skill. There are hundreds of regional variations. You must make layer upon layer of honeyed pastry and alternate it with sweetened cream or custard, then cover the outside of the cake with pastry crumbs. It is incredibly labor intensive. The tsarina, Elizabeth Alexeievna, gobbles it up whenever it's served."

Lagrasse's eyes widened. "You've dined at the emperor's court?"

Anya bit her lip as she realized her slip. "Oh, well, I went there a few times, certainly. With my mistress, Princess Denisova. I would go down to the kitchens and sample the leftovers."

The chef nodded, apparently satisfied by her explanation. "Very well. You may bring me recipes."

"Thank you, Monsieur Lagrasse. I know you will rise to the occasion."

Anya turned on her heel and swept back up the stairs, confident Wolff would follow.

"That," he said, when they'd reached the safety of the hallway, "was masterful."

The undisguised awe in his tone made her preen a little.

"I have medals from my military campaigns, Miss Brown. I have faced Bonaparte's canons and cavalry. But even *I* would hesitate to suggest to a Frenchman that he bake a Russian cake."

Anya sent him a triumphant grin. "You speak French?"

"Well enough to know that you're wasted as a secretary. You should be a diplomat. I've never seen such soothing of ruffled feathers. When you mentioned Ude, I thought he was going to stab you with a bread knife, but you played him like a fiddle."

"We have a saying in Russia: 'you catch more flies with honey than vinegar.'"

Wolff smiled. "Or in this case, with honey cake. Where are you going to find the recipes? Can you write them down for him?"

"Oh. I don't know any by heart. Perhaps I could go—"

"You're not going anywhere," he countered, reading her mind with infuriating ease. "If you need anything, I'll send someone to get it."

Anya gave a huff of frustration. She'd hoped to be allowed out to a bookshop or library, at least. "Very well. Send someone to look for a book of recipes at Hatchards, or in one of the antiquarian book sellers on Publisher's Row. It can be in Russian. Or French. I can always translate."

Wolff stopped walking and turned, so she stopped too.

"You are a woman of many hidden talents, Miss Brown," he said with a smile. "And those desserts sound delicious." His gaze dipped to her mouth, and he let out a low chuckle that made her stomach flutter. "I am longing for a taste."

Chapter 16.

Wolff left the house shortly after their visit to the kitchen. Anya heard the slam of the door with a slight twinge of resentment, but she was saved from boredom by the arrival of a package and letter from the dowager duchess.

> *Oxfordshire is deadly dull without you, my dear. You will be relieved to know that John Coachman is none the worse for our adventure on Hounslow Heath. I'm sure Sebastien is guarding you well; do try to restrain the urge to strangle him, despite what I'm sure will be endless provocation. His methods may be unorthodox, but I have complete faith in his abilities, as does my good friend Sir Nathaniel Conant at Bow Street. I imagine you're feeling quite cooped up; I've sent you our little project to keep you amused.*

Anya opened the illustrated book of fairy tales that had accompanied the letter and began to read.

Three hours later, she'd been swept away to a world of beautiful women, brave princes, dark woods, and wondrous animals. She'd read of Baba Yaga the witch and Vasilisa the Beautiful. Of the Tsarevna Frog, and Tsarevich Ivan, the Firebird and the Grey Wolf. Of Father Frost—Ded Moroz—and the Snow Princess Snegurochka.

Perhaps she was sensitive about the subject, but she noticed that many of the tales featured people hiding their true nature. Princes hiding as frogs. People cursed into golden birds or fearsome bears. She quashed a guilty twinge. She was hiding her *own* identity for a perfectly good reason: self-preservation.

There were lots of wolves in the tales too. One helped Ivan catch the firebird, but more often than not, the creature's role was ambiguous at best. They could be noble and fearless—or pitiless and sly. Of course, wolves featured in the stories of many other countries. The English book Tess had been reading told of Red Riding Hood's encounter with a wicked, predatory beast.

Anya wrinkled her nose. She'd always had a soft spot for the wolf in that tale. What if he were really a man trapped in the body of a beast? What if he fell under the spell of the beautiful girl? What if she tamed him? He'd be the very best protector. She let out a soft laugh at her own foolishness. Wasn't that what every woman dreamed? That she'd be the one to gentle the beast? No doubt they believed it right up to the moment they were eaten up for dinner. She wasn't such a fool.

After lunch, she made her way down to Wolff's library. She tried to snoop through his desk, but most of the drawers were locked. Disappointed, she nevertheless found a small tin of watercolor paints, a pencil, and some blank sheets of paper and entertained herself by sketching instead.

Before long, she'd drawn a whole host of vignettes. There was her family's *dacha*, their summer house in the country outside Moscow, complete with stables and orchard. A wave of nostalgia hit her as she remembered climbing the trees and picking fruit for *vareniy*, a kind of liquid jam, with Dmitri and her parents.

She sketched some of the dresses she'd worn in Paris, then Petya, her pet wolfhound who'd lived to the ripe age of fifteen before he'd succumbed to old age. She didn't try to draw Dmitri or her parents. Already their familiar features seemed indistinct in her mind; to capture them on paper was more than her artistic ability allowed.

Lastly, she drew the tiara she'd destroyed. The design formed in her mind with guilty clarity. Two rows of graduated diamonds formed the top and bottom borders, *kokoshnik* style. More diamonds suspended like drops of rain within an open lattice of anthemion leaves, alongside sapphires the bottomless blue of a Russian lake.

She allowed herself a little artistic license. If she ever won a fortune at cards, she would take this drawing to a jeweler and ask him to remake it. Money would be no object, so she'd have the gems set in white gold or platinum instead of the original yellow gold. The silvery color would made the diamonds shimmer like sunlight on snow, the perfect diadem for the ice princess they'd once called her.

She shook her head at such fantasy. Of all the diamonds she and Elizaveta had hidden in their flight from Paris, only a handful remained. The rest had been used to pay for their passage from Ostend to Dover, for food and rent when they'd reached London. They'd received far less than the stones' true worth on several occasions; there were always unscrupulous characters ready to take advantage, but they'd been desperate and unwilling to attract attention by making too much of a fuss.

The last time she'd been forced to sell a gem, she'd followed Charlotte's suggestion and gone to the royal jewelers, Bridge & Rundell. The proprietor, the elderly Mr. Rundell, had treated her with the kind of polite disdain at which the English so excelled. He'd given her shabby dress and practical boots a knowing glance and accepted her story of being given them by her deceased employer with subtle incredulity and silent disapproval.

It was clear that he suspected her of being a demimondaine selling the favors given by a lover, or at the very least of having dubious associates, but his eyes had brightened when he'd realized the gems were of the highest quality, and he'd paid her a fair sum.

Anya had no doubt they'd end up around the wrist or neck of some man's lady love. She liked to imagine they'd be bought by a doting husband, but life had taught her to be cynical. From what she'd seen of society, whether in Moscow, Paris, or London, most men barely tolerated their wives, let alone bought them expensive baubles. It was the mistresses who received the expensive trinkets.

She wondered how many pieces Wolff had bought for women over the years.

The sound of the back door opening and Mickey's deep growl welcoming his master had her sitting straighter in her chair. The two men conversed for a few moments, too low for her to hear, but she heard Wolff's inquiry after her whereabouts.

"Your study, sir," Mickey said, and she braced herself as Wolff strolled down the hall and into the room.

He was dressed, as ever, in exceptionally well-fitting clothes. His dark jacket molded faithfully to his broad shoulders, his buff breeches outlined his slim hips and long muscular thighs. His hair was rumpled from the wind and his face glowed with health and vitality. Anya swallowed. Why did he have to look so damned appealing? It wasn't fair.

She did not stand to greet him. He'd lent her no such courtesy.

He sauntered over to the desk and glanced at the pages in front of her. "What are these?"

"Just some idle sketches." She tried to slide the drawing of the tiara under the pile, but he leaned one hip against the desk edge, reached out, and pulled the papers toward him.

Anya felt an embarrassed heat mount in her cheeks.

"These are very good," he said, and the genuine admiration in his tone warmed her even more. He tapped the sketch of the tiara. "Is this a design you have imagined, or a reproduction of an existing piece?"

"It was real. It belonged to Princess Denisova's grandmother."

"Did she leave it back in Russia?"

"No. It was destroyed. A casualty of war."

A sudden flash of memory assailed her, her mother wearing the tiara to some great state banquet, laughing and carefree on the arm of her handsome father. She quashed a wave of sadness. Family tradition held that every Denisova bride should wear the tiara on her wedding day. She'd certainly put an end to *that*. Not that she had any plans to marry, anyway.

Wolff accepted her explanation. He reached into his coat and withdrew a gold signet ring.

"You recall that Russian I mentioned, murdered down at Blackwall? He was wearing this. There's a crest. How do I find out which family it belongs to?"

Anya studied the engraved central stone. The armorial showed a plumed helmet, a shield with a single dagger, and a crescent shaped dash. "As a matter of fact, I know. This is for the Orlov family. Count Grigory Orlov was a lover of Catherine the Great. He's famous for presenting her with the Orlov diamond, a stone as large as half a chicken's egg. It's set into the imperial scepter. There are numerous Orlovs in Moscow and St. Petersburg."

Anya bit her lip, afraid she'd displayed too intimate a knowledge of the Russian court. Orlov's grandson, Count Pavel, had proposed to her once, but he'd been several years younger than herself, and almost a foot shorter, and she'd declined his offer. She preferred tall men. Like Wolff.

She gave herself a mental slap on the head.

"Thank you, Miss Brown. That is most helpful."

He stood and glanced at the gilt clock on the mantel-piece. "Lagrasse is almost ready for our first taste test. I managed to procure a few recipes for him to try from the Austrian ambassador, Prince Esterhazy. His wife, Prin-cess Maria Theresia, is a patroness of Almack's."

Anya schooled her expression into one of polite inter-est, despite the fact that she'd met the prince and princess several times back in Russia. Plump, dark-haired Maria Theresia was only a year younger than herself. She'd been married at seventeen. Now twenty-one, she was al-ready a fixture in London society.

"Dinner will be served in half an hour. I trust you can be ready by then?"

His expression suggested the same polite disbelief as Mr. Rundell. He clearly thought women needed hours of primping.

Anya gathered her papers and stood. "Of course. Am I to expect the pleasure of your company, my lord?"

"You can indeed."

"How nice," she said with faint irony. "You'll excuse me if I don't change for dinner. I'm afraid my wardrobe is somewhat restricted."

She looked down at the blue dress she'd been forced

to don again that morning. It was too extravagant for daytime; the bodice was scandalously low, but there had been no sign of her lavender gown. She had a horrible feeling Wolff had ordered Mickey to dispose of it.

"I thought of that." His smile was instantly suspicious. "I had to go to Bond Street anyway, so I visited a few modistes while I was there. You'll find a selection of dresses in your room." He brushed an invisible speck of lint from the sleeve of his already impeccable coat and lifted his brows in clear dismissal.

Anya bit back a retort and swept from the room.

She found no fewer than four new outfits on her bed. In addition to two day dresses, there were two more evening gowns, some scandalously sheer silk chemises, and a collection of accessories like scarves and gloves. The sight of the gloves made her heart beat faster. Was Wolff going to let her go out? She hoped so. She was sick of being cooped up indoors.

She suppressed a groan of delight as she stepped into one of the new gowns. The deep claret color was flattering, the workmanship exquisite. What was Wolff's game? Was he trying to buy her affection, her capitulation, with dresses? Did he, in his mind, already see her as a kept woman, a mistress he could dress—and undress—at will?

The thought made her shiver, and she stiffened her spine. She would not accept charity. Nor could she be bought. Even if she had to sell every one of her remaining diamonds, she would pay him back.

Chapter 17.

Seb caught himself drumming his fingers on the table and forced them to still. What was wrong with him? He'd stayed out of the house all day to avoid being under the same roof as his irritatingly beguiling guest, but now he couldn't wait to see her, to spar with her again. His blood pounded in anticipation.

He shouldn't have given into the impulse to buy her clothes, especially not ones that wouldn't have looked out of place in a high society ballroom. But the sight of her in that shabby lavender gown had caused him something close to physical pain.

He told himself it was purely aesthetic preference. A woman that beautiful shouldn't be dressed in threadbare, styleless garments. It was an affront to the natural order of things.

Thanks to his half-Italian parentage, he possessed an eye for beauty that stemmed all the way back to the Renaissance. His ancestors had doubtless patronized artists like Caravaggio and Donatello in the same way he enjoyed buying his boots from Hoby and his coats from Weston.

He wasn't a tulip of fashion, like the ridiculous dandies who flounced about town in pale satins and silks, but he made no secret of the fact that he enjoyed the sybaritic pleasure of a well-cut coat and a perfectly tied neckcloth. Benedict and Alex never stopped mocking him about it.

His love of beauty extended to his choice of bedpartners too, but despite his reputation as a rake, he'd always been discerning. Beauty alone wasn't enough to hold his interest. He required intelligence, a quick wit, and a sense of humor from his paramours too.

His "guest" had all those things, and more.

The dining table had been laid for two. With a start, Seb realized he couldn't recall the last time he'd actually dined at home. He'd taken to eating with Benedict and his wife, Georgie, or Alex and his wife, Emmy, or grazing from the buffet in the public half of the Tricorn. More often than not, he'd asked Mickey to bring him a plate of food in his study so he could eat with one hand and read a report from Bow Street with the other.

No wonder Lagrasse scowled at him. He hardly noticed what he was eating most of the time.

Tonight he would savor every bite, just as he would savor the company of his guest. She was a woman of contradictions. She liked caviar and knew the tsarina's favorite cake, but she was also friends with some of London's most expensive courtesans. None of it made sense.

He'd set Jem Barnes, one of Bow Street's youngest informants, to the task of listening out for news involving any more Russians in the criminal underworld. If there were plans afoot to capture his reluctant houseguest, he wanted to hear of them.

He sucked in a breath when she appeared in the doorway. Why in the name of all that was holy had he bought her a dress in such a provocative deep red? It was hard enough to keep his thoughts and his hands off her as it was. It would be well-nigh impossible now he'd seen her in that fever dream of a dress.

The low-cut bodice displayed the perfect globes of her breasts and the soft architecture of her shoulders and throat. She'd piled her hair up on her head, but a few thick tendrils brushed her collarbone and skated temptingly close to the valley between her breasts, like a trickle of honey. One he wanted to trace with his tongue.

Seb cleared his throat and gestured to the place setting opposite him. "Good evening, Miss Brown. Have a seat."

He did not rise or pull the chair out for her as he would have done for a woman of higher social rank. He watched her for a reaction, to see if she was irritated by the omission, but she didn't appear to expect it. She seated herself without fuss and sent him a polite smile across the snowy white linen.

"Good evening, my lord."

Her scratchy-yet-prim tones sent a jolt of desire straight to his groin, and he placed his napkin across the straining fabric in his lap. She took a tentative sip of her wine. Her throat dipped as she swallowed, and he wanted to taste her skin. He had a brief vision of sweeping everything to the floor, the flowers, the silverware, the glasses, the porcelain, of pulling her clean across the table for a kiss beyond all civilized bounds. Of putting his mouth between her breasts and—

"This is excellent wine," she said demurely.

Seb coughed. Thankfully Mickey entered carrying a tray, followed by the tiny stomping figure of Lagrasse. The disparity in height between the two men was comical. Mickey could have used the chef as an armrest.

"What do we have here?" Seb managed hoarsely. God, his voice was deep.

Lagrasse ignored him and sent Anya a dazzling smile. "To begin, madame, I 'ave prepared you ze beetroot soup."

Her eyes gleamed as Mickey placed a small bowl of liquid the precise color of her gown before her. "Oh! Borscht! How clever of you! Are you serving it hot or cold?" She picked up her spoon and skimmed the surface away from her. Her manners were impeccable.

"'Ot for you tonight, madame, wiz ze dill and a soupçon of sour crème."

Seb gave an inner snort. The soup wasn't the only thing hot for her tonight. He was burning up.

She took a delicate sip and closed her eyes. "Delicious."

The little Frenchman beamed in pleasure, and Seb quelled the impulse to tell him to leave so he could have her reactions all to himself. He wondered what else he could do to put such a satisfied smile on her face. Several depraved options came to mind.

A polite silence reigned as they both sampled the soup, and Seb, to his surprise, discovered it wasn't half as bad as he'd expected. He'd had some pretty disgusting meals during his time around France and Spain, including a revolting cabbage stew somewhere near Cadiz, but this was far better.

At Lagrasse's nod, Mickey uncovered a second dish.

"As the lady requested, we 'ave ze blini. Wiz 'oney and crème."

The chef proudly placed a selection of the tiny pancakes on Anya's plate and stood back to await her verdict.

"I'll serve myself, then, shall I?" Seb muttered, half amused, half irritated by the fact that he seemed to have been forgotten in his own dining room. Clearly *his* opinion counted for nothing.

Mickey sent him a dry look and scooped some of the remaining blinis onto his plate. "'Ere you go, sir."

All three of them watched in rapt fascination as Anya

ignored her knife and fork, picked up one of the little pancakes, and brought it to her lips. She ate it in two delicate bites then licked a smear of honey from her fingers.

Seb almost groaned aloud. This was pure, erotic torture. He wanted to blindfold the other two men. But Mickey seemed impervious, and Lagrasse appeared more nervous than aroused. He shifted his weight from one foot to the other.

Seb ate his blini in one bite. It was bloody good, so he polished off six more in quick succession, which earned him a glare from Lagrasse, presumably for not taking the time to savor the things properly.

He watched Anya eat another and a wisp of pleasure curled through him at her obvious enjoyment. Her happiness was like a warm cloud around her. He felt his mouth curl in an answering smile.

She finally pursed her lips. "Hmm. Perhaps a tiny bit more salt to balance out the sweetness of the honey? But other than that, perfection, Monsieur Lagrasse. As good as any I tasted in Russia. Thank you."

Lagrasse let out a relieved breath. "*De rien, madame.* It is a pleasure to cook for someone 'oo appreciates the skill of an artist like myself." He sent Seb a superior, chiding glare, apparently forgetting who paid his extortionate salary every month.

"You may leave us," Seb drawled.

He took another sip of wine as the two men filed out and caught her gaze, making no attempt to hide the sensual hunger he was feeling. "Hold still."

He rose from his seat, reached across the table, and used his finger to swipe a smudge of honey from the corner of her mouth. She inhaled sharply. He held his finger in front of her lips, silently commanding her to take it into her mouth. Her eyes widened, but she parted her lips and he sent her a simmering smile of approval. She took the very tip of his finger into the hot cavern of her mouth and his cock gave an insistent throb as she flicked away the honey like a cat licking cream. His knees almost buckled.

Her chest was rising and falling in sweet agitation, but she never dropped her gaze from his. He found himself falling, drowning in the fathomless blue of her eyes.

Then she pulled back, breaking the spell, and sent him a demure smile, although her voice when it came was rather breathless.

"Blini are extremely popular in my homeland. There's a whole week, Maslenitsa, every year when we celebrate our love for them. Maslenitsa means 'butter week.' The little blini symbolize the sun; by eating them, people consume its warmth and energy."

Seb sat back down and took a fortifying sip of wine. "Fascinating."

Color rose to her cheeks as she realized he wasn't referring to the information, but to her.

Conflicting emotions warred in his chest. He wanted her with a hunger that was breathtaking. Would it be dishonorable to seduce her? Would he be taking advantage of his position? She was supposed to be under his protection—shouldn't that also mean protecting her from himself?

He'd never felt anything but contempt for men who dallied with their servants. A governess or parlor maid would fear for her job if she refused her master's advances. He'd never manipulate a woman like that.

But Miss Brown was not his servant. Technically she was an employee of his great-aunt, and heaven knew he had little enough influence over that old battle-ax. Even if he petitioned for Anya to be let go, he doubted Dorothea would listen.

Besides, why should he feel guilty about wanting to

sleep with her? She'd said she didn't have much experience with men, but he doubted she was still a virgin. And while he usually preferred women who knew what they were doing in bed, he'd be more than willing to make an exception for her. The thought of continuing her education left him breathless. He'd start by addressing her woeful lack of experience when it came to kissing—

"I have a favor to ask of you, my lord."

Seb raised his brows, his pulse pounding in anticipation.

"How may I be of service, Miss Brown?" He could think of any number of wicked ways. God, he couldn't wait.

"I would like to go out."

"My pleasure. Wait—what?"

Chapter 18.

"You bought me gloves," Anya said. She glanced longingly out of the window. The mews yard was in shadow, but it was still relatively early in the evening. "It won't be dark for at least another hour, and I've been stuck inside these past two days. Can't I take a quick ride in park?"

Wolff opened his mouth, and she spoke quickly to forestall a refusal.

"Hardly anyone will be out at this hour. I won't be seen." She sent him an imploring look and swallowed her pride at having to beg. "Please."

He frowned. "You can't ride. I don't own a sidesaddle."

"I don't need one. I can ride astride."

"Not in skirts you can't."

"Then lend me some breeches."

His brows lifted in either shock, disapproval, or interest. "Breeches?" He glanced down at his own athletic frame and his lips twitched in amusement. "I hardly think you'll fit a pair of mine. Or Mickey's."

She held his gaze stubbornly. "Well, you must have a

stable lad. I'm sure a man who works for Bow Street can improvise at short notice."

She could scarcely believe she was suggesting something so scandalous, but Wolff already considered her the worst sort of hoyden anyway, so what did it matter?

His lips twitched again at her challenge. "Very well. I'll see what I can do."

He rose and she matched the move, unwilling to stay seated with him looming over her.

"You may return to your rooms, Miss Brown."

Less than half an hour later, Mickey delivered a pair of clean brown woolen breeches, a white shirt, a shapeless brown wool jacket, and a pair of scuffed knee-high riding boots to her chambers.

With a spurt of excitement, Anya put them on, remembering all the times she'd borrowed Dmitri's clothes to romp around the forests with him when they were children. The boots were a little big, but not enough to signify. She plaited her hair into a single thick braid and pinned it in a coil to her head, then shrugged into the jacket. It, too, was too big, but it disguised her curves, which was the aim.

Wolff was waiting for her at the bottom of the stairs. He glanced up as she descended and narrowed his eyes, taking a slow inventory. A simmer started in her blood and her step faltered. In contrast to her scruffiness, he looked impeccable. His boots gleamed, his greatcoat fell in heavy folds almost to his ankles. He held a black riding crop in his hand; he tapped it impatiently against his thigh. The sight made her pulse leap.

She waited for some rude comment, but he simply nodded once and strode to the door. She followed him out into the stables where two mounts had been saddled. The dark horse was the one he'd been riding when he'd come to the rescue on Hounslow Heath.

He indicated the second horse, a handsome grey with liquid eyes. "That's Borodino, and this"—he patted the bay—"is Eclipse."

"Borodino? After the battle?"

"Yes. I had him shipped back from the Peninsular. He's so used to noise that nothing disturbs him, not barking dogs, brawling street vendors, or rattling carts. He never flinches. You'll be safe with him." He frowned down at her. "Are you sure you want to go? It's cold."

Anya chuckled. "If you'd ever faced a Russian winter, you wouldn't call this cold. I'm used to snow several feet deep, my lord. I'll manage."

He plucked a cap from a nail on the wall and tossed it to her. "Cover your hair."

She tugged the peak low over her brow, then put her foot in the stirrup and mounted without his assistance. She caught a brief look of surprise on his face at her skill. Presumably he was accustomed to women who needed to use a mounting block or to be lifted up into the saddle by a man. Well, she was no damsel in distress.

She adjusted the reins as he mounted his stallion with a fluid movement that spoke of endless familiarity, and they urged the horses out into the mews yard. Wolff watched her for a moment to see how she handled her mount then led on, apparently satisfied.

"Stay behind me. You're dressed as a groom. You must act as one. If anyone sees you, they'll assume you're exercising the grey."

Anya nodded meekly, unwilling to do anything to make him change his mind.

"We'll go to St. James's Park, it's closest."

Within minutes, they rode through the gated east entrance of the park and started along one of the tree-lined paths designated for riding. As expected, the place was almost deserted.

"We can't stay long. This place is dangerous at night, no matter how genteel it appears in the daytime. It's a notorious haunt for prostitutes."

"I thought the gates were locked at night?"

"They are. But it's estimated there are over seven thousand keys in private possession, so it might as well be left open."

She brought her mount level with his and glanced up at the sky. "It smells like it's going to snow."

He shot her an amused glance. "You can smell impending snowfall?"

"Of course! You can sense it in the air." She shrugged. "Perhaps it's a Russian thing. We're clearly experts. Just as no two snowflakes are alike, so no two snowfalls are alike. There's wet snow. Slushy snow. Dry, powdery snow. Snow that's perfect for making snowballs. We have at least four different words for a snowstorm. *Metel* is wind-driven snow. *V'yuga* is a common literary term. *Buran* is a regional word, used in Siberia. And *Purga* is more like a blizzard."

He shook his head with a chuckle. "Well, you're not likely to see a blizzard here in England. The most we usually get is a light dusting. Winters used to be much colder a century ago, so I'm told. The Thames regularly froze over, and each time it did, a Frost Fair would be held on the ice. All kinds of stalls would pop up, with tradesmen selling everything from spiced ale to gingerbread and roast oxen."

"It sounds wonderful."

"The last one was two years ago. I was off fighting in Portugal, but Dorothea said they led an elephant out by Blackfriars Bridge to prove the thickness of the ice."

"I would have loved to see that. We're so used to frozen rivers in Russia, we never do exciting things like that. I suppose the novelty has worn off. Still, they say it was the harshness of our winter that defeated Napoleon when he invaded with his *Grande Armée*. He was beaten by General January and General February."

Anya's smile faded as she recalled the grim statistics that had been reported in the news sheets at the time. "I heard he lost hundreds of thousands of men on that campaign."

"He did indeed," Wolff said. "Poor bastards. I wouldn't wish that on anyone, even the enemy. I'd rather be shot than freeze to death."

Anya's chest tightened at the memory of Dmitri. She supposed she should take some slight comfort from the fact that his death had been relatively quick.

They rode on in companionable silence as the shadows lengthened. Anya took a deep breath, glad of the fresh air despite the chill, and cast around for a less depressing subject. Wolff probably had hundreds of unpleasant memories from the war. No need to dwell on them.

"I'm translating a book of Russian fairy tales for the dowager duchess," she volunteered. Her breath made a dragon's breath white puff in the cold air.

"Do you have a favorite?"

"Of course. The story of the ice maiden Snegurochka, a beautiful girl made out of snow. *Sneg* is the Russian word for snow. She's always described as wearing a long silver-blue robe edged with arctic fox fur, and a crown made of snowflakes."

"You have a cloak like that."

"Yes." She'd forgotten his unnatural perceptiveness. "It, ah, used to belong to the princess. She gave it to me."

"So what did this ice maiden do?"

"She's the daughter of Spring the Beauty and Ded Moroz, old Father Frost. She was immortal, but lonely, and she longed for the companionship of humans. She used to spy on every human she could find, and in time, she fell in love with a shepherd boy named Lel."

"Of course she did." His tone was dry. "A girl can't always find a titled, moneyed prince to fall in love with."

Anya glanced sideways at him and felt her heart turn over in her chest, despite his cynicism. In the lengthening shadows, he embodied masculine grace and strength. He was exactly the kind of human a foolish immortal would fall in love with.

She cleared her throat. "There are several versions of the story. In some tales, the very act of falling in love warms Snegurochka's heart so much that she melts and disappears in a puff of water vapor."

Wolff snorted. "That's unfortunate. A cautionary tale for avoiding romantic entanglements, then."

"But *another* ending has it that falling in love does not kill the princess," Anya continued. "Instead, she falls into a deep decline because she knows she can never be with her mortal love. Her mother, Spring, asks whether she would forfeit her immortality to be with Lel, and she answers without hesitation, 'Of course! I'd rather live a short and happy life with Lel than spend eternity without him.' Seeing the depth of her daughter's love, Spring grants Snegurochka her wish. The Snow Maiden becomes mortal and marries her shepherd, and they have a long and happy life together."

"She gave up her privileged position for love?" Wolff raised his brows. "No wonder it's a fairy tale. Which ending do you prefer?"

Anya wrinkled her nose. "I suppose the first one's the most realistic. Love certainly has the power to destroy those unlucky enough to encounter it."

Apart from Elizaveta, all the people she'd ever loved had left her; her parents of illness, Dmitri from war. Her heart still felt bruised. It made sense to enclose it in a layer of ice so thick, it could never be melted. They'd called her the ice princess back in Russia, because she'd kept most of her suitors at a frigid, polite distance. She hadn't minded the sobriquet.

"You seem a little young for such a cynical outlook."

Anya shrugged. "I'd like to believe in the second ending. One should always hold out hope, after all." She risked another glance at Wolff, certain he would be mocking her, but his face was impossible to read.

They'd reached the edge of a large pond. Several swans and ducks floated serenely on the surface, but Anya squinted at a large, unfamiliar bird with a long yellow beak. "What is that?"

Wolff's teeth flashed white as he smiled. "Have you never seen one? It's a pelican. They're not native to these shores. In fact, I believe one of your countrymen was responsible for it being here."

"How so?"

"According to legend, some Russian ambassador presented King Charles the second with a pair of pelicans back in the 1600s. Those birds there are the descendants of that original pair. Occasionally one creates havoc by pouncing on a passing pigeon and swallowing it whole."

"Oh dear! I suppose that might strain diplomatic relations between our two countries. At least the ambassador didn't give King Charles a white elephant to bankrupt him."

Wolff's amused gaze flicked over her, and she immediately felt self-conscious. She was sure her nose was pink with cold. He, in contrast, looked as handsome as ever. His lips didn't look pinched, they looked sinfully tempting. Would they feel cool beneath her own? Or warm?

He cleared his throat. "We should get back to the Tricorn. I'm going to need a glass of brandy to warm me up."

Anya gathered her scrambled thoughts. "Do you find it cold here, after the heat of Portugal and Spain?"

He tilted his head, considering. "The heat was nice. But I'd still rather be here, without bullets flying at me. Better cold and alive than warm and dead."

She nodded. *Better an impoverished companion than a princess without options too.*

"The dowager duchess said you'd lost your hearing during the war," she said carefully. "But you don't seem to have any particular difficulty."

He shrugged, an elegant lift of his shoulders that reminded her of the physical power banked in his frame. "A canon blast at Waterloo. It only affected my left ear, thankfully. Sometimes I have to angle my head a little when it's particularly windy or there's a lot of chatter, but it's not a great inconvenience. It's quite useful at parties, actually. I can't tell you how many times I've literally turned a deaf ear to some gossiping harpy or boring politician."

He sent her a teasing smile that knotted her stomach. "Remember that when you're whispering sweet nothings to me, Miss Brown. Right side only, if you please."

Anya straightened in the saddle and sent him a haughty look. "There will be no whispering, Lord Mowbray. Sweet or otherwise." She turned the grey and kicked it to a trot.

His deep chuckle echoed after her.

Chapter 19.

It was dark by the time they got back to the Tricorn. Mickey must have been watching for them, because he came out and took the horses.

"Delivery came from the wine merchants, sir. I've placed it in the study. There's a nice fire in there too."

"Thank you, Mickey."

Wolff strode inside. Anya followed him into the burgundy salon and went straight to the fire to warm her icy hands. They tingled painfully with the returning circulation. A wooden crate, stamped in Cyrillic, had been placed on the sideboard.

"Vodka!" Anya read in delight.

Wolff lifted the lid to reveal a dozen bottles of clear liquid nestling in the straw-filled interior. "I've no idea if it's any good or not. I have far more experience with brandy."

"I know a little."

"You?"

His tone was pure skepticism, and Anya smiled to

herself. Her family owned an entire vodka distillery back in St. Petersburg. She knew the manufacturing process from field to crate. Not that she'd admit that to *him*.

She shrugged. "In Russia, everyone drinks it. Wine made from grapes is so expensive that only aristocrats can afford it, but vodka's available everywhere. It's called 'bread wine' because it's made from wheat, rye, or barley. And sometimes 'burning wine' because it makes you feel like your throat and stomach are on fire."

She sent him a challenging look. "I've tasted the very good and the very bad. I can certainly tell you if it's good enough to serve to your guests."

He pulled forward two cut glass tumblers, opened a bottle, and poured a thimbleful of liquid into each glass. Anya only just refrained from scoffing at his frugality.

"Any host who doesn't offer plenty of drink is considered unfriendly," she scolded. "And not emptying your glass is a sign of disrespect."

"Really?"

"Yes. We Russians take our vodka very seriously. There are rules for *everything*. You should always pour for others before yourself, and you should never pour a single shot just for you." She took the glass he offered with a smile. "It is never sipped, but downed in one gulp, ice-cold."

"I'll bear that in mind," he said dryly. "Anything else I should know?"

She lifted her glass and took a tentative sniff. "It should be flavorless and odorless."

He sniffed at his own glass. "So far, so good."

"Most importantly, vodka is never, ever drunk without a reason." She sent him a stern look. "An everyday dinner in Russia is not accompanied by vodka the way an everyday dinner in France or England comes with a glass of wine. Russians only drink when there's an 'occasion.' Conveniently, we find something to celebrate in almost everything." She gave an impish chuckle as she listed the items on her fingers. "Weddings, funerals, the birth of a child, signing a business contract, religious holidays, a successful harvest. All perfectly appropriate reasons to drink."

"Good God," Wolff said with a choked laugh. "It's a wonder any of you are ever sober. So, what shall we drink to?"

Anya tilted her head. "The first toast, traditionally, is 'to our meeting.'"

"Very well."

They both lifted their glasses and swallowed the contents, and she gasped as the liquid stole her breath. Warmth burned down her throat and made her eyes water. Wolff lifted his brows at her in silent demand for her verdict.

"That is very good vodka," she said truthfully. She held her glass forward again. "Our next toast should be to our families."

He poured another inch into her glass and refilled his own. "Our families."

They both drank.

Anya quashed a twinge of grief. She didn't have any close family left. The loss of Dmitri was like a dull ache that resurfaced at the most unexpected of moments. But she must not get maudlin. She still had dear friends in Elizaveta, Charlotte, and the dowager. They were like family too.

"The next is to our health." She offered her glass again and Wolff, after a slight hesitation, refilled it. "*Za zdarovje,*" she said solemnly.

He matched her drink, and Anya let out a deep sigh. She'd forgotten this taste of her homeland. It was certainly doing its job of warming her up. Her stomach felt as if it were glowing, and her senses were tingling pleasantly.

"Of course, the more eloquently you can express the occasion, the more it confirms that it's special. For example, my brother always used to say, 'May we have as much sorrow as drops of vodka left in our glasses.'" She sent Wolff a contented smile. "That's nice, don't you think?"

"It is." He carried the bottle over to one of the chairs positioned by the fire. "Come, sit down."

He sat, but Anya ignored the other chair. Instead, she sank to the floor, grateful she still wore breeches. They allowed much better freedom of movement than skirts. She raised one knee and leaned back against the front of the chair with a happy sigh.

Wolff lifted the bottle and sent her a questioning glance. She offered forward her glass.

"So what's *your* favorite toast?"

She raised her glass and met his eyes. "To tables breaking of abundance and beds breaking of love." She tipped her head back and drank.

He downed his own shot. "An excellent sentiment. Might I propose one more?"

"Go ahead."

He leaned forward and his hand was slightly unsteady when he poured. Or perhaps it was her hand that was swaying? Either way, a splash of vodka trickled onto her wrist.

"Oops!" Anya chased the drop around her hand. She caught it on her tongue and turned laughing eyes to Wolff to share the silly moment, but the naked hunger in his gaze made her levity vanish like woodsmoke. A swirl of excitement replaced it. His expression was ardent, his gaze burning. He looked like he wanted to gobble her up. Heat flashed across her skin.

"What was your toast?" she managed hoarsely.

"To friendship."

A knot of emotion caught in her throat. "Are we friends, my lord?"

"We're certainly not enemies."

Anya tossed back the vodka and rested her head against the seat of the chair. The combination of the warm fire and the alcohol was conspiring to make her drowsy and languid. The room was starting to spin. "Maybe you're trying to get me so drunk I'll spill all my secrets? *In vino veritas*, and all that."

"Maybe," he agreed pleasantly. "Is it working?"

"A little." Anya smiled. She was, in fact, feeling wonderfully informal. The only person she'd ever been this relaxed with before was Dmitri. A bittersweet pang of memory assailed her as she remembered the way they used to lounge about on the floor like puppies when they were younger, reading in front of the fire. The feelings she was having toward Wolff, however, were decidedly unsisterly.

"Don't get too close to the fire, Ice Princess," he murmured. "You might melt."

Her heart missed a beat. He couldn't possibly know how close that teasing nickname was to the truth.

"Hic!"

She clapped her hand over her mouth but couldn't stop another involuntary squeak escaping. "Hic."

Wolff's chuckle filled the space between them. "You appear to have hiccups, Miss Brown."

"So it would seem."

"Do you Russians have rules for those too?" he teased. Anya glared at him, but her chiding was ruined by another undignified hiccup. "Hic! Yes we do, actually. If you have hiccups, it means someone is thinking of you. The fastest way to—hic!—get rid of them is to start naming people. If they stop at a certain name, that person was the one thinking of you."

"You'd best start naming people, then."

"Hic!" Anya frowned in exasperation. "Very well. The dowager duchess."

They waited.

"Hic! No, not her. Elizaveta?"

She held her breath. Three seconds passed. "Hic! Not her either."

Anya bit her lip. Wolff's gaze dropped to her mouth and the hungry, sleepy expression reappeared.

She pressed her lips together. "Vasili Petrov?"

His expression darkened. A muscle ticked in the side of his jaw, and something dangerous flared in his eyes. He glared at her as long moments ticked by, almost daring her to make a sound.

"Hic."

Anya let out a relieved breath, even though it was only a silly game. She didn't want Vasili thinking of her, ever.

Wolff leaned forward in his chair, and she sucked in an unsteady breath as he continued to stare at her. "Sebastien Wolff," he prompted softly.

"Sebastien Wolff," she echoed.

The silence stretched. And held.

Her eyes widened. "It worked! You're thinking of me! What are you thinking?"

He set down his glass with quiet deliberation. "I'm thinking about kissing you."

Her pulse was rushing in her ears, desire swirling through her bloodstream. This was a test, a battle of wills to see who would capitulate first. Well, it would not be her. She was thinking about kissing him too.

She placed her empty tumbler carefully on the rug. In the most subservient move of her life, she prowled toward him on hands and knees, like a cat. When she neared his chair, he sat back like a king on his throne, hands resting loosely on the arms, and widened his legs in unmistakable invitation for her to come between them.

Anya stood, holding his gaze, even though her knees trembled. She stepped between his thighs and placed her hands on the back of his chair, one on either side of his head. Her face was inches from his own. She could see the fine grain of his skin, the dark stubble on his jaw, the tiny laugh lines at the corner of his eyes. The scent of him filled her nose, a hint of vodka mixed with a woodsy, masculine fragrance and a tang of leather and horse.

Her stomach swooped in excitement, but she sent him her most superior ice-princess look to remind him who was in charge. "This seems like *me* kissing *you*," she taunted softly.

He lifted his head and pressed his mouth to hers.

His lips were soft, unhurried. Anya closed her eyes and kissed him back, clinging, shaping, exploring the contours of his mouth. Her tongue snaked out and encountered his, and she gasped, then did it again, wanting to taste.

The world fell away and clicked into place at the same time. His tongue darted over and under hers in a way that made her light-headed and his muffled groan was the sweetest sound she'd ever heard. His hands found the curve of her hips. He tugged her closer, then slid them around to her bottom, and Anya squirmed in delight as he squeezed her through the fabric of her breeches.

She was hot, hotter than the fire, melting like an icicle under his hands. Desperate, she grasped his hair in her fists and bent her knees, straddling him in the chair.

A jolt of shock rocked her as her core nestled over the solid bulge of his arousal.

She pulled back and stared down at him. Both of them were panting. He stared right back at her, his gaze so open, so direct, she felt the connection all the way down to her soul. He was hard and hot beneath her, indecently close. Only a few layers of cloth separated them. She wanted them gone.

His fingers tightened on her bottom, and he lifted his hips to press himself even closer to the center of her body.

"That's where I want to be," he rasped, and his low growl vibrated from his chest into hers. "Right there. Inside you." His heavy-lidded gaze studied her for a long moment—and then he shook his head with an almost disbelieving sigh. "But not tonight."

Anya blinked. "What?"

His lips twitched, even though his humor seemed self-directed. "Oh, we *will* finish this, Miss Brown, I promise you." He rolled his hips again and a tremor crackled through her body like summer lightning. "But I have rules too."

"Rules?" she parroted, like an imbecile.

"You're drunk," he said softly. "And as tempted as I am, I refuse to take advantage of you in this state." His dark gaze held hers as he slid her off his lap and pulled her gently to her feet. He stood, holding her against his body for a moment as she swayed.

"When I take a woman to bed, I want her sober." His eyes burned into hers with erotic intent. "So she remembers all the wicked things we do."

Before Anya could protest, he bent down and swept her into his arms, cradling her against the hard wall of his chest.

She bit back a moan of disappointment. He was refusing

her? Unfair! She might be a little tipsy, but she wasn't *drunk*. Still, it had a certain neat symmetry. She'd turned him down at Charlotte's, after all.

The stupid man had clearly made up his mind to be noble. She closed her eyes as he carried her into the hall and up the curving staircase to her rooms. He jiggled her in his arms and managed to open the door, then strode through to her bedroom and deposited her gently on the bed.

Anya glared up at him. "I'm really not drunk."

"You're not entirely sober either," he countered, with irritating logic. "And whatever else you can say about me, I've never slept with a woman who didn't know exactly what she was doing." He bent and pressed a chaste kiss to her forehead. "I'll see you in the morning, Miss Brown."

Anya let out a groan of utter frustration as the door clicked closed behind him.

Chapter 20.

Anya woke with a pounding head and uncomfortable memories of the night before. Kissing Wolff had been glorious, but she shouldn't have let down her guard. What if she'd let her secret slip?

When she asked Mickey about his whereabouts, she learned he'd gone out, but had left her a note:

> *Several Russians from the delegation will be attending the club tonight, including Prince Trubetskoi. My colleague hasn't found a Russian speaker to mingle with the guests, so I have a request: Will you do it? You can wear a mask to hide your face. I shall expect your answer when I return.*

Anya frowned down at the paper. Venturing out in a crowd would be a risk, certainly, but she was desperate to escape the confines of the living quarters again, even for a few hours. There was little chance of anyone recognizing her if she did as Wolff suggested and dressed as a masked courtesan. Most men, in her experience, only saw what they expected to see. Especially when it came to women.

And perhaps doing her captor a favor would be no bad thing. If he was in her debt, he might be persuaded to do something for her in return.

A short while later a knock sounded at the door, and she turned to see Mickey ushering in the elegantly clad figure of Charlotte Haye.

"Charlotte! What are you doing here?"

Charlotte returned her hug and stepped back with a wide smile. "I've come to see how you're holding up, of course. And don't worry. Elizaveta told me you're concerned about meeting that brute Count Petrov again. I made certain nobody was watching the house or following me. I even changed carriages three times and went all the way to Limehouse and back, just in case. It was quite the adventure!"

She held Anya at arm's length and studied her through narrowed eyes. "I do hope you don't mind me coming. We've all been *dying* of curiosity."

"Not at all! I've been in dire need of female company. And you've come at a most opportune time. I need help dressing like one of your girls."

Charlotte's eyes widened in scandalized interest. "And why is that? Please tell me you've changed your mind about seducing Lord Mowbray?"

Anya felt heat rushing to her cheeks. "No! At least, I don't think I have."

Charlotte sent her an amused look. "That doesn't sound like a definite no. What's going on?"

"Mowbray is letting me visit the Tricorn's gaming floor tonight. But since the only women who attend are . . . less than respectable . . . that's what I need to be."

Charlotte gave a crow of delight. "How marvelous!

I've been itching to get my hands on you and your far-too-practical wardrobe for months! Show me to your bedroom. I can't wait to get started."

A little dazed, Anya led her up the stairs and into her set of rooms. Charlotte looked around approvingly, and when Anya showed her the gowns Wolff had provided, she gasped in delight.

"Mowbray bought you these?" she breathed, wide-eyed. "Darling, you're going to look ravishing! Now strip."

Anya did as she was told.

The evening gown Charlotte selected was a superb example of the dressmaker's art: watered silk, with tiny puff sleeves and a neckline that left Anya's shoulders scandalously bare. The provocative color changed from peacock blue to kingfisher green in the light, and the material made a satisfying swish, like a whispered secret, whenever she moved.

The front was cut so low, it almost showed her nipples, and Anya resisted the urge to try to cover herself. An ingenious built-in corset held everything in place and would—hopefully—avoid disaster.

"Who would have guessed you were hiding a bosom under there!" Charlotte teased.

As a princess, Anya had clothes that had always been of the highest quality, but they had, by and large, been quite demure. This dress was neither of those things. It was a daring, silent statement that proclaimed the wearer a powerful, confident woman. And Wolff had chosen it for *her*. Was that how he saw her? It was hard not to be flattered.

"Never underestimate the importance of clothes in a woman's arsenal," Charlotte said, her tone serious. "In the right setting, satins and silks can render you as invulnerable as armor. Knowing you look good, that you have the power to bring grown men to their knees, is a valuable asset."

She gave a mischievous smile and led Anya to the dressing table so she could brush her hair. "Sensible men can be persuaded to do a great many foolish things when under the influence of a revealing bodice and a trim waist. I once persuaded the Chevalier d'Anveau to buy me a matched curricle and pair, thanks to a particularly well-cut décolletage."

Anya smiled. Charlotte's opinion on the importance of fashion was rather similar to Wolff's.

She sat still as Charlotte pinned her hair into an elegant upswept style and added the blue ostrich feather plume that had come along with the dress. To Anya's eye, she looked underdressed without a tiara on her head and a glittering necklace at her throat, but still, it had been a long time since she'd made such an effort over her appearance.

Since she'd felt so attractive.

A teal-colored opera mask would cover her from forehead to nose, and her worry dissipated at the anonymity it would provide.

Charlotte opened her reticule and extracted a pot of rouge, which she dabbed sparingly onto Anya's lips and cheeks, then stood back to admire her handiwork.

"Perfect! You'll break hearts tonight, Madame Incognito. I guarantee it." She collapsed gracefully onto the side of the bed. "So, tell me everything. Has Wolff kissed you again?"

Anya fought a guilty flush. "What do you mean, *again*?"

Charlotte sent her a chiding look. "He kissed you that night at my house. Don't think I didn't notice, young lady! The atmosphere in that room was crackling. He didn't take his eyes off you the entire time. Until you looked at him, and then he looked away. The whole thing was vastly entertaining. Better than watching an opera."

Anya sighed. "Yes. He did kiss me that night. And he's kissed me again since then."

So very thoroughly.

"And you enjoyed it," Charlotte predicted, with a gleeful bounce upon the bed.

"Yes. Very much." Anya couldn't stop the smile that sneaked across her lips at the memory.

Charlotte tilted her head. "You naughty girl! Are you going to take him as your lover? He wants you, I'm certain of it. And that's not all. I've seen all the ways men look at women—with lust, with pride, with covetousness, with hopeless longing. He looks at you with more than just desire. There's something else there, something real. Something rare."

"I'm very tempted," Anya confessed. "But I've never taken a lover. I always assumed I'd wait until I found someone to marry, but I'm twenty-two now, and the chances of that happening are growing more and more remote. Perhaps I ought to see what all the fuss is about?"

The girls at Haye's had tried on countless occasions to explain to her that women could experience just as much pleasure as men, provided one's partner was skilled enough. Anya was beginning to think it was time she discovered the truth for herself.

"It's just like riding a horse," Charlotte said with a wry smile. "You need a little practice until you learn how to control your mount, but you'll quickly gain confidence and discover the right positions. And then—it's marvelous. Think of how much you like riding a horse; the breathless thrill of a fast gallop, the swoop of excitement as you clear a fence. Good sex is even better."

Anya considered her words. There was no question that she desired Wolff. Her body crackled to life whenever he was near. Along with his confidence in his own abilities, and the fact that he clearly desired her too, he was the perfect candidate if she wanted to take a lover.

A pang of guilt seized her. Neither Charlotte nor Wolff knew she was a princess, however. Would they treat her any differently if they knew?

Charlotte's advice would probably remain the same, even if she discovered her secret. She fully believed in a woman taking control of her own pleasure, whatever her station in life.

But Anya doubted Wolff would see her in the same light, as a potential bed partner, if he knew her background. He'd probably balk at deflowering an aristocratic virgin, no matter how willing that virgin was. It was shamefully dishonest not to tell him, but she'd come to a decision; she wanted him.

"Do you think a man can sleep with a woman without feeling anything for her other than physical attraction?" she asked.

Charlotte met her eyes. "Honestly? Yes, I do. For many men it's just scratching an itch with the nearest available body. Women, on the other hand, need their *mind* made love to, not just their limbs."

She folded her hands in her lap. "One of my theories is that men love with their eyes, while we women love with all of our senses. We like to have our brains stimulated by clever conversation and witty repartee. We like to hear a man's laugh, to have our stomach tighten when we catch a whiff of his cologne, to feel the prickles of his jaw." She gave a laughing sigh. "Men, in general, just need a pair of breasts shoved in their face and they're raring to go."

Anya chuckled and glanced down at her own exposed décolletage. "In that case, I'd say I'm perfectly attired for a successful seduction."

Charlotte stood and caught Anya's hands in her own. "Bravo! It's your decision, my darling. Do whatever makes you happy." She pressed a gentle kiss to her cheek. "I must be getting home. The girls will be wondering where I am. Good luck with whatever you decide."

Chapter 21.

Anya heard Wolff's return an hour or so later, and the tempo of her pulse increased. She heard the door to the adjacent suite open and close, and waited an extra half hour to give him time to get dressed for the evening. Then she slipped on her shoes, collected her mask, and made her way along the hall to his chamber, excitement warring with nerves in her chest.

He opened the door—clearly expecting Mickey because his gaze swiftly readjusted downward about eight inches to her face. And then his eyes swept the rest of her, and Anya held her breath. His chocolate-brown gaze seemed to devour every inch of her, and her skin heated in response.

He smiled, a lazy smile that caused his cheek to crease into that almost-but-not-quite dimple, and her heart gave an irregular kick. He was so full of vitality, so ludicrously handsome, that she felt momentarily dizzy. The stark black and white of his formal evening clothes made him look both commanding and slightly wicked. Like Lucifer on his best behavior.

"You look exquisite, Miss Brown."

Anya dropped him a pert little curtsey. "Why, thank you. Charlotte came and gave me some help to get ready. We both approve of your choice."

She peered around his body, trying to sneak a glimpse of his rooms, but he placed both hands on the doorframe and leaned forward, denying her entry to what he obviously considered his private, inner sanctum.

The move only increased her desire to see it.

He leaned close enough for her to catch a faint whiff of cologne and warm skin, but she ignored the traitorous clenching of her stomach.

"I take it, from your outfit, that you've decided to lend me your assistance this evening."

"That's what I wish to discuss with you." Anya ducked neatly beneath his outstretched arm and slipped past him into his room. He turned with a muttered curse, and she bit back a smile.

"So *this* is the lair of the big bad Wolff," she teased. "I must confess, I've wanted to see it." She studied the red leather-topped desk and overstuffed armchairs with a chuckle of delight. "Hmm. Rather disappointing. I was sure there'd be more ravished virgins and piles of human bones."

He crossed his arms and sent her a look that was part amused, part exasperated.

"Make yourself at home," he said dryly. He prowled toward her and she took a retreating step back. "So what was it you wanted to discuss?"

"If you want me to help you spy on my countrymen, you need to give me something in return."

He raised his brows. "You want payment?"

"Of a kind. Skills. I've realized I need to be more proficient in certain areas."

His mouth twitched, and she flushed as she belatedly realized the potential for misinterpretation in her words.

"And you want me to teach you?" he drawled.

"I do." She quashed the highly improper thoughts his words had summoned. "At first I thought of asking you to teach me to shoot a rifle or a pistol, but then I realized that's not very practical. I'm unlikely to ever need to know such things. You *could* teach me some ways to defend myself without a weapon, however."

The memory came, unbidden, of Vasili's hands on her wrists, of his mouth grinding upon hers. Of how powerless she'd been. She never wanted to be in that position again.

"Knowledge is power," she said softly. "Please show me."

He gave a slow exhale. "Right now?"

She nodded.

"I'm not sure there's much you can do while wearing that dress," he said. "But I suppose I can show you a couple of basic moves."

He took another step and stopped less than an arm's length away.

"Because of your height, you're at an immediate disadvantage. So you'll need to be inventive when it comes to bringing down your opponent."

"How?"

"Fight dirty. Hit him in the crotch," he said baldly. "Or punch him in the throat. If he can't breathe, he can't fight."

Anya nodded earnestly.

"Pull his ears, or better still, bite them. Jab at his eyes. And if you can grab his nose, snap it to the side. It'll bleed like the devil."

Anya's gaze automatically went to the perfect line of

his nose. Considering the number of battles in which he'd been involved, she'd have thought it would have been broken a time or two. The man was clearly charmed.

He smiled and Anya returned the gesture, delighted with this new information. Even Dmitri hadn't discussed this kind of thing with her. Then she jumped as Wolff reached out, caught her fingers, and raised their joined hands between them. Her blood pulsed in her fingertips as he intertwined their fingers and then bent hers back with gentle force.

"Bend his fingers back," he said softly, and his voice was lower, a rough murmur that seemed suddenly far more intimate, despite the gruesome subject matter. He increased the pressure, just to the edge of pain. "You might break a few bones that way."

He released her, only to bring his hands up to her shoulders, left bare by the cut of the dress. Anya sucked in a breath.

He slid his hands upward to encircle her neck. A shiver of awareness slithered down her spine as his fingers disturbed the fine hairs at her nape beneath her upswept hair. His palms were warm against her skin as he applied just the slightest pressure.

His gaze snagged hers. "If someone's trying to throttle you, put your hands together and bring your arms up and out, over his. That should break his hold. Try it."

Anya did so and was pleased when the instructions worked. He let his arms fall back to his sides, but his gaze dropped to her mouth and awareness thickened the air between them, a bright, expectant tension, like the hush before a thunderstorm.

Anya could feel the warmth radiating from his chest; her body felt like melting wax.

"We should get down on the floor."

Her eyes widened. "What?"

"The gaming floor," he clarified, with a thoroughly wicked chuckle. "Get your mind out of the gutter, Miss Brown."

He stepped back and strode to the door, then shot her a challenging look over his shoulder. "Come on. Let's put you to work."

Chapter 22.

The noise from the Tricorn was an audible murmur from behind the connecting door. Wolff pushed it open and a wave of sound assaulted them as they stepped into a picture-lined hallway. Mickey stood at the far end at a podium, greeting guests who entered through the front door.

"The gaming rooms are on the upper level." Wolff took her elbow and led her up an impressive curving double staircase. At the top, he paused and took two glasses of what appeared to be champagne from a tray on a stand. He handed one to her.

"For courage. But only one glass." His gaze clashed with hers and his lips gave a devilish quirk. "Tonight, I want you sober."

Anya took a deep gulp. Sober because she needed her wits about her to listen to her countrymen? Or sober because he wanted to make love to her in that state, as he'd promised last night?

Her heart pounded at the thought.

They crossed into the main salon, and Anya looked around with interest. This half of the Tricorn was more opulent than the private apartments, as luxurious and tastefully decorated as Haye's. As ornate as her own residences back in Russia. Wolff nodded to a couple of acquaintances. Despite the early hour—it was only around nine o'clock—the place was already busy.

Guests gossiped and tried their hand at games of chance at the green baize tables. Anya had forgotten what it was like to be in such a crowd. She'd missed it: the laughter, the heightened sense of excitement that went along with the rattle of dice and the swish of cards. People drinking and enjoying themselves. It was a sight to gladden the heart.

She stayed close to Wolff, intensely aware of him beside her, of the occasional brush of their bodies as the crowd jostled them together.

They made a slow traverse of the room, and she listened in to the various conversations as they passed. The topics were the same as any salon in St. Petersburg or Paris; people seeking power and influence, jockeying for position. Bragging—who knew what, who owned what. The women they passed were elegant and animated, cheering their escorts with rouged lips and painted cheeks.

Wolff greeted several people, shaking hands and patting shoulders, while never relinquishing his grip on her arm. He didn't introduce her to anyone, and the men slid knowing glances at her exposed skin and drew their own conclusions. Clearly it was not unusual to encounter a woman on Wolff's arm.

They ended up at the far end of the room near a quartet of musicians, and Anya smiled as he turned his deaf ear to them.

"I think *you* would make an excellent diplomat," she

said. "You make everyone comfortable enough to spill their secrets."

"That's the aim. To gather information."

"You enjoy your work for Bow Street?"

"Yes. It feels like I'm doing something useful. My older brother, Geoffrey, has a seat in the House of Lords, but making laws holds no interest for me. Government moves too slowly for my taste. I prefer situations that yield more immediate results."

Anya nodded. She understood that. Justice was sometimes best served outside the strict parameters of the law. "What games are played here?"

"Faro. Cribbage. Ecarte, loo, whist, vingt-et-un, piquet. Rouge et noir. Whatever the clients want."

"Do people try to cheat?"

He gave a dry chuckle. "All the time. Cardinal Mazarin used to call it 'making the most of the game,' I believe, but we don't tolerate it here in any form. We employ those who know what to look for."

"Such as?"

"Someone with an accomplice who looks at their opponent's cards over their shoulder and sends a signal to give an advantage. Last month a chap tried to use the reflection in a silver snuff box to sneak a look at the cards as they were dealt. There are numerous other ways: weighted dice, marked cards."

"How do they mark cards?"

"You make a tiny scratch with your fingernail so you know which one is a queen, for example. Or you give it a 'wire edge' by scraping the side to make it rough. You can get cards that have been cut so there's a slight difference in size or dimensions so one is singled out— that's called *biseauté*. Some are convex or concave in the middle, but only by the smallest amount."

"That's amazing."

"Some cheats rub certain cards with soap to make them slick, or with resin to make them sticky, so they're identifiable when being dealt or handled. I've seen cards pricked with a pin so they have a tiny hole. The raised bump is indistinct to the naked eye, but you can feel it with your fingertips."

Anya shook her head in wonder. "Goodness! And do clubs ever cheat their guests?"

"Sometimes. You can tip the odds in the house's favor by having roulette wheels with black segments slightly wider than the whites, to increase the chances of the ball falling into them. Or you can slip some coins beneath one leg of the table to tilt it and make it favor certain numbers. But we never resort to underhand tactics like that here. Anyone with a basic understanding of mathematics would realize we don't *need* to cheat. The bank holds the advantage in any game of chance, thanks to the laws of averages. We get a steady return on investment."

Anya glanced around at the opulent décor. "So I gather."

Wolff leaned closer. "I've become quite adept at spotting liars and cheats, Miss Brown. It's a necessary part of this business." The subtle warning in his voice made her shiver. "People often give just as much away with their bodies as they do with their mouths."

She exhaled nervously. "What do you mean?"

He tilted his head to indicate a young man at the nearest table. A woman stood at his side, leaning over to see the outcome of the dice throw. Like Anya, she was masked.

"Let's take Lord Naseby and his companion over there as the perfect example." A slight, cynical smile flickered over his mobile mouth. "He wants everyone to think he's brought along a courtesan, but I rather suspect that's his sister, Lady Penelope."

"Why do you say that?"

"Look at the way he's touching her. His arm's around her waist, but there's nothing lover-like about it. He's shielding her, protecting her, but not in a jealous way. It's more solicitous than sensual." His warm breath tickled the bare skin of her shoulder as he bent closer, and her body tingled in awareness. "There's a big difference between the way a man touches his sister and how he touches his lover, Miss Brown. Surely you know that. A lover would be proud to have such a woman on his arm, favoring him with her company. He'd use small, proprietary touches to signal to every other man in the room that she's with him."

His voice dropped even lower, and Anya felt her breath quicken.

"A lover would want to touch her skin. He'd put his hand at the small of her back. He'd lean in and kiss the exposed nape of her neck."

His own breath ruffled her hair by her ear and his lips ghosted across her skin. Goose bumps broke out all over her body.

"You're very observant, my lord," she managed.

"Indeed, I am. And I'm sorry to say that I don't believe you're being completely honest with me, Miss Brown."

Anya gulped, but was saved from having to answer when he spoke again.

"You want me to teach you a real life skill? I'll teach you how to lie convincingly."

She lifted her brows. "How?"

"When you think about it, we lie to people all the time, especially in the *ton*. Little white lies. We say, 'Delighted to meet you,' and 'You're looking well,' when we really mean just the opposite. But those are easy. We do them without thinking, with the intent to make the recipient feel better or to spare their feelings. It's the big lies, the serious lies, that I'm talking about."

"Go on."

He leaned closer. "The trick is to always put a little truth in with the lie."

"How do you do that?"

"Well, let's say I ask you, 'Are you a courtesan?' You can easily answer 'yes,' if you silently add some extra bit of truth in your own mind to clarify; you can think *but only for tonight, in this room.* That will make the lie far more believable."

"I see."

"Let's try another example, and I'll show you what I mean. Ask me something to which you know the truthful answer."

"Do you live here in the Tricorn Club?"

"No," he said easily. "I don't live *here* in the Tricorn Club, *in the gaming room. I live next door, in my own apartments.* Your turn, Miss Brown." The corner of his mouth curled upward. "Do you want me to kiss you?"

Anya's breath caught. Oh, he was wicked. "You think you know the answer to that?"

"We'll see. Tell me the truth or a lie. Your choice."

"In that case, no," she lied evenly, maintaining eye contact with him even though her pulse beat a reckless tattoo in her throat. "I don't want you to kiss me." *Not more than fifty times a day,* she added silently.

His smile widened. "That was excellent. I really can't tell if you're lying or not."

He looked as if he would say more, but a disturbance from the card room broke the spell. He gave a deep sigh of irritation. "Let's see what that's about."

He ushered her across the floor and growled deep in his throat when he spied a pair of young men slumped at one of the tables. Both were clearly well on the way to inebriation, judging by their loud, slurred conversation and heightened color.

"Here's another life skill," he growled. "How about I show you how we get rid of troublemakers here at the Tricorn?"

"Doesn't Mickey just pick them up by their collars and throw them out into the street?"

"It's tempting, but no. I have a more subtle method."

He beckoned to one of the hovering staff members. "Evening, Tom. I see Alvanley and Stoke are already in their cups and starting to get annoying. I think it's time for them to leave."

The thin man smiled. "Very good, sir."

Anya sent Wolff a confused glance as the servant slipped out of the room and returned moments later with two glasses filled with what looked like more liquor. He delivered them to the troublemakers' table with a polite bow.

"What's this?" The red-faced man with a disordered neckcloth peered upward, angry at the interruption to his card game. "I never ordered these."

"On the 'ouse, gents," Tom said calmly. "Compliments of the establishment."

Stoke, or Alvanley, whichever one it was, softened visibly. "Oh. Well. Mighty kind of you."

Both gamblers accepted their drinks and downed them in a drunken toast.

Wolff smiled. "Watch this. In five minutes, they'll be asleep."

Anya gasped. "You've drugged them?"

"Just a few drops of mandrake tincture in their brandy. Not enough to cause any lasting harm, just temporary insensibility. Lagrasse has the recipe."

Sure enough, not five minutes later, both men began to yawn. Stoke—or Alvanley—sagged in his chair, while the other one slowly slumped forward until his forehead came to rest on the card table. He let out a snore. Tom leapt forward and caught the glass from the man's limp hand before it could fall to the floor.

"That was particularly quick because both of them were already six sheets to the wind. It takes a bit longer on someone who's sober," Wolff explained.

"Amazing!" Anya murmured. "That's far better than using force."

Just imagine if she'd had something like that when dealing with Vasili. Obviously, as a means of defense, it still relied on getting the target to ingest it, but she would have felt far safer, knowing she had the ability to render him—or any other threat, for that matter—unconscious in a matter of minutes.

"Do you think I could have some of that stuff?"

Wolff sent her a skeptical look. "And have you use it on me? I think not."

She frowned. "I promise on my life I will never use it on you, nor on any of your staff. You *did* agree to provide me with means to defend myself without weapons, remember?"

"In exchange for you listening in to your countrymen. Which you have yet to do."

He led her back into the main room and indicated a group of four men dicing at a table with Lord Naseby. "That's Prince Trubetskoi, one of the Russian envoys. Go and see if you can hear anything useful."

Anya nodded, and he slipped away through the crowd. She'd actually met Trubetskoi on several occasions back in Russia. She didn't know him well, but he would doubtless recognize her if he saw her unmasked. Still, she was sure she looked so different now from the prim and proper ice princess he'd met in St. Petersburg that she'd be safe.

Russians had a saying: *Listen more, talk less,* and certainly some of the Tricorn's guests should have heeded that advice. Anya hovered close to the group, and as Wolff had suspected, they were chatting freely in Russian between themselves. She quickly learned that the one called Kutzov was on a prolonged losing streak, that Krupin was pining after a well-endowed girl named Misha, and that all four of them planned to visit Haye's later that evening.

Anya smiled at the thought of Charlotte's delight at having five such good-looking new customers.

Unfortunately, her loitering did not go completely unnoticed. The man named Kutzov slid over and caught her playfully around the waist.

"Gut evening, pretty lady," he breathed in heavily accented English, and Anya caught the fog of vodka on his breath. "Give Mika a kiss for good luck?"

Anya twisted her head away. As the man undressed her with his eyes, she resisted the urge to give him a setdown and instead, tried to imagine what Tess or Jenny would say in the situation. She gave a coquettish giggle and tried to mimic the accented tones of the Covent Garden flower sellers.

"Oi! Easy, sir. I'm wiv anuvver gent tonight. 'E might not take kindly to you breathin' all over me."

She wriggled free of his arm and stepped back, only to bump into a large body positioned directly behind her. The newcomer caught her arm.

"Leave her alone, Kutzov," the man said easily in Russian. "There are plenty more where she came from. No need to piss off the locals by stealing a cheap whore."

Anya's blood turned to ice, and with a sickening sense of dread, she turned to see the man from whom she'd been hiding for more than a year.

Chapter 23.

Vasili Petrov looked exactly the same. Anya glanced into his pale eyes and felt a wave of fear and loathing. His gaze was cold, as dead as a Siberian winter.

Unlike the others, he was dressed in his military uniform, all gilt braid and pale-blue jacket, exactly as he'd been the day he'd told her Dmitri was dead. His hair and blond mustache were neatly trimmed, and he flashed her a charming, meaningless smile, unaware that she knew he'd just insulted her.

She was reminded of a quote from Shakespeare: "O what may man within him hide, though angel on the outward side." Vasili hid a heart that was blackened and corrupt. Cruelty simmered beneath the surface, soul-deep.

Desperate to escape, she ducked her head and swirled away, thankful for her concealing mask. She threaded her way through the crowd and found Wolff near the doors to the dining room. He was talking with an elderly gentleman, but when he saw her, he held out his arm in a gesture of welcome and drew her into his side.

The older man sent Anya an indulgent smile and nodded at Wolff. "I'll keep you informed, Mowbray. And cede the field to this delightful young lady who desires your company."

He walked away, and Anya turned her body into Wolff's chest, savoring the sensation of safety. She placed her hands on his shoulders and went up on tiptoe to whisper in his ear. "Petrov is here!"

He sent her an easy, polite smile. She stared at him in confusion.

He bent his head to nuzzle her temple and despite the fact that her heart was still pounding in fright, she felt a traitorous curl of desire ripple through her. His lips skimmed her cheek and his nose brushed the pulse below her ear.

"I can't hear you with that ear," he whispered softly. "What did you say? If it was 'Take me to bed, Sebastien,' I'm all yours."

A shiver of longing pebbled her skin even as she felt his muscles tense. With a heavy sense of inevitability, she dropped her arms as she saw Vasili and Prince Trubetskoi advancing on them. She thought she might be sick. God, had Vasili recognized her?

Wolff's arm snaked around her waist, and she was glad of the support. Her legs felt like water.

But neither Vasili nor the prince flicked her more than a passing glance. Instead, the prince said, "Lord Mowbray? It's a pleasure to see you again. May I introduce a colleague of mine, Count Petrov? We worked together at Vienna, during the talks."

Vasili gave a stiff, formal bow. "My compliments on the excellent Russian fare you have provided tonight, my lord. The blini with caviar were most excellent." He paused and lifted one brow in what Anya supposed was meant to be a friendly tease. "One might almost think you had a Russian helping you plan it."

Her stomach lurched, but Wolff gave an easy laugh. His hand stroked her back, kneading the tense muscles there. "No. My chef, Lagrasse, is French. But the recipes are authentic. I'm glad they meet your exacting standards."

Vasili flicked a glance over at her, but there was no recognition in his gaze. "So, this pretty piece is yours, is she?" He chuckled, but it was more malicious than amused. "No wonder Kutzov had no luck."

Wolff slid his finger down her arm to the sensitive skin at the bend of her elbow in an unsubtle display of ownership. "There are plenty of other women to keep your friend company," he said pleasantly. "I'm afraid this one's engaged for the evening."

He bent and placed an easy kiss on the bare skin of her shoulder, and Anya almost jumped out of her skin.

"Go wait in my rooms, sweetheart. I'll be along in a few moments." He patted her playfully on the bottom, playing the part of eager lover to the hilt.

Anya stretched her lips in a parody of a smile and grasped the excuse to leave. Ignoring Vasili and the prince, she leaned in and pressed a kiss to the very corner of Wolff's mouth. "Hurry," she murmured, trying to emulate Charlotte's throaty purr. "I'll be waiting."

She turned and walked away on shaking legs, certain Vasili was going to call out to her, but she made it down the curved staircase and back into the private wing unchallenged. Once there, she leaned heavily on the door and closed her eyes. Dear God, that had been close. But her disguise had worked. Vasili was still none the wiser.

She made her way back to her own suite. Despite what Wolff had said, he didn't truly expect her to go to his chamber. Did he? But what of his promise last night to make love to her if she was sober?

Anya untied her mask and let it drop onto the desk. She was sober now. Her blood was still pounding in her ears, her hands shaking in reaction to the near miss. She felt full of pent-up energy, like an overwound clock.

A masculine tread sounded outside her door. She swept it open and came face-to-face with Wolff, his fist raised to knock. He dropped his hand and studied her face. "Are you all right?"

"Yes. Petrov didn't recognize me. But you'll have to find someone else to do your spying in future. I won't tempt fate again."

"Agreed." He reached into his jacket pocket and pulled out a tiny cork-stoppered bottle. "I have a present for you."

Anya took it. It was barely an inch long, the kind of bottle used for perfumed oils, with a thin glass tube protruding down into the clear liquid it contained. Anya sniffed it. "What is it? Perfume?"

"No. It's a measure of Lagrasse's tincture."

Anya smiled in delight. "For me? Thank you! You don't know how much safer I'll feel, knowing I have this on my person."

"My pleasure." His gaze roved over her and an appreciative smile curled his lips. "Have I mentioned how fetching you look in that dress?"

"I believe so."

"You'd look even more fetching out of it."

Anya sucked in a breath, and his wicked gaze clashed with hers.

"You're sober tonight, Miss Brown. Will you let me show you pleasure? I promise you I can."

How was any woman supposed to refuse an offer like that? Anya wanted nothing more than to throw herself into his arms and scream "yes!" but a thread of conscience nagged at her. If he knew she was highborn, he'd probably run a mile in the opposite direction. She shouldn't bed him under false pretenses.

Yet this was the perfect opportunity to take what she wanted without fear of repercussions. Unlike every other man who'd made advances toward her, he wouldn't be sleeping with her to improve his social standing or to trap her into marriage. There was no ulterior motive. His only goal would be to give and to experience pleasure.

She swallowed. At least she could tell him some part of the truth. "I . . . I once had a bad experience with a man."

His eyebrows met in a dark scowl. "Who? When?"

"It doesn't matter. But it made me . . . cautious."

A muscle ticked in his jaw. He looked furious on her behalf. "Did he force himself on you?"

"No. But he would have, if my friend hadn't come to my aid. I was made very aware of my own helplessness. I didn't like it."

Anya stared into his eyes and spoke from the heart. "I don't think you men truly understand the enormous level of faith women put in you at any given moment. With very few examples, you are stronger. You can simply take what you want. So any time a woman is alone with a man, she must trust that he won't use his superior strength to take advantage. She must hope that he has a core of honor, of decency, not to abuse his position."

"Do you trust *me*?"

She didn't hesitate. Maybe she couldn't trust him with the full truth of her identity, but with her body, yes, she trusted him implicitly.

"Yes."

"Good. Because I would never do anything to hurt you. We can go as fast or as slow as you like."

Anya took a deep breath. "Then, yes. Show me pleasure. Please."

Wolff exhaled, then sent her an amused look from beneath his brows. "We'll get on a lot better if you actually
let me into your room."

With a start, she realized he was still standing out in
the corridor. She took a step back.

He crossed the threshold and closed the door.

Chapter 24.

"Why don't we start with the basics?" Wolff said softly, stepping close.

Anya nodded.

"I believe I've told you how much I like kissing. You should know I've made quite a study of it." He moved closer. "Historically speaking, we have the Romans to thank for the widespread practice of it. In Roman society, when, where, and how you kissed someone was an important indicator of social status."

His boots brushed her skirts. "They describe kissing in three forms. First, there's the *osculum*, which is a friendly peck on the cheek." He bent and pressed a chaste kiss just below the cheekbone. Her stomach quivered.

"Next, we have the *basium*, a more erotic kiss on the mouth."

He matched his words with a featherlight brush on her lips. It was only a casual touch, but Anya felt it right down to her toes. She was enchanted, a prisoner of sweetness, completely focused on where he touched her.

She sucked in a shaky breath. "And the last kind?"

"The *savium*. The most passionate of kisses."

He gazed hungrily at her lips and her blood thundered in anticipation. Unable to bear the suspense, she rose up on tiptoe and fused her mouth to his. His arms came around her and he answered her demand with a thrilling ardency, angling his head for better access. Desire scalded through her blood.

"Very good, Miss Brown," he groaned after long, drugging minutes. "You're proving to be an excellent pupil."

His fingers grazed her bare skin above the low back of the dress, leaving goose bumps in their wake. He stared deeply into her eyes. "I give you my word that I will do nothing unless you expressly allow it. I want you to explore at your own pace. My body is yours."

Anya expelled a shuddery breath, amazed at his generosity, his understanding. How many other men would have been so accommodating? "Thank you."

A wicked light of mischief gleamed in his eyes. "If it will put your mind at ease, I have a set of handcuffs in my rooms. You can restrain me, if you really want to."

A frisson of something hot flashed through her at the very idea of him bound and helpless, at her mercy. "Why would you do that?"

"Because I want you to touch me. I want it so badly, I'll give you complete control and take whatever scraps you're willing to give."

Anya could barely breathe. If he were bound, he couldn't overpower her as Vasili had tried to do. He couldn't force her to do anything. But he was nothing like Vasili; she trusted him without the need for such drastic measures. He was inherently decent. Honorable to the core. She wouldn't force him, any more than he would force her. If they were going to do this—and they *were* going to—then it would be as equal partners.

"I don't need you restrained," she said. She stepped back, her stomach tight with excitement, her blood singing with nervous energy. "But I do want you to put your hands behind you until I say."

She could hardly believe her own daring. She reminded herself she was a princess, accustomed to ordering people to do her bidding, and indicated the chair in front of the desk with an imperious flourish. "Sit down and hold the chair."

She tensed, thinking he'd refuse, but all he said was, "Can I remove my coat first?"

"Of course."

Her heart pounded as he tugged at his cuffs and shrugged out of his evening jacket. It took some contortion; the fit was very snug. He swiveled the chair on its front legs and turned it to face her, sat down, and reached behind him to clasp the back legs. He lifted his brows in haughty inquiry.

Now what?

Anya swallowed. She stepped forward until her knees bumped his, then pulled out the single gold-and-diamond stick pin that secured the front of his cravat. She placed it carefully on the desk, avoiding his heavy-lidded gaze, untied the white linen of his neckcloth, and unwound it from around his neck. She dropped that to the desk too.

He was left in a white shirt, black breeches, and top boots. Without the cravat to hold it together, the neck of his shirt fell open, revealing an exciting glimpse of tawny skin. Fascinated, she stroked her fingers over the jut of his collarbone and the intriguing hollow at the base of his throat. His skin was warm. Smooth. Delicious.

And hers to explore.

Gaining confidence, she let her hands skim the bunched muscles of his shoulders, pulled taut by the unnatural position of his arms. He shuddered under her touch and spread his knees. She stepped between his muscled thighs.

"Take off my shirt," he commanded hoarsely. "Touch me."

With hands that were not quite steady, she tugged his shirt from the waistband of his breeches, avoiding the prominent bulge clearly visible beneath. "You may release the chair," she breathed. "For a moment only."

He lifted his arms. She raised the cotton up and over his head and tossed it to join the cravat on the leather desktop. "Hands back on the chair."

He made a soft groan but did as he was told, and her breath caught as she studied him. His torso rippled with muscle and narrowed to a lean waist with a line of dark hair that arrowed from his navel down beneath his breeches.

Good lord, the man was *beautiful*—if such a word could be used for someone so undeniably male. He was like one of those marble statues she'd seen in a museum in Paris, carved by those same ancient Romans who classified their kisses into types. He was the embodiment of power, willingly restrained, and Anya felt her throat tighten in gratitude. What a man. What a gift.

She circled him and he regarded her warily, like a wolf trapped in a snare, unsure whether she meant to free him or dispatch him. She stepped behind him and, giving in to impulse, kissed the nape of his neck. She heard his sharp intake of breath and smiled against his skin. Next, she placed her lips to the slope of neck and shoulder and flicked out her tongue to taste. His skin was slightly salty, and her nose filled with his heady, masculine scent. Her pulse thundered in her ears as she ran her hands greedily over the swell of his bicep then down the long sinews of his forearms.

"Anya," he breathed softly. A warning and a plea.

She reached around and slid her flattened palms over his chest, then down his stomach. His muscles jumped in responsive relay. She stopped at the waistband of breeches.

"Lower," he demanded, turning his face into her hair. "Or come back around here and kiss me."

She stepped back around the chair.

"Closer, between my legs."

She did so, and saw his arm muscles twitch as he fought the impulse to release the chair. The control he was exerting was remarkable. It would be so easy for him to take her in his arms, but voluntary resistance was a piquant part of the game.

"Not yet," she teased. "Not until I say."

His hot glare promised retribution of the most sinful, pleasurable kind. Her knees felt weak. Who'd have thought playing with fire could be so much fun?

"This is killing me," he groaned.

She bent and touched her mouth to his. He tried to devour her, to impress his will on her through his kiss, so she drew back and sent him a laughing look of silent admonishment.

He growled, deep in his throat. "Fine. As slow as you like."

She kissed him again. And again. A steady rain of kisses, longer and deeper until she put her hands on his shoulders and stroked up his neck to tangle her fingers in his hair. His corded muscles strained for release. She cupped his face and drank him in, lost in the darkness, the heat.

She slid her hand down between their bodies and over the bulge in his breeches, exploring the amazing contours of his body. He sucked in a breath and hissed out a curse.

She stepped back, panting, astounded by the ferocity of her own reactions. Her breasts felt achy and the flesh between her legs throbbed with need.

"Yes," he said fiercely. "Undo my breeches. I want to feel myself in your hand."

She wanted that too. She fumbled a little with the button at his falls, but then he sprang free, hot and hard in her palm. He groaned and tilted his head back in apparent bliss. "Wrap your fingers around me. Tighter."

She did, amazed at the texture of this most masculine part of him, at the mat of curly dark hair that surrounded it. She gave a little squeeze and glanced up to gauge his reaction. His eyes rolled back in his head.

"God yes, perfect."

She'd heard Charlotte's girls talk about this. About having a man in your hands, or in your mouth. She'd thought the whole thing sounded quite strange, unpleasant, even, but now she began to see the appeal. She wanted to give Wolff pleasure, wanted to touch and taste.

She pressed his knees apart and dropped to the floor between his thighs. His head snapped back up. She gazed up at him earnestly. "I want to see what you taste like."

He gave a groan of wholehearted assent, and she was filled with sudden tenderness. There was something wonderful about having such a physically powerful man reduced to a begging, quivering mess. This was what she'd wanted forever—a power of her own, something completely unrelated to her position as a princess.

She ran her fingers over him, marveling at the bead of clear fluid that had appeared, then bent and flicked her tongue experimentally against him. He tasted clean and bright, like the sea. His hips bucked and he nearly arched off the seat.

"Hands on the chair," she reminded him sternly, thoroughly enjoying her position of mastery.

He shuddered. "Again. Do it again. Please."

She was happy to oblige. She licked him, tiny laps of the tongue, gratified by his response. Growing bolder, she opened her mouth over him.

"Fuuuuuck!"

He thumped his booted heels on the floor, and she suppressed a little smile of feminine triumph. She, Anya Denisova, did this to him! He, who was no stranger to women, was finding pleasure in her touch. She licked him again, and he moaned.

"That's so good. Don't stop."

He tilted his hips and pushed himself a little farther into her mouth. "Stroke your hand up and down," he instructed hoarsely. "Tighter. Grip tighter. Close—God, I'm so close. You should—I can't—"

She didn't stop. She wanted to see him lose control, wanted to be the one to push him to the peak of pleasure.

"Anya, I'm going to—"

She lifted her head and stroked him as his entire body went rigid. He pushed himself hard into her hand, every muscle straining and shaking. Spurts of viscous white liquid jetted over her fingers, his stomach, cooling rapidly in the air.

Anya felt almost dizzy, her heart filled to bursting. She took her hand away and rested it on his thigh, savoring the feel of the corded muscles twitching beneath the fine cloth. "You can release the chair now, Mr. Wolff," she croaked.

He was panting, his chest rising and falling in great gusts as if he'd been running. His member lay against his stomach in the open fall of his breeches, only marginally smaller now that he'd found release. He gave a deep, contented sigh and stretched his arms out in front of him, then brushed her hair back from her face with a tender caress. He used his shirt to clean her hand and his stomach, then rebuttoned the fall of breeches.

Anya rose shakily to her feet. He opened his arms to her.

"Come here."

He drew her down onto his lap and buried his face in her neck. "Thank you. That was incredible. Like nothing I've ever experienced."

She nestled her head into his shoulder, suddenly shy, and he pressed a kiss to the top of her head.

So that was the male climax in all its glory. She'd been surprised, certainly, but not disgusted. He'd obviously received great pleasure, and she'd enjoyed giving it to him. Her entire body was filled with a thrumming, restless energy.

He pulled back to look at her and gave her a smile that heated her blood even more. "Now it's your turn."

Chapter 25.

What the hell had just happened?

Seb felt as if he'd been taken apart and put back together in a completely different configuration. Never had he allowed himself to be so vulnerable during a sexual act, so completely at the mercy of another. Usually it was *him* taking charge, issuing commands to direct his bed partner with cool, practiced assurance.

Not this time. He'd never realized how sexy it would be to cede control. He'd liked it. No, more than liked it. He'd *loved* it.

Anya's hands and mouth had been gently questing. Instead of firm competence, she'd been sweetly tentative, and it had been the most erotic experience of his life.

He'd meant to put her at ease, to give her the power to explore him after her admission of a prior bad experience, but he'd been the one to receive the gift. The fact that she'd placed her trust in him was profoundly gratifying; he felt honored that she'd chosen him to help her past her misgivings.

Having a woman finish him with her hand or her mouth was usually something he did to take the edge off before engaging in full sex, but on several previous occasions, he'd caught himself looking out of the window, thinking of something else, as if he weren't fully present in the room.

That certainly hadn't been the case this time. His attention hadn't wavered for a moment. He'd never forgotten who was with him. Anya. An extraordinary, infuriating enigma. A puzzle he *would* solve . . . as soon as he returned the favor.

Sebastien—it seemed ridiculous to call him Wolff after what they'd just done—helped her to her feet and stood. Without a word, he took her hand and led her through the doorway into her bedroom.

Anya went, unresisting. Who would have thought, when he'd propositioned her back at Charlotte's, that he would end up being her first lover in truth? She had no misgivings. He was the perfect man to relieve her of her unwanted virginity. He was gentle, despite his size, honorable, despite his reputation.

No lamp had been lit. The four upright posts of the bed loomed out of the darkness. He turned her by the shoulders so her back was to him.

"This dress is very fetching, but I'd prefer to see you out of it."

His fingers were swift and sure as he unbuttoned her as efficiently as any lady's maid. The bodice of the dress was boned to act as a corset too, so when she peeled it off her arms and let it fall to the floor in a puff of teal, she was left in only her silk chemise and drawers.

The cool air on her skin was a thrilling contrast to the warmth of his breath on her shoulder, and a wonderful confusion swirled in her belly, the promise of secret delights. She shivered, but not from cold.

She was no longer an ice princess, untouched by earthly desires. Anya could feel herself warming, melting like the fictional Snegurochka. The problems with that were obvious; she couldn't afford to care for Wolff any more than she already did. Even now, she was dangerously attracted to him, not just physically, but emotionally too. She respected him, trusted him. He was a good man, fiercely loyal to those he loved, dedicated to his work for Bow Street and to making his business a success. He was strong enough, and cynical enough, to protect her from men like Vasili.

But their brief liaison couldn't possibly last. They were like two ships blown together by a freak storm. They would part company soon enough. But at least for tonight, they could enjoy each other's company to the utmost.

The heat of his chest warmed her back through the thin silk of her chemise. He slid his hands to her hips and tugged her back against him, soft against hard, and she marveled at the difference in their size. He was huge, hot and muscled, but she felt nothing but worshipped as he bent and kissed her neck, her jaw, the sensitive hollow behind her ear. She tilted her head to grant him better access, a wordless demand.

"Do you like that, Miss Brown?" he teased with a low laugh. "You'll like this more."

He shaped her waist then slid his hands upward to cup her breasts. Anya gasped. They seemed to swell into his palms, heavy and aching as he squeezed them gently through the silk. He brushed his fingers over the sensitive peaks, and she moaned in delight at the strange, wonderful abrasion.

She turned in his arms and ran her hands greedily over his skin, exploring the contours of his chest. His heart beat strong and steady beneath her fingertips, and he sucked in a breath as she skated her fingers over his flat male nipples. Filled with a devilish impulse, she leaned into him and flicked her tongue over one. His fingers tightened in her hair.

"Wicked girl." He peppered hot kisses over her face—her cheek, the corner of her eye, then found her mouth again and kissed her long and deep. "Two can play at that game."

In a lightning move, he lifted her chemise over her head and lowered her to the bed. Anya gasped at the feel of his chest bare against hers. He kissed his way down her throat then rubbed his lightly stubbled jaw over the soft skin of her breasts, creating a shiver-inducing friction that had her squirming in delight.

He trailed his tongue in a lazy, ever-decreasing circle around one rosy peak, and when he captured it between his lips, she gave a soft, startled cry of wonder. All sensible thoughts fled. His hand slid over her hip, bunching the silk of her drawers, and despite her excitement, she stiffened.

He lifted his head and caught her gaze. "Relax. Let yourself get accustomed to my touch."

His voice, deepened by desire, made her shiver. Still holding her gaze, he stroked his palm over her stomach, then lower still, between her legs, petting her through the silk. To her mortification, she felt dampness there, the evidence of her desire. She put her hand down to try to shield herself, but his impassioned groan made her pause.

"No, sweetheart, it's all right. It's perfect. You're perfect. God, please let me."

He slid down her body and used his broad shoulders

to nudge her knees apart. Anya's eyes grew wide as he slid one hand beneath her bottom to lift her hips and pressed a kiss there, right at the hot center of her body. She sucked in a slow scandalized breath.

His chuckle was a wicked sound. "Nice? Tell me what you want, Miss Brown."

She caught his hair and pushed him back down. "More. More of that."

"My pleasure. *Your* pleasure."

His breath warmed her, then his tongue pressed against her, soaking through the thin layer of silk, smoothing the fabric over the soft folds. Hot, like dragon's breath.

She could scarcely catch a breath. He found the little bud and the narrow parting beneath, his clever tongue flicking and teasing until she was a writhing mass, entirely his. He was a master, building a fever by slow degrees, and she was dissolving into a puddle, disappearing in a puff of hot steam. She didn't care. Such joy was worth disintegration. She clutched his hair and urged him on.

She barely noticed when he drew down her drawers and discarded them. She was simply naked, and he was there, between her thighs. She arched as his fingers and mouth joined forces to drive her insane. He lapped at her hungrily, as if he wanted to devour her and ease her at the same time, to satisfy her every wicked craving.

He worshipped her. She twisted and writhed as he found the entrance to her body and entered her slowly with his finger. She gasped, then relaxed, trusting him completely. He did it again, and again, his fingers moving in tandem with his tongue. Hot delight and spiraling darkness. The tension built and built until it was almost unbearable, but before she could do more than gasp, her entire body simply . . . exploded.

She let out a shuddering sob, a cry of incredulous wonder. Her inner muscles squeezed his finger, clenching and releasing with beats of glorious sensation.

Anya fell back against the bedspread with a sigh of utter contentment, dimly aware of him rising from the bed. She heard the rustle of clothing as he stepped out of his breeches, but by the time she opened her eyes, he was lying next to her, and the feel of his lean, muscled frame, completely naked, was the most incredible sensation.

Her heart was thundering against her ribs, and she was panting with exertion. He cupped her jaw and pressed a reverent kiss to her mouth then pulled back and gazed deep into her eyes.

"Beautiful," he murmured.

It was impossible to ignore the hard evidence of his desire. It pressed against her thigh, hot and insistent, and with a start, Anya realized he was ready for more despite what she'd done to him in the chair.

He raised his brows at her in laughing question. "Feeling relaxed now, Miss Brown?"

"I am indeed, Mr. Wolff."

"Think you can take more?"

She held his gaze. "Yes. I want everything."

He made a sound of pleasure and moved over her. She reveled in the glorious weight of him pressing her into the bed. She'd never felt more cherished, more protected.

He propped himself up on his forearms to relieve her of some of his weight, and his hair-roughened thighs slid against hers as he settled between her hips. With a shudder, she felt him, slick and solid at the entrance to her body. He took her hands, laced his fingers through hers, and spread them wide against the bed. It should have been alarming, a position of utter submission, but instead, Anya felt powerful, beautiful, like some glorious sacrifice to the pagan gods. She'd chosen this, desired it above all else.

"Yes."

He pressed into her, just a fraction. Anya arched up in instinctive reaction to the strange, stretching sensation. He was bigger than his fingers. It felt odd, a little uncomfortable, but not painful. She released her breath and relaxed, and he slid in deeper. He buried his face in her neck, and she could feel the shudders racking his body as he fought to slow his pace.

"God, you're so tight," he groaned. "So good. Feels so good."

She couldn't help a tiny inward smile at the sound of the sophisticated, worldly Sebastien Wolff reduced to panting monosyllables. His voice was ragged with longing. At least she wasn't the only one losing her mind.

A ball of unexpected emotion tightened her chest. *Hers.* Even if it was only for tonight, this glorious man was hers. She arched beneath him. "More. Give me more. Don't stop."

He let out a shaky, laughing exhale. "Whatever the lady wants. Your wish is my command."

He slid back, then forward again, and she felt the glowing embers of her previous climax flutter back to life. He set a lazy pace but soon it wasn't enough. Anya clutched his shoulders and urged him on as his steady rhythm gradually became more urgent. Her body fit his like an exquisite glove, yielding sweetly as the sparks of pleasure grew.

Control began to spiral away. She lost the ability to speak English. She reverted to Russian, panting, issuing hoarse commands and pleas in her native tongue.

"Yes, there . . . no, wait!—yes, more . . ."

It wasn't modest or restrained. It was wild, perfectly abandoned. He caught her thigh and drew her leg up, around his hip, and the slight change in angle sent her one step closer to oblivion. He drew her on a breathless, upward arc until another crest of pleasure crashed over her, beating against the confines of her body in a sparkle of scarlet and black.

With a hoarse groan, he withdrew from her body and pressed himself against her belly. Every muscle in his body went rigid. Anya clutched him tight, savoring the sweat-slicked heat of him, the glorious masculine weight as he spent himself against her.

Panting, she blinked up at the ceiling, drowning in the aftermath of sensation. No longer a virgin, but she didn't have a single regret. She'd never felt so replete, so utterly boneless. Making love with Sebastien Wolff was like being caught in a tempest or a blizzard, a sublime force of nature. She felt shaken and yet oddly peaceful.

He rolled aside with a deep sigh of repletion. "God in heaven, woman, that was good."

The bed creaked as he lifted away from her and left the bed. She could only just see him in the light that filtered in from the study, but it was enough to appreciate the sight of him totally and unashamedly naked. She stared at his beautiful broad shoulders, the long line of his back, the hollowed indents on the sides of his buttocks. Her mouth went dry.

He poured water from the pitcher into the porcelain bowl on the washstand, dipped and wrung out the washcloth, and brought it back to her, utterly unself-conscious. Anya felt heat rise in her cheeks as he gazed down at her with a smile.

"Here. Use this."

Pretending she'd done this countless times before, she used the cloth to clean the pearly fluid from her skin, glad that he was being so matter-of-fact about the whole process. He was clearly used to such casual intimacy.

The thought that he'd done this with other women sent a shaft of jealousy through her, but she pushed it away. Tonight, he was hers.

He tugged back the covers and she slipped beneath them. Would he leave her now?

He slid in beside her and gathered her in his arms, turning her so her back was curved into his chest, and Anya let out a deep sigh of contentment. She'd never been naked with another person before, but it felt so natural to be with him like this. She smiled into the darkness and closed her eyes.

The heat generated between their bodies was incredible. He pressed a kiss to the top of her head and her heart gave an odd, panicked flutter. She might have been ice before, but she was well and truly melted now.

Chapter 26.

Wolff wasn't there when she awoke, but Anya couldn't recall him leaving during the night. Pale light filtered through the window, and she realized it was only just past dawn.

What was she to make of his absence? Should she be insulted? Grateful? Relieved?

A sliver of apprehension wormed its way into her belly. Last night, it had been so easy to lose herself in the moment, to forget that morning would come. But she'd have to face Wolff sooner or later. Would he treat her differently today? Would he carry on as if nothing had happened?

She needed to think, to consider all the ramifications, but she couldn't do it here, not with the scent of him on the sheets and the memory of his kisses still fresh on her skin. Just the thought of him scrambled her brain. She would go to the stables. The unjudgmental presence of the horses would be a welcome comfort.

She tugged on the breeches and shirt she'd worn to

the park, then slipped down the stairs and let herself out into the mews yard without encountering anyone. The grey, Borodino, tossed his head and whickered in greeting, and she stroked his velvety nose.

"It's all right," she crooned. "Whatever horrors you've seen, they're behind you now. You're safe here."

Her heart contracted sharply. The horse was lucky indeed to have been rescued by such a kind-hearted man. Sebastien had provided a safe haven for the traumatized animal. He must have seen equally dreadful things himself during the war. Did he, as many soldiers did, experience nightmares that plunged him right back into the hell of battle? Who did he have to comfort *him*?

With a jolt, Anya realized she wanted it to be her. She wanted to make him laugh in honest enjoyment, to be the one he came to when he couldn't sleep. She wanted to be his friend and his confidante. The one who lightened his days and eased his nights.

She felt more for him than mere liking. More than simple lust. She understood him, with a soul-deep recognition. It was far too easy to imagine herself living here at the Tricorn, becoming a permanent part of his world.

It could never happen, of course. He saw her as nothing more than a temporary diversion, and surely Vasili wouldn't be staying in London for much longer. She had a few weeks, at most, to enjoy being with Wolff before she'd have to return to Covent Garden and slip back into her dreary life.

A shuffling step in the straw made her turn, expecting the stable lad, but a larger figure entered the barn. He looked vaguely familiar, and Anya's stomach dropped in sudden dismay as she placed him: the third kidnapper from Hounslow Heath, the one who'd ridden away.

He smiled as he advanced, showing several missing

teeth. "Good morning, Princess," he said in Russian. "I've been looking for you."

Anya backed up, cornered. "Who are you? What are you doing here?"

His smile was ugly. "You know what I'm doing here. Count Petrov is most anxious to see you, little dove." His gaze flicked lasciviously over her body, immodestly displayed in the shirt and breeches.

"I'm not going anywhere with you." She sidestepped and snatched a leather lead rein from a nail on the wall, brandishing it in front of her like a whip.

Eclipse whinnied and kicked his hooves against his door in the next stall, picking up on the tension in the air, but the placid Borodino paid them no attention. He was used to people flailing and arguing near him.

"You were fortunate to receive help before." The man's lip curled in a sneer. "Your savior killed my brother and my friend. But this time, you won't be so lucky. Count Petrov does not take kindly to those who fail him."

Anya swung the leather, trying to hit him in the face, but he blocked the move with his forearm and caught the strap in his fist. He yanked her toward him and she stumbled, falling to her knees in the straw, and when she opened her mouth to scream, he grabbed her by the hair and pulled hard enough to make her eyes water. She gasped in pain. He clapped a dirty palm over her mouth so she bit him, hard, and he swore as she twisted and thrashed.

She managed to let out a panicked shout. "Help! Sebastien!"

Eclipse reared again and let out the equine version of an enraged roar. His hooves thundered furiously against the wooden boards as he tried to get to Anya.

Anya tried to remember the advice she'd been given. She aimed for the man's nose, tried to elbow him between the legs, but he managed to evade all her attempts. He caught her around the waist and dragged her toward the stable entrance.

The back door banged, and she gasped in relief when both Sebastien and Mickey burst into the mews yard and skidded to a halt on the cobbles.

"Take your hands off her this instant," Wolff commanded.

The deadly calm of his voice should have been an indication to the man holding her to run. Unfortunately, the simpleton didn't take the hint. He pulled a knife from his belt and held it to her throat. Anya froze.

"No. The *printsessa* comes with me."

Her heart missed a beat. For one brief, hopeful moment she thought Wolff wouldn't register the Russian word for princess, but of course he missed nothing. His eyes narrowed.

"Princess? What are you talking about?"

"Princess Denisova," the man repeated. "She comes with me."

Wolff actually smiled at what he thought was the other man's mistake. "I hate to break it to you, old man, but you've got the wrong girl. That's not the princess. That's her maid. Anya Ivanov."

Her captor let out a belly laugh of genuine amusement. "A maid? Is that what she's told you? By the saints! I can see why you would think it, with her dressed in these clothes like a common whore, but I make no mistake. This is Princess Anastasia Denisova. Cousin to the tsar."

Anya stared at Wolff, mutely pleading with him to dismiss the claim, but the look he sent her dashed any hope. She saw the exact moment he drew the correct conclusion. His eyes narrowed and his jaw tightened in fury.

"Princess Anastasia Denisova," he repeated, and the

name was like an accusation on his lips, practically dripping with disdain.

He returned his attention to the man holding her. "Put the knife down and let her go. I don't want to have to hurt you. Go and tell your master the princess is under my protection."

The knife pressed more firmly to her throat and her captor's arm squeezed her belly in warning. "I'll cut her."

"No, you won't. Petrov won't want her harmed."

"Step back, Englishman."

Anya wasn't sure what happened next. Wolff's hand shot out and caught her assailant's wrist, forcing the knife away from her. The arm holding her waist slackened, and she stumbled forward into Mickey's beefy arms.

She turned to see the Russian slash the knife in a wild arc toward Wolff, who ducked and then dealt the man a punishing blow to the temple and another to the underside of his jaw. The knife clattered to the ground, but the big Russian wasn't beaten. He put up his fists in a boxing stance and the two men traded jabs. Wolff managed to land a hit on the side of his head, but received a punishing left to the cheekbone in return. He staggered, but didn't go down.

Then the Russian changed tactics and lunged forward, catching Wolff around the waist in a bear hug and hurling them both to the ground. The two of them rolled over and over, fists and curses flying, and Anya had to stop herself from crying out in dismay at the ferocity of the attack.

Wolff finally ended up on top of the larger man. He straddled his body and delivered a barrage of brutal punches to the man's face. The man's nose broke with a sickening crunch, and he finally went limp. Panting, Wolff unfisted his grip on the man's shirt and let the body drop back onto the cobbles. With a final curse, he stood and brushed down the front of his shirt, now smeared with blood and dirt.

Mickey gave a grunt of congratulation, then straightened Anya and, with his giant paws, dusted off the straw sticking to her back.

Wolff turned to her and the look of fury on his face was enough to make her chest squeeze in fright. He looked wild. Utterly ferocious, with his hair a disordered mess and his cheekbone already turning an ugly shade of scarlet from the blow he'd received.

He crouched down to inspect the unconscious man's outstretched hand. A gold signet ring glinted in the pale morning light. "The Orlov family crest," he said grimly. "Just like the dead man down at the docks." He stood and dusted his hands.

"The Orlovs have been allies of the Petrovs for centuries," Anya said quietly.

Sebastien ignored her. "Mickey. Take this idiot over to Bow Street and lock him up." His eyes flashed back to Anya and her heart missed another beat. "And you?" he bit out. "My study. Right now."

He turned and stalked away, fury evident in every long stride.

Anya gulped. For a cowardly minute, she imagined leaping up onto Borodino and galloping back to the dowager duchess, but that would only delay the inevitable confrontation.

"Better go, miss," Mickey said gently. "'E don't like to be kept waiting."

Anya nodded glumly. Now there would be hell to pay.

Chapter 27.

"Princess?"

Seb strode to his desk then pivoted on his heel, fury scalding his insides. "You're the bloody princess? Cousin-to-the-tsar, wear-a-crown-to-bed *princess*. Christ alive, woman!"

The gorgeous wretch sidled into his study and hovered just inside the door. He clenched his fists against the urge to release every profanity he knew, one after another.

"I don't wear a crown to bed," she said coolly. "As you well know. I don't even have a tiara."

Her reminder of his monumental mistake didn't help cool his temper.

"Should I bow?" he growled with deep sarcasm. "Your Majesty."

"I believe 'Your Highness' is the correct form of address."

He scowled at her equally sarcastic tone and gave a bitter, self-recriminatory laugh. "You're a bloody little liar, that's what you are! All this time, pretending to be something you're not."

She gave a dainty shrug. "We're all pretending to be something we're not. You, for example, pretend to be a rational, sensible human being. If you'll just let me—"

"Does Dorothea know?" He didn't wait for an answer. "Of course she does, the old schemer."

God, he'd been so stupid. He should have realized who she was straight away. All the signs had been there. Her haughty demeanor, her polished manners, her strange worldly innocence. The way Dorothea had been oh-so-keen to throw them together.

He'd been set up.

By a septuagenarian battle-ax.

She frowned. "I don't see why you're getting so angry—"

"I slept with you!"

"So?"

"So? You came to me under false pretenses."

She crossed her arms. "And what difference would it have made if I'd told you?"

"I never would've slept with you! I do not seduce well-bred—" He stopped short and glared at her. "Oh, God, you were a *virgin,* weren't you?" The guilty look on her face was enough to incriminate her, and he swore again, furious at himself as much as her. "Christ alive! I don't bed virgins. Ever. I bed wenches. Actresses. Widows. Tarts."

Her eyes widened at that, but she lifted her chin in that haughty way he should have realized came from a lifetime of privilege.

"Well, now you've fucked a woman who outranks you. Congratulations."

His jaw dropped at her shocking use of profanity, but she wasn't finished.

"I'm glad I didn't tell you. I'm not ashamed of what we did. I wanted you. You wanted me. I fail to see the problem."

"Fail to see the problem?" he echoed in disbelief. "I've ruined you! You're the lost princess. You're—"

"I'm not *lost*," she countered, equally incensed. "I'm not a parcel! I know exactly where I am. I *chose* to come here to England. I chose to give myself to you." Her expression took on a cynical slant. "What? Will you fight Vasili in a duel over my 'lost honor'?"

Seb glared right back at her. "Hardly. I never fight duels."

"Why not?"

"Because I'd kill my opponent." He shrugged at her raised eyebrows. "That's not false modesty. I spent three years in the Rifles. I'm a bloody good shot. It would be unfair advantage. I've seen too many men die for important principles to indulge in a petty squabble at Chalk's Farm over a woman. Besides, duels are outlawed, technically."

"I hardly think it would be the first law you've broken," she sniped.

"I've never broken a law. Merely bent them on occasion."

Seb squeezed his temples with his hand, trying to banish the tension that was pounding in his skull. His knuckles stung from the fistfight, and his cheekbone throbbed with every pulse of his heart.

He strode to the sideboard, poured himself a large measure of brandy, and downed it. His hand wasn't entirely steady. He did not offer any to her, despite the fact that she looked like she could do with it. He wasn't feeling that charitable. God, what a mess.

"What the hell was a princess doing in a brothel?" he growled.

"I'm Charlotte's neighbor. I'm teaching some of her girls to read and write."

He let out a snort of self-directed humor. "Her neighbor. In Covent Garden. Oh, bloody brilliant." He took another steadying draught of liquor. "You do realize we'll have to marry now, don't you?"

Her mouth dropped open in shock. "Don't be ridiculous! There's no need for that. You haven't ruined Princess Anastasia. You've ruined secretary Anna Brown, whom nobody cares about in the least. Princess Anastasia doesn't exist. She's dead."

He pinned her with a level stare. "I'm honor bound to do the right thing."

She looked a little panicked, and Seb felt a stab of malicious pleasure. Good, the little pretender ought to be afraid. Her subterfuge had landed them both in a situation that would ruin the rest of their lives.

"I'm not marrying you," she said crossly. "I'm not marrying anyone. As soon as Vasili returns to Russia, I'll go back to working for the dowager duchess."

"Dorothea will expect us to marry, even if nobody else in the *ton* knows who you are. Do you honestly think she'd let me seduce you and then abandon you without the protection of my name?"

"You didn't seduce me! We seduced each other. And you didn't"—her face turned a delicious shade of pink—"that is to say, you finished—" She trailed off again in acute embarrassment, and Seb was more than happy to let her squirm. "There's no chance that I could fall pregnant from the encounter," she finished stiffly.

He shrugged. "It's the principle of it."

"I don't care about principles. You don't want to marry me. And I have no desire to wed someone who's only offering because he feels guilty or because of some misplaced sense of honor. Nobody will know what happened between us, not even the dowager, unless you tell her. Because I'm certainly not going to mention it."

Seb raked his fingers through this hair. He didn't *want* to marry the infuriating woman, of course, but her strident refusal still stung. "Tell me the truth about Petrov. Is he really your fiancé?"

"No. Never. He wants what I am, what I stand for. A title. A fortune. Generations of good breeding." Her lips curled in disdain. "But what is a princess? Nothing! Polite conversation and perfect manners. A brood mare for little princes. I was worse than useless. At least here in London I've learned some practical skills. I can light a fire. Sew a seam. I've taught the girls at Haye's to read."

She tilted her chin, and Seb fought the sensation of drowning in the cornflower blue of her eyes.

"Do you know what happened when Napoleon arrived in Moscow four years ago?" she said fiercely. "The inhabitants burned their own beautiful city to the ground rather than let him take it. And I would rather kill myself than let a brutal pig like Vasili take *me*."

Seb frowned. He had no answer to that.

"He wants to marry me to ensure my silence because he thinks I have evidence that he's a spy."

"Do you?"

"No. I told you. If my brother found anything, he never sent it to me. I assume it was on his person when he was killed at Waterloo and was buried with him."

She shuddered, and Seb quelled the ridiculous impulse to cross the room, take her in his arms, and comfort her. He had similar haunting memories from his years in the Rifles, images of friends dead or dying that he could never erase from his brain. She looked so small, so vulnerable in those ridiculous boy's clothes, like one of the scrappy street urchins he used to run messages and gain information for Bow Street.

"Perhaps there *was* some evidence, and he managed to hide it before he was killed?" he said.

"If he did, I can't imagine where you'd look for it. If it was hidden in his belongings wherever he was staying the night before the battle, it's been looted or destroyed by now."

Seb pulled out the chair behind his desk and sat, striving for some semblance of normalcy. "So. Petrov knows where you are."

She leaned back against the closed door and her slender shoulders sagged in defeat. "Yes."

"You can't keep on hiding forever. And I have a business to run. I can't drop everything to be your personal bodyguard twenty-four hours a day."

She sent him an irritated glare. "Nobody's asking you to."

He ignored that. "It's time to put an end to your little farce. Princess Denisova must be resurrected. You can be introduced to the *ton* as the protégé of my great-aunt. Nobody will dare contradict the Dread Dowager Duchess."

"What? No! How will that keep me safe from Vasili?"

"You'll be more difficult to reach if you're surrounded by members of the *ton*. Society will shield you, just as it shields every unmarried young woman from the unwanted attentions of men. You'll have a chaperone. Constant companions. You'll have to face Petrov, but it will be in full view of a hundred witnesses. You can deny you were ever betrothed."

Her skin paled. "He'll be furious."

"What can he do in a room full of people? He's too conscious of his own social standing to make an ugly scene. I know men like him. How he appears in public is very important to him."

She shook her head. Several wisps of straw still clung to the strands, blending in with her honey-colored hair. She looked like a rumpled dairymaid. One he still wanted to tumble, damn it.

"He's relentless," she said wearily. "He'll try something."

"We'll make it clear you're under Bow Street's protection."

An odd expression flitted over her face, one Seb couldn't identify. It almost looked like hope. Eagerness. "So I would remain here?"

"No. You'll stay with Dorothea. Alex, Benedict, and I will take it in turns to guard you there."

"Oh." She seemed almost disappointed, but he must have been mistaken. She was probably regretting she ever let a rogue like him anywhere near her royal personage.

Of course she'd refused him. He wasn't good enough for her. He hadn't been good enough for the likes of Julia Cowes a decade ago, and even though he'd made a fortune and gained a title on his own merit since then, he was still no fit mate for *a bloody princess.*

She needed to go and marry some charming European aristocrat—one with a spotless reputation who didn't go around propositioning strangers in brothels and getting into fistfights—and end up as queen of some balmy Mediterranean principality.

Seb drummed his fingers on the leather desktop, imagining and discarding ways out of the ridiculous situation. "If Petrov thinks you have incriminating documents, perhaps we take can advantage of that. We can set a trap for him."

"How?"

"We'll force his hand. He'll get desperate and make a mistake—he'll try to get to you, or try to get the evidence back. And when he does, we'll be ready."

"I don't want to meet him. Either in a ballroom or a back alley. He's dangerous."

Seb narrowed his eyes. "Do you think I'm not?"

She had the grace to flush and look away, and he nodded, mollified. "I protect what's mine."

She gave him that haughty look he'd come to detest. "I'm not yours, Lord Mowbray."

"Yes, Princess." He drawled the title like an insult, a deliberate bastardization of the term of endearment. "For now, you are."

He lifted his brows, just daring her to argue, but she wisely held her tongue. He cast what he hoped was a scathing glance at her boy's attire. The sight of her slim legs and the hint of her breasts beneath the fabric made him want to throw her over his shoulder, carry her upstairs, and lose himself inside of her, princess or not.

Damn her.

"I'll have Mickey bring you a valise. Pack your things. We'll leave for Dorothea's house in thirty minutes."

"Isn't she's still in the country?"

"No. She returned to Grosvenor Square last night. She sent me a note."

Chapter 28.

The dowager duchess took one look at Anya's stony face and turned to Seb. "I do hope you've been treating Miss Brown with the utmost care and respect, Sebastien?"

Seb sent her a dry glance as he removed his gloves. "You can dispense with the charade, Dorothea. I know exactly who she is."

"You do? Oh, well, that makes everything so much easier, doesn't it?"

"Does it? I'm rather of the opinion it makes everything that much worse."

She frowned. "I see. You're in one of *those* moods, are you? Not that I'm not delighted to see you both, but what are you doing here? Has the odious Petrov left town?"

"He has not. But it's no longer practical for the princess to be at the Tricorn. From now on, she'll be staying here."

"But what about the danger to her?"

"I will arrange for armed guards from Bow Street. In in ten days' time, you will host a ball to present the newly discovered Princess Denisova to polite society."

The dowager raised her thin brows in an expression remarkably like Anya's. "Only ten days, Sebastien? Are you mad?"

"I have every faith that you can accomplish it. You will invite the whole world, and they will come."

"And Petrov?"

"Invite him too. And you must hint that there's a mystery surrounding the princess. That will get people talking."

Anya finally spoke. "To what purpose?"

Seb glanced at her and his chest tightened. She'd changed into one of the morning gowns he'd bought for her, a pale sage green that clung to her figure and made her look like some woodland sprite or naiad. He could hardly bear to look at her. Already she seemed different, more self-possessed, more unapproachable, as if an invisible shield had formed between them. An image of her, pink and tipsy in front of the fire, assailed him, but he tamped it down. There would be no more evenings like that.

"Petrov will start to sweat, wondering what we have on him and whether we're about to expose him in public."

"And will you?" Dorothea asked.

"If my guess is correct, it won't come to that." Seb inclined his head at the two women. "I'll leave you to work out the details. I'm off to Bow Street to see about someone to watch over you both. Don't leave the house until they get here."

Anya looked as if she would protest, but in the end, she said nothing at all, so he turned on his heel and left. He ignored the feeling that he was abandoning her, that he ought to keep her by his side. The niggling thought that no one, not even his best friends Alex or Benedict, could protect her as well as he could, followed him out the door.

It was too dangerous for him to stay. There was only so much provocation a man could endure, and he knew his limits. Alex and Ben would be immune to her infuriating charms, each one being fatally in love with his own wife.

"A Russian princess?" Benedict repeated for perhaps the twentieth time. "You're joking."

Seb rolled his eyes at his friend's continued incredulity. "I only wish I were."

"Do you think she wears a crown to bed?" Alex chuckled. His eyes held an inquisitive gleam and Seb cursed inwardly. Alex had a mind as sharp as a razor, and he loved ferreting out secrets. It was why he was such an asset to Bow Street.

"I wouldn't know," he said crossly.

Alex sent him a frankly disbelieving look, but thankfully didn't pursue the subject.

The three of them were at Manton's, the shooting gallery on Davies Street. Seb had sent a note around to Bow Street, asking Ben and Alex to meet him there. It was where he always went when he had something to sort out in his mind. The concentration needed to shoot accurately usually pushed everything else from his head. At least temporarily.

With their trusty Baker rifles in tow, they made their way to the long gallery, which was conveniently empty at this early hour, since most of the members didn't rise before noon. Seb had already given them a brief rundown of his adventures on Hounslow Heath and Anya's near misses with Petrov's thugs.

"I need you to help me guard her. I'm going to set a trap for Petrov, and I don't want her to be in any danger."

"You think he's our spy?" Ben asked.

"It's more than likely, from what Anya—from what the princess says."

Ben and Alex exchanged an eyebrows-raised look as they caught his unintentional slip.

Seb cursed himself again. It was hard to think of her as a title when he'd held the real woman in his arms. She wasn't some abstract concept. She was a warm, beautiful, sensuous—

No. No no no. Even thinking of her in that way was probably treasonous.

Annoyed with himself, he shrugged out of his coat, loaded his firearm with brisk efficiency, and took up position on his stomach on the ground, propped up on one elbow, leg raised at a right angle toward his hip to act as balance. Alex and Ben did the same, on either side of him.

He rested his cheek on the wooden stock and looked down the sight on the top of the barrel. With his left eye closed, he positioned the upright pin in the middle of the *V* and aimed at the paper target at the far end of the room.

He cleared his mind. He became aware of his pulse, his breathing. He slowed his breaths, waiting for the pause between heartbeats before he squeezed the trigger. The paper target quivered as the shot hit the center. He reloaded with brisk efficiency.

Bloody woman. She'd lied to him, manipulated him. He hated to be controlled, either by others or his environment. That was one of the reasons he'd joined the Rifles instead of the regular army. As a Rifleman, he was, more often than not, in control. The one with the target in his sights. The balance of life or death hinged on the pressure of his finger and the accuracy of his eye.

He enjoyed the same feeling of omnipotence overseeing

the gaming floor at the Tricorn, watching those below risk it all on the turn of a card. Such foolish whimsy was not for him. He liked being master of his fate.

And yet when it came to Anya—no, *Princess Denisova*—he had no control whatsoever. The bloody woman had played him for a fool. He'd been her little experiment, a panting dupe to relieve her of her unwanted virginity and to satisfy her sexual curiosity.

The fact that it had been the best sex of his life infuriated him even more, since there was clearly no hope of a repeat performance. Not now, not ever.

He hit the target again, dead center.

The deceitful little charlatan would appear next week as the virtuous Princess Denisova, as pure and untouched as the driven snow. Men would slaver over her, line up to fill her dance card.

Only he would know how beautiful she looked with her hair spread across his pillows like a river of honey, how her lips grew puffy from kissing. Only he would know the sweet sounds she made when she neared her climax, the scrape of her fingers against his scalp urging him on—

He missed the target completely.

"Bollocks."

Beside him, Ben chuckled softly. "Finding it hard to concentrate, are we? Something—or someone—on your mind?"

"Bugger off," Seb grunted.

The problem was, he and Anya were remarkably similar. She was determined to be mistress of her own fate. And while he might deplore her methods, he couldn't really fault her desire. Not when it burned so strongly in himself. Having met Petrov, he could even understand her need for subterfuge.

Seb sighed. The worst thing about this whole situation

was that for one bizarre moment, back in his study, he'd actually imagined himself married to her . . . and it hadn't felt wrong at all.

Which it was, of course. Completely wrong. He didn't want to be married to *anyone*, least of all a prickly ice princess who smelled like jasmine and tasted like perfection. Compatibility in bed wasn't enough to base a marriage on. He only needed to look at the example set by his own parents for a case in point. They were certainly no shining example of matrimonial bliss.

Seb frowned at the distant target. He certainly desired Anya physically, but honesty compelled him to admit that what he felt for her was more complicated than mere lust. He *liked* her, with her quick wit and her ridiculous superstitions. He admired and respected her, despite her stubbornness—or maybe because of it. He loved the way she challenged him. She fed his soul, met his energy with her own. In a paradoxical way, she both stimulated and calmed him.

He yearned for her.

"Well, you know we're with you, whatever you need us to do," Alex said.

Ben nodded in agreement.

"Sounds like you had quite the week with her at the Tricorn," Alex prodded. "The princess sounds like a fascinating woman. Brave, too, if she was willing to risk exposure to help us listen to the delegates. I'm sure Emmy and Georgie would get along famously with her."

Seb let out a noncommittal grunt. "They'll get to meet her at the ball. And she's not fascinating; she's irritating. Always issuing demands and ignoring my orders. I spent the entire week trying not to strangle her."

With a flash, he remembered Alex and Ben urging him to find some gorgeous someone who irritated him enough to want to strangle her. Seb blinked. Anya was that *someone*. He wanted to scold her and hug her simultaneously. He wanted to show her off to the world and keep her all to himself.

Bugger.

He had to stop thinking about her. There could be nothing permanent between them. Their one night had been a brief, glorious interlude—one he would probably dream about for the rest of his natural life—but it was over. From now on, it would be purely business. He would keep her safe from Petrov because he was a Bow Street Runner and it was his duty to protect and serve the inhabitants of the city.

And he would watch from the sidelines when she chose some less tarnished, more suitable partner to marry and disappeared out of his life forever.

Chapter 29.

Wolff was correct in his assessment that the late invitation would have no effect on attendance, Anya thought. Acceptances flooded into the Grosvenor Square mansion, and she read each one aloud to an increasingly ecstatic dowager duchess. A few guests tried to deliver theirs in person, to sneak a peek at the newly discovered princess before the night itself—as though she were some strange animal just introduced at the Royal Exchange—but all callers were denied by the stone-faced Mellors.

The prospect of throwing open the house had invigorated the dowager. Anya's middle finger developed a callused bump on one side from transcribing a myriad dictations: orders for flowers and wine, for musicians and beeswax. The staff had been whipped into a frenzy of polishing and dusting, and even the duchess's cook, a no-nonsense Scotswoman named Mrs. MacDougall, had been prevailed upon to cede her kitchen to the world-famous Lagrasse for the night. He was promising "an unparalleled dining event."

Of the Tricorn's three owners, Anya saw only two. Benedict Wylde and Alex Harland, both equally charming, had taken turns to guard her. They'd regarded her with keen interest, as if intrigued to see the difficult woman their friend had been saddled with at the Tricorn, but neither had spoken to her any more than was strictly necessary. They'd loitered unobtrusively during the days and presumably hovered, unseen, during the nights.

Of Wolff himself, there was no sign. Anya told herself she didn't care, but her chest ached with a strange undefined yearning, and at night, in the sumptuous bedroom she'd been assigned, she dreamed wicked dreams—of his mouth at her ear and his hands on her skin, fulfilling the melting promise of his words.

Bond Street's most celebrated modiste, Madame Cerise, had come in person to measure her for a gown "fit for a princess." Anya had stood still as an ice sculpture as she'd been prodded and pinned, even as she felt herself retreating behind a wall of cool reserve.

The resulting dress was a magical confection, a dazzling dove-grey satin shot through with silvery threads that made the skirts look like a mercury waterfall frozen midstream. Metallic embroidery on the bodice and hem created the illusion of thousands of tiny ice crystals and added a sparkling richness that made even Anya catch her breath.

She sent another note to Elizaveta, to let her know she was well. A scrappy urchin named Jem Barnes was enlisted to deliver the note without being followed, and Anya was delighted to receive a prompt reply from her friend.

I'm more than well. Elizaveta had written. *I'm engaged! Oliver and I went for a walk in Regent's Park yesterday and—after dropping the ring in a flowerbed, poor darling!—he asked me to make*

him the happiest of men and be his wife. Of course
I said yes! I know that you will wish me happy,
my dearest friend, and I cannot wait to see you
in person. I'm so glad that you're staying with the
duchess now and have the protection of the men
from Bow Street, but I still worry for you. I won't
rest easy until Petrov is back in St. Petersburg and
far away from both of us. With love &c, Eliz.

Anya's happy tears at Elizaveta's engagement had
mingled with a gut-wrenching, bittersweet grief. Elizaveta, her childhood rock, her other half, her faithful
companion and youthful confidante, was leaving her.
And while she was so happy for her friend, she couldn't
shake the feeling that everything was changing, and not
necessarily for the better. Everything she'd once taken
for granted, everything safe and secure, was slipping between her fingers like sand through an hourglass. Soon,
she would be left with nothing but memories and thin air.

She didn't want to examine her feelings for Wolff
too closely. They were too complicated, too contradictory. He'd seen her as nothing more than a duty to be
discharged. He'd washed his hands of her as soon as he
could.

Anya gave a mournful sigh. He was also generous,
unselfish, and honorable to the core. When she'd given
herself to him she'd thought it only physical attraction,
but somewhere along the way a whole host of deeper
emotions had become engaged. Now she was both furious with him for abandoning her—and desperate for a
glimpse of his surly, handsome face.

The night of the ball finally arrived. Anya accepted the
ministrations of the friseur to arrange her hair and allowed Tilly, the duchess's timid maid, to lace her into her

dress and apply a fine coating of silvery powder to her skin with an enormous powder puff. Her shoulders and chest shimmered in the lamplight like pale moonbeams, and Anya studied the stranger in the mirror, searching for some hint of recognition.

She was every inch the poised, perfect princess. Her blue eyes looked huge in her pale face, her rouged lips a striking contrast to the silver dress.

This was not the same carefree girl who'd left Russia eighteen months ago. There was a sadness in her eyes now, an understanding that the world was both more cruel and more wonderful than she'd ever imagined. There was determination too, and pride, and a new, distinctly feminine awareness.

Tonight, her first foray back into "polite society," would be an ordeal. It would have been far more bearable with Wolff at her side, poking fun at the pomp and circumstance and staring down those who would challenge her right to be there. Without him, she felt as cold and frozen as a bulb beneath the surface of the soil. He was the warmth she needed to thaw the ice and coax her into the sunlight. He'd taught her to glow, to burn.

But he was not in the drawing room when she joined the dowager duchess before their grand entrance to the ballroom. A few select guests had assembled, and Anya felt all eyes upon her as she paused in the doorway.

"Princess!" Dorothea came forward to take her hand. "You look wonderful, my dear. Come and meet everyone."

A tall man with sandy hair and a friendly face stepped forward.

"Princess Denisova, allow me to present my eldest great-nephew. This is Geoffrey, Marquis of Cranford."

Sebastien's half-brother.

The man bowed low over her hand. "Delighted to meet you at last, Princess."

Anya studied him. There were few physical similarities between the two men, apart from their height. Geoffrey's hair was a lighter brown. And unlike Wolff, who
only had to look at her to melt her into a puddle, Geoffrey's eyes were soft and unthreatening. His ready smile
reminded her of Dmitri, and Anya felt an instant affinity.

"I hear you like to ride?" he said. "Seb tells me you're
an excellent horsewoman."

Her stomach twisted at the thought that Wolff had
complimented her, albeit in her absence. "Yes, I do."

"Then perhaps you'll do me the honor of meeting me
in the park sometime? We can exercise our mounts together."

"I would like that very much."

He presented her with a small box wrapped in ribbon. "It is customary to give young ladies a token on
the eve of their first official ball." He smiled. "I'm
aware that this is not your first ball, Princess, but it is
your first *English* ball, and I hope you'll accept it in the
spirit of friendship."

Anya tugged open the ribbons to reveal an exquisite
silver beaded evening bag.

"It's a reticule," Geoffrey said unnecessarily. "I'm
sure you've a hundred already, but I'm told ladies can
never have enough. You can keep coins in it, or hand-
kerchiefs, or whatever else it is you like to cart about
with you."

Anya smiled up at him in genuine pleasure. "Thank
you! It matches my dress. But I do hope you've already
placed a coin inside?"

"A coin?"

"It's a Russian superstition. If you give someone a
purse or any other kind of money holder as a gift, you
must put some money inside. If it's empty, it's said to
cause bad financial luck." She shrugged wryly. "It's

'seed money'—the belief is that it grows and attracts even more money."

"That's a nice theory." He reached into the pocket of his waistcoat, pulled out a gold sovereign, and handed it to her solemnly. "Here you go. May it multiply into a vast fortune for you, my lady."

The dowager chuckled at their antics.

"Any more superstitions I should know about?" Geoffrey asked with a smile. "Have I, perhaps, been putting my feet into my boots in the wrong order this whole time? Should rice pudding only ever be eaten during a full moon?"

Anya laughed. His dry sense of humor was rather like that of his brother. "Oh, there are hundreds. We Russians are a superstitious lot." She gestured toward a vase of flowers on the side table. "For example, while it's never a mistake to take a bouquet of flowers when invited to someone's home, you *must* make sure that bunches for festive occasions have an odd number of flowers. Bouquets with an even number are reserved for funerals."

"Heavens!" the dowager said lightly. "I had no idea. One, two, three—" She began counting the blooms then let out a sigh of relief. "Thank goodness, fifteen. I feel so much better now. Our ball is a guaranteed success." She turned toward a shadow in the doorway. "Ah, Sebastien. There you are."

Chapter 30.

Seb's gaze found Anya the moment he stepped into the room, and all the air left his lungs in a rush. He'd had the same sensation when he'd taken that artillery blast at Waterloo: a roaring in his ears and a squeezing of his chest that almost knocked him backward.

She was wearing some silver concoction and smiling up at his brother, and Seb had never seen anything so blindingly beautiful in his life.

The past week had been hell. The Tricorn—usually his one place of comfort and repose—had been dull and empty without her. She'd breathed life into it, despite the short time she'd been there. He'd found evidence of her occupation everywhere: a stack of papers piled haphazardly in the library, half-read books left lying, spine up, on tables. The tantalizing scent of her perfume in the air. Every time he entered a room, he was haunted by images of her defying him, teasing him, challenging him.

The servants had noticed her loss too; Lagrasse had

been grumbling about "unappreciative audiences" for days and even Mickey had been unusually morose.

Tonight, Seb was as edgy as before a military push. Dorothea had done an excellent job of intimating that there would be some kind of revelation, and the ballroom was already uncomfortably crowded with guests all waiting to meet the silvery goddess in front of him.

The presence of so many people made him nervous. It would be difficult to protect the princess when Petrov made his move—as Seb was sure he would. The Russian would doubtless come to repeat his demand for the "evidence" he thought she possessed. Seb had sent Anya strict instructions to stay inside the ballroom, no matter how overheated it became. There would be no chance of the Russian getting her alone.

He'd had agents following Petrov all week, but the man had done nothing out of the ordinary. The runners watching *this* house had reported a figure lurking in Grosvenor Square yesterday evening, but the man had slipped away before he could be identified. Had it been one of Petrov's minions? Seb had men stationed around the perimeter, just in case.

That Petrov might decide to silence Anya with a sniper was not beyond the realm of possibility. A good rifleman—one as skilled as Alex, Ben, or Seb himself—could hit a target through a window from a hundred yards away. The thought of a bullet passing anywhere near her made his blood run cold.

Anya turned as Dorothea announced him, and he watched the smile she'd given Geoffrey fade, replaced with a polite, wary expression, and for the first time in his life, he was conscious of being jealous of his brother. He'd never begrudged Geoffrey the title, or the responsibility of running the estate he'd one day inherit. But he hated him stealing a smile from Anya.

Geoffrey was a marquis. He'd be Duke of Southwick when their father died. He'd be a suitable match for her. Seb clenched his jaw.

"What have you there?" Dorothea glanced with undisguised interest at the leather-covered jeweler's box he'd collected earlier from Ludgate Hill. Seb forced himself to step forward and offer it to Anya with a casualness that belied the emotional weight of the gift. Already he regretted the foolish impulse.

"If you're going to go out in the *ton*, you should dress the part," he said stiffly.

Their gloved fingers brushed as she took the box, and even that slight contact was enough to send a shiver of awareness through him.

A gasp escaped her as she opened the lid.

"I took your drawing to Bridge & Rundell," he said.

The tiara was perfection, the physical embodiment of her elevated status. He'd meant it to serve as a reminder of the cavernous gulf that separated them—the Bow Street Bastard and the fairy-tale princess. A reminder of just how different they were. But his heart still pounded against his ribs as he waited for her response.

Tears sprang to her eyes. "Oh, I—" She seemed at a loss for words.

"You had one just like it, you said."

Her throat bobbed as she swallowed a knot of emotion and blinked rapidly. "Yes. The Denisov tiara. I had to break it up to get enough money to come here."

Her brows twitched into a frown and a wave of panic swept through him. Every other time he'd given a woman a piece of jewelry, it had been as a parting gift, a "thank you" for a few weeks of mutual pleasure. Would she think of it as a *douceur*? They'd only shared one night, but he prayed she wouldn't interpret it as a crude attempt at payment. There weren't enough jewels in the world for that.

But her fingers skimmed over the sapphires and diamonds like a lover's caress, and he found he could be envious of inanimate objects too. Then her glistening eyes lifted to his and the rest of the world fell away.

"Thank you," she managed huskily. "This means . . . so much to me. You have no idea."

He had a fair idea. The yearning and rapture on her face was reward enough for the foolish, quixotic gesture, even if it revealed the depths of his regard for her to anyone with a pair of eyes. He wasn't wearing his heart upon his sleeve—he'd put in it a bloody jeweler's box and handed it to her with a roomful of witnesses.

Shit. He should have bought her a fan or a silver card case—some meaningless, less sentimental trinket that would have left him less emotionally naked. Less exposed. But he'd wanted to see that smile of hers, and restoring some small part of her family heritage had seemed like a good way to do it.

"It's almost exactly as I remember it," she breathed softly. "Except for the setting. The original was gold. I like this better."

He managed a careless shrug, as if it weren't the most expensive gift he'd ever given. As if he hadn't paid a king's ransom for it and bullied and threatened Rundell for the past week to have it ready by tonight.

She pressed her lips together. "It must have cost a fortune. How can I ever rep—"

"There's no need for repayment," he growled, and she flinched at his unintentionally gruff tone. "It's a gift, freely given. Take it."

Her eyes searched his, looking for God knew what, but then she inclined her head. "Then, thank you, Lord Mowbray. You're very kind."

His lips twitched. "That's not my reputation."

"Oh, my!" Dorothea sighed, craning her neck to peer at the tiara on its bed of crushed black velvet. She glanced approvingly at him. "I must say, Sebastien, whatever your faults—and they are legion—you do have the most exquisite taste."

"Why thank you," he said dryly. "But I can't claim credit for this particular design. Rundell merely re-created what the princess had already drawn."

"Come, let me help you put it on." Dorothea dragged Anya toward a pier mirror. She stood motionless as the tiara was placed on her hair, then turned her head this way and that to inspect it from different angles. The diamonds flashed tiny rainbows across the room, and the dark sapphires threatened to suck all the available light into their cobalt depths. Fathomless darkness and eternal light, the entire universe in one glittering headpiece.

Seb exhaled softly and quelled the urge to applaud. *Bravo, Princess.* He'd never been much for poetry, but the fragment of a verse came to him, something he'd read a few years ago by one of those opium-addled fools like Byron or Coleridge.

She walks in beauty, like the night
of cloudless climes and starry skies,
and all that's best of dark and bright,
meet in her aspect and her eyes.

It seemed entirely apropos. She was an ice princess brought to glittering life. Her upswept hair revealed the elegant nape of her neck. The delicate bumps of her spine looked like a row of natural pearls. He wanted to trace them, to undo the tiny buttons at the back of her dress and peel back the silk until he found the sweetly rounded curve of her—

No. No no no.

Business, not pleasure.

Princess. Out of bounds.

He cleared his throat, pasted a polite smile on his face, and gestured to the open doorway. "Our guests await. After you, Princess."

He caught Geoffrey's amused look, one that simultaneously appreciated and mocked the extravagance of his gift. It was a look that clearly said: *Oh, you've done it now, little brother. And I will tease you mercilessly as soon as we're alone . . .*

Seb sent him an answering scowl, just daring him to comment. Anya and Dorothea filed out of the room. He quashed the impulse to catch Anya's wrist and prevent her from entering the ballroom, to carry her up to the nearest bedroom instead. Nobody could hurt her if she were locked away with him. He could keep her safe forever in his arms.

He shook his head. What utter bollocks.

Mellors's dulcet tones echoed through the hall as the doors to the ballroom were thrown open, and Seb glimpsed a sea of expectant faces all turned toward them.

"The Dowager Duchess of Winwick and Her Highness the Princess Anastasia Denisova."

Seb blinked. Anastasia. He'd never even given her full name a thought. She was simply Anya. The girl who made him imagine ridiculous, impossible futures. The girl who drove him mad.

He had to get a hold of himself. The private world they'd created at the Tricorn had been a temporary illusion. This was the reality. She was public property; he had to share her with the world.

He frowned, struck by a sudden revelation. Good God, was this what it felt like to be *married*? Was sharing your partner only made bearable by the knowledge that you were the one who got to take her home? The only one to receive her private smiles. The only one who got to see her naked. Did husbands savor those private moments, like a dragon hoarding treasure, just so they could endure evenings like these?

He'd never know. He was here for her protection, to do his duty.

That was all.

Chapter 31.

"Princess, may I introduce the Earl and Countess of Ware, Benedict and Georgiana Wylde."

Anya tried to ignore the unnerving effect of Wolff's hovering presence at her side and extended her hand to the couple who'd come over to greet them. "Delighted."

The pretty brown-haired woman sent her a friendly smile which put Anya instantly at ease. "Please. It's Georgie and Benedict. We really don't stand on ceremony."

Anya returned the smile. "Neither do I, usually. Please call me Anya."

She'd seen Benedict Wylde often over the past week as he'd patrolled the house and gardens. He was tall and handsome, with brown eyes and hair a few shades lighter than Wolff's. She'd thought him quite lofty and fearsome, but the softening of his features whenever he happened to glance at his wife made her revisit that opinion.

"Georgie runs Caversteed Shipping," Wylde said.

"It's quite the international enterprise." His expression of unashamed pride made Anya envious. "Her ships trade with Russia all the time. I'm sure she's dying to discuss such boring details as international tariffs and shipping routes with you." There was a teasing chuckle in his voice.

His wife elbowed him playfully in the ribs. "Benedict! You make me sound like the dullest woman in the room!"

He raised his brows with a chuckle. "Never. I love it when you talk commerce. It makes me feel more intelligent just by association. And it might not be a bad idea to look into expanding your trade in Russian spirits. I tried some of the vodka Seb trialed at the Tricorn last week, and while I can't see it ever being more popular than our native gin, there might be a market here if you import it."

"As a matter of fact," Anya said, "my family have all sorts of commercial interests back in Russia. I actually *own* a vodka distillery."

She felt, rather than saw, Wolff stiffen at her side, and suppressed a snort of laughter. She wondered if he was remembering her comments the night they drank together. She'd admitted to knowing a little about the stuff. He probably wanted to strangle her right now.

The thought brought a disproportionate amount of delight. For some reason, annoying Wolff was the most enjoyable thing ever.

She turned her head and slid him a teasing smile and enjoyed the way his eyes narrowed with the promise of retribution. Her stomach flipped. If he wanted to punish her, he'd have to get her alone. And she wanted that more than anything.

Georgie Wylde's grey eyes widened in interest. "You do? That is fascinating. I do hope you'll come and visit my warehouse sometime. I'd love to get your opinion on the quality of the Russian goods I've been importing. If you wouldn't be too bored, that is," she added quickly.

"It sounds very interesting. I'd love to come, thank you." A warm glow settled in her chest at the olive branch of friendship the other woman was offering.

Another couple joined them; her second guard, Alex Harland, and a woman Anya assumed to be his wife. She was petite, with almost elfin features, and a smiling mischievous look about her. Anya liked her immediately. She looked like the kind of girl who would be a lot of fun.

Wolff shifted at her elbow. "And this is Earl Melton and his countess. Alexander and Emmeline Harland."

"Alex and Emmy," the girl said immediately. "Really, Seb, there's no need to be so formal." She turned back to Anya. "My grandmother, Camille, Comtesse de Rougemont, is good friends with the Dread Dowager Duchess." She indicated a stylish older woman chatting with Dorothea across the room. "And my brother, Luc, is somewhere around here too, with his new wife, Sally. They just got married last month."

Her gaze flicked to Anya's tiara. Her eyes widened in appreciation and a smile spread over her face. "Those," she said reverently, "are exceptionally fine diamonds."

Her husband gave a little snort of amusement. "You would know, my love."

She shot him a chiding glance and smiled back at Anya. "I'm a great lover of diamonds."

"And emeralds and rubies and, well, most jewels in general, really," her husband finished drily.

Benedict and Georgie both chuckled. Alex pulled his wife closer to his side and tucked a tendril of her hair behind her ear in an affectionate, unconscious gesture. "Do try to recall your promise, darling. What do we do with jewels?"

Emmy rolled her eyes. "We look but we don't touch,'" she parroted, in the flat tone of one who'd repeated the phrase *ad infinitum*.

Alex smiled down at her. "Exactly."

She let out a dissatisfied sigh. "Is it from Bridge & Rundell? It looks like their work." She sent a sideways glare at her husband. "I haven't been there in ages. I'm not allowed within thirty paces of the place."

Anya frowned in confusion. "Because your husband's worried you'll bankrupt him with your purchases?"

They all laughed at that, and Anya had the feeling she was missing an inside joke.

"That's not the reason," Harland said.

Anya lifted her brows in question at Wolff.

"Emmy here used to have an unusual vocation," he said softly. "She was, ah, an importer and exporter of precious stones."

Anya turned to the girl in interest.

"What he's too polite to say," Alex added in low tones, "is that until recently, my wife was a criminal mastermind who 'liberated' certain jewels from their unlawful owners."

Anya stared at Emmy in doubled fascination, and the other girl sent her a cheeky grin.

"Alas, my career was foiled by those dutiful gentlemen at Bow Street." She laughed, her gaze sliding from her husband to Wylde to Wolff. "They put an end to all my adventures."

Alex sent her a wicked, knowing look. "Oh, not *all* your adventures, surely?" he purred.

A pretty blush rose to her cheeks.

Anya smiled at the teasing and obvious affection between the two couples. It was refreshing to encounter some society marriages where the partners hadn't married for either convenience or duty. Her own parents had looked at each other that way, and her chest ached in longing for something similar for herself.

She glanced around the room, looking to see if Vasili and the rest of the Russian delegation had arrived, but while she recognized Prince Trubetskoi and two of the men who'd been with him at the Tricorn, there was no sign of Petrov.

She sensed Wolff shift at her elbow. "Dorothea's beckoning me. Excuse me."

Anya watched as he crossed the room, admiring his broad shoulders and long legs. Halfway across, he was accosted by a stunningly beautiful brunette. He bestowed a wide, genuine smile on the woman and bent to kiss her hand, and Anya quashed the spike of jealousy that stabbed through her as the woman gazed up at him adoringly.

"She's very beautiful, isn't she?" Georgie said without malice.

Anya jumped, caught in her surveillance, and tried to brazen it out. "Who?"

The other woman sent her a dry, knowing look. "The woman talking with Seb. Her name's Caroline Apsley. I believe the two of them were, ah, romantically linked before the war."

Anya's chest squeezed tight. "You mean she was his mistress? They're still on friendly terms, clearly."

Georgie nodded. "She's a widow now. She has high hopes to reel him in."

Anya tried to school her expression into one of polite interest. It was none of her affair. She had no claim on Wolff. But still, it felt like betrayal.

"He's not interested, though," Benedict murmured, having shamelessly eavesdropped on the conversation.

"Why do you say that?" Anya tried to keep the eagerness out of her voice. She was pathetic.

"Because I know Seb. I spent three years with him, day and night, all around the Peninsular. I've seen him smile at countless women like he's smiling at Caroline right now. He's charming and gallant, and it doesn't mean a thing."

Anya lifted a shoulder. "If you say so."

"Ben's right," Alex added. "Seb smiles at every woman that way. Every woman but one."

Anya turned to look at him, caught by his sly tone. "You're right. He scowls at me."

"And buys you outrageously gorgeous jewelry," Emmy added on a laugh, her eyes back on the tiara.

"You know how particular he is about his clothes," Anya said lightly. "He wanted me to be well turned out."

"Well, if that's what you get for Sebastien Wolff's scowls, he can scowl at me any time he likes!" Emmy chuckled.

Alex swatted her playfully on the bottom. "Might I remind you that you're a happily married woman, Emmeline Harland?"

Emmy twinkled up at him. "I don't need reminding."

Alex bent his head and Anya just caught his intimate whisper. "Leaving me, princess?"

"Never."

Anya turned away. Alex's teasing endearment for his wife was clearly another private joke. Anya really *was* a princess, but Wolff had never spoken it to her in that way, as an endearment. The Harlands' easy laughter was a world away from what she and Wolff had attained.

Chapter 32.

"Sebastien, you must dance with the princess."

Seb slid a sideways glare at Dorothea. She was in fine fettle tonight, enjoying her position at the epicenter of the social whirl. He hadn't seen her so animated for years.

"Sorry," he said blandly. "I can't hear you."

She let out a snort of irritation. "In that case, you look like hell. And the cut of your jacket is hideous."

"It is not!"

"Aha! So you can hear me. You aren't deaf in *both* ears. You're just willfully ignoring me. Really, Sebastien, sometimes I think you use your injury as an excuse to avoid speaking to people you don't wish to speak to."

He didn't bother to deny it. "I'm certainly deaf to insults. And stupid ideas."

"You only hear what you want to hear," she sniffed. "And there's no need to be testy with me. You must see why I sent Anya with you. I was certain the two of you would get along famously. Was I mistaken?"

He didn't miss the glitter of curiosity in her eyes. He glared at her. "Yes. You were. Completely. I only helped her out of duty."

She seemed to deflate a little. "Hmm. Well, it's my ball, and as the hostess's close relative, it still behooves you to lead her out in the dancing. You're an earl, aren't you? She ought to have at least an earl for her first dance."

He ground his teeth.

"If you won't do it, I'll ask Geoffrey—"

Seb growled.

Dorothea sent him a knowing smile. "Oh, never mind. Look, Prince Trubetskoi's beaten you to it."

Seb's head snapped around. Sure enough, Anya was accepting the arm of her fellow countryman and letting him lead her onto the dance floor. He made a conscious effort to unclench his fists.

The prince was a good-looking bastard. Tonight, he was wearing full military uniform with a row of colorful campaign medals glittering on his chest. His eyes gleamed and his lustrous black mustache twitched as he laughed down at something Anya said.

Seb never trusted a man with a mustache. Petrov had a mustache, didn't he? And really, who wore full dress uniform to a private ball? Seb could have worn his own medals too—if he'd wanted to look like a vainglorious prick. Anya wasn't impressed by all that military bollocks. Was she?

He'd chosen a jacket of the deepest navy, so dark it looked black, and a diamond-and-sapphire pin for his cravat. The choice had been deliberate, a subtle masculine echo of Anya's blue and clear gems. As if something so insignificant could bind them. He was a fool.

He couldn't tear his eyes away from the dance floor. Trubetskoi was holding her so close, he'd be breathing in her perfume, that gorgeous jasmine and rain scent. It would be swirling in his brain, making him fevered. How could he possibly resist her?

His hand lingered on the silken skin of her back, and Seb tried not to scowl. Why should Trubetskoi get to touch all that creamy softness? He watched the Russian's gaze linger on her alabaster smooth shoulders and her perfect breasts and quelled the urge to throw him through the nearest window, international diplomacy be damned.

Dorothea sent him a shrewd, amused glance. "I've already heard several gentlemen announce their intention to offer for her. Marrying an Englishman would cement the ties of friendship between our two nations. But of course, with her connections, she could marry into any noble family in Europe."

Seb couldn't hold back a grunt of annoyance. "She's a woman, not a bloody peace treaty. And I have it on good authority that she doesn't want to marry anyone. They're all fortune hunters—even the gouty royal dukes."

Dorothea shrugged. "There aren't many men who can match her fortune, it's true. She has all sorts of commercial interests back in Russia. Textile mills, printing shops. Why, she even owns a vodka distillery!"

Seb ground his molars together as Anya's laughing voice echoed in his memory. *I know a little bit about vodka*. The wretch.

"Having her tiara remade was a very generous gesture."

"She's a princess. Society expects it."

"For someone who claims to have no feelings for her other than duty, I'd say it was above and beyond. You must have paid Rundell a small fortune to have it completed in such a short time."

He shrugged.

THE PRINCESS AND THE ROGUE

"I suppose it would be vulgar to inquire how much it cost?"

"It would. I can afford it."

Dorothea regarded him thoughtfully. "I'm sure you can. In monetary terms."

He didn't even want to ask what she meant by *that* cryptic comment, so he pretended not to hear and disengaged himself as swiftly as possible. "Do excuse me. I think Alex is trying to catch my attention."

Dorothea's derisive snort indicated she saw through his cowardly retreat, but she let him slip away without further comment.

Ben and Alex were temporarily without their wives. Seb sidled up next to them and the three of them stood in companionable silence for a few moments. They'd stood this way countless times during the war, surveying the land or fortifications before them for possible danger. Seb felt a deep sense of gratitude that they'd survived to stand here now, as free men. The only terrain he needed to survey now was the ballroom, the only potential threat that of ambush from matchmaking mamas and enthusiastic widows.

He ran his hand through his hair and his fingertips touched the raised ridge of scar hidden behind his left ear. He'd been so lucky. There were far worse injuries he could have received. Alex's new brother-in-law, Luc Danvers, had lost the lower part of his leg at Trafalgar. At least Seb hadn't lost a limb or received dreadful scarring. Other men he'd served with had gone mad, unable to reassimilate into civilian life after everything they'd seen. They tried to lose themselves in drink or gambling, ruined their minds in opium dens, or even ended up incarcerated in asylums like Bethlehem. He had nothing to complain about. No reason to feel so frustrated and dissatisfied.

"You know," Benedict mused suddenly, "Coleridge once said the happiest marriage he could imagine would be the union of a deaf man to a blind woman."

Seb gave an amused snort. "Sounds about right."

Ben levelled him a significant sideways look that made him lift his brows.

"Do you have a point?" Seb asked.

"You might be deaf, my friend—"

"Only on the one side."

Ben continued as if he hadn't been interrupted, "—but the princess isn't blind to your faults. She sees them and likes you anyway. It's inexplicable, but there you are. You'd be the greatest fool in London if you didn't do something about it."

Seb frowned at him. "I already *did* something about it. I asked her to marry me. She said no."

Alex and Ben shared a look that made him want to bang their heads together. Smug bastards. "Since when did you two become the experts on matchmaking?" he growled. "God, you're as bad as Dorothea."

"We're not experts on matchmaking. We're experts on *you*. We've never seen you like this with any other woman."

"Like what exactly?"

"Irritable." Alex chuckled.

"Frustrated," Benedict added with a grin.

"Discombobulated. It's a joy to watch."

Seb ground his teeth again. At this rate, he wouldn't have any molars left with which to chew.

"Ask her again," Alex insisted. "It's a woman's prerogative to change her mind, after all."

"Not a chance. She's given me her answer."

Seb glared across the room to where Anya still swirled in Trubetskoi's arms. She looked gorgeous, happy. Perfectly at ease. Scores of men were hovering at the periphery, all eagerly waiting to claim her for a dance.

None of them knew her. All they saw was that beautiful face, those glittering diamonds. Seb was the only one who realized her polite smile never reached her eyes. Who'd seen her laughing at the pelicans in the park, or downing vodka like a hardened criminal in front of the fire. He closed his eyes. He still wanted her. It was like a sickness in his blood. A constant, gnawing ache.

"Fine. I'll ask her to dance."

The crowd parted like the Red Sea before his glowering expression. He strode forward and waited, arms crossed, at the edge of the dance floor until Trubetskoi swirled her to a laughing, breathless stop. A couple of idiots tried to step forward and claim her attention, but Seb fixed her with a determined glare, just daring her to accept anyone else, and shouldered them all out of the way.

He held out his hand. "My dance."

Her eyes widened at his commanding tone, but she sent Trubetskoi a polite smile and grasped his fingers. The contact burned, even through her elbow-length gloves. Seb turned her as the musicians struck up a waltz and slid his free hand down to rest at the lower curve of her spine. With the faintest pull, he drew her toward him, and she inhaled sharply, as if the light touch heated her blood too.

He swung her into the first turn.

She trod on his foot.

Her long skirts covered the misstep, but Seb enjoyed the hectic blush that flooded her cheeks. She wasn't as composed as she wanted to appear. *Good.*

"Quick!" she blurted out in a panicked whisper. "Now you have to step on *my* foot."

"What?"

"It's a Russian superstition."

He rolled his eyes. "Not another one. Don't tell me, we have to sacrifice a chicken and spread its entrails in the street or something equally ludicrous."

She narrowed her eyes at him. "Nothing so gory. The person who was stepped on just needs to return the favor."

"Why?"

"Because if you don't, we'll be enemies forever."

He sent her an ironic look. "We've been at odds for the entire time we've been acquainted, Your Highness. Do you really think it would help?"

She met his eyes, and he felt the punch right down to his gut. "Not the entire time," she said softly.

His body hardened to the point of pain. Bloody woman. As if he needed reminding.

"Step on my foot!" she hissed again through her teeth, pretending to smile for the benefit of their interested onlookers.

"I'll hurt you."

"You won't."

"It's ridiculous."

"Just do it."

He exhaled a put-upon sigh. "Fine."

Using the cover of her skirts, he waited until the dance slowed and very gently pressed the toe of his boot onto the top of her foot, acutely conscious of the fact that she only wore the flimsiest of dancing slippers beneath her skirts. That, naturally, led to him imagining everything else she had on under there, from silken stockings to soft-as-a-snowdrift skin.

Seb sucked in a breath. Dancing was a mistake. Just being in the same room with her was a mistake. He almost wished Petrov would appear and make his move and put an end to this torment.

Almost.

"You look very beautiful tonight," he said, praying she didn't hear the ridiculous combination of resentment and longing in his tone.

She glanced up at him, and he had to remind himself to breathe. Her eyes sparkled. "Thank you. So do you."

"I don't think a man can be *beautiful*, per se," he countered sternly.

She tilted her head, as if considering the notion. "How should I compliment you, then, Lord Mowbray? Should I call you handsome? Noble? Irresistible?" Her lips parted on a teasing smile and he resisted the urge to say: *Mine. You should call me mine.*

"Any of those will do," he said lightly. He cast around for a safer subject. "Have you been enjoying yourself with the dowager duchess?"

She nodded, and he cursed the fact that they were reduced to speaking of such inane things. God, they'd be discussing the weather next, or the dancing. Inches separated them, but it might as well have been a hundred miles.

"Geoffrey gave you a reticule," he said, and could have kicked himself for sounding like a jealous fool.

"He did. It's lovely. Although I prefer the gift *you* gave me."

"The tiara?"

She shook her head, making the item in question catch the light like hoarfrost in the dawn.

"No."

She saw his surprise and hastened to explain. "The tiara is, without doubt, the most wonderful present anyone's ever given me, but I wasn't thinking of that." She sent him a secret, confiding smile. "I meant the vial of sleeping potion you gifted me at the Tricorn."

Seb lifted his brows. "You prefer *that* to Geoffrey's reticule?"

"I do. Unless I hit someone over the head with the reticule, it's of very little use in terms of defense. The tincture, on the other hand, makes me feel invulnerable. It is potential. A chance to control my destiny. It is *freedom*."

Seb tried to ignore the disproportionate amount of gratification her words gave him and failed miserably. The way she said it, so reverently, made him want to give her a vat of the stuff. Hell, he'd order Lagrassse to cook nothing but mandrakes for the next month. She could bathe in it if she wanted to.

The sudden scorching image of her in the bath, flushed and dripping, assailed him, and he almost stumbled.

"All that in a little bottle," he managed lightly.

She nodded, her eyes bright. "I carry it wherever I go."

"Even tonight?" he teased. His eyes flicked over her chest. "I can't imagine where, in that dress."

"It's in the pockets of my skirts," she whispered.

"Well, just remember you swore never to use it on me."

She laughed up at him. "Of course not."

They made another swirl around the floor, and Seb realized with a start how effortlessly they danced together.

"I enjoyed meeting your friends," she said. "They were extremely interesting."

Seb made a noncommittal sound.

"I should like to meet them again."

He bit back a silent groan. That was all he needed. For her to be everywhere he went, laughing with his friends, posing an impossible temptation at every turn. Reminding him of everything he wanted and couldn't have. Napoleon himself couldn't have devised a worse torture.

The Harlands and the Wyldes stood to one side of the ballroom, watching Seb and Anya dance.

Georgie took a thoughtful sip of her champagne. "No wonder Seb didn't want to stay for dinner with us the other night. He had all that temptation waiting for him back at the Tricorn."

"They do make a beautiful couple." Emmy sighed.

"Like a fairy-tale prince and princess," Georgie added, her eyes shining.

Their husbands both rolled their eyes.

"You're blind," Alex said. "And delusional. They're arguing. I can tell from here."

Emmy tilted her head, studying them carefully. "No, I don't think so. There's tension there, but it's not animosity. It's more like . . . passion. Barely contained."

Georgie lifted her brows. "You think they—"

"Failed to contain it?" Emmy chuckled. "Oh, come on, *look* at them. Of *course* they did."

"So, what went wrong?" Georgie asked. "They're clearly at odds now. Do you think Seb got bored? Is that tiara his idea of a parting gift?"

Alex shook his head. "He hasn't lost interest, believe me." He sent Benedict an amused glance over Georgie's head. "He's been like a bear with a sore head all week. Whoever said 'absence makes the heart grow fonder' was way off the mark. In Seb's case, absence makes the heart grow moody and irritable."

"Poor Seb," Emmy chided. "You could be a bit more sympathetic."

Alex stifled a snort. "'Poor Seb,' my arse. He did nothing but take the piss out of the two of us when we fell in love with you two. He deserves everything he gets. It's about time someone gave him a run for his money." He caught Benedict's eye again. "Do you remember what he said to me at Manton's?"

"What?"

"He said he wanted to strangle her.'"

Emmy looked mystified. "Is that a good thing? It doesn't *sound* like a good thing."

Alex slid his arm around her waist and drew her into the cradle of his body. "Oh, it is, my little thief. It most definitely is."

Georgie and Emmy shared a look.

"Men are incomprehensible," Georgie declared.

"We think the same thing about you women." Her husband chuckled. He glanced over at Alex and raised his brows. "The question is, of course, whether the stubborn idiot is going to do anything about it?"

Chapter 33.

Anya's heart was beating painfully fast as she and Wolff swirled around the dance floor. His proximity was playing havoc with her composure. Even his slightest touch enflamed her. Part of her resented it. Why *him*? Why not someone less complicated, more suitable?

Still, she savored the sensation of being in his arms, even at such a frustratingly polite distance. The scent of him teased her nostrils, and her fingers tightened involuntarily on his shoulder. His muscles were reassuringly solid beneath the exquisitely cut coat.

The warmth radiating from him sent tremors of recognition through her, and a blush rose in her cheeks as she vividly recalled the feel of his body within her own—the heat and abandon, the exquisite combination of friction and glide. His strong body shuddering in ecstasy.

She wanted her gloves gone so she could feel the heat and the texture of his skin. She wanted to slide her hand up the slope of his neck, to thread her fingers through his hair and tug him down for a passionate kiss.

She wanted to lead him out of this stuffy, overcrowded ballroom and into somewhere dark. A room, the moonlit garden, anywhere private, to slake the thirst and hunger she had for him.

He caught her eye and gave her one of his lazy, intimate smiles, as if he guessed the direction of her thoughts. The strength of her own desire shocked her. It was something primitive, uncivilized. It came from somewhere deep within, a place where she was not a princess, but simply a woman.

She couldn't believe he'd had her tiara remade. Did he appreciate the enormity of it? Did he understand what it meant to her to have her family's history restored? In one fell swoop, he'd erased her past misdeed in destroying it and had given her a new symbol of hope to pass down to future generations.

She thought perhaps he did comprehend it. Then she reminded herself not to read too much into his gesture. He enjoyed beautiful things. Perhaps having the tiara reconstructed was no different from him demanding culinary excellence from Lagrasse or ordering the finest pair of dueling pistols from Manton.

The music came to an end on an uplifting series of chords, and she forced her hands down to her sides. She tried to think of something to say, but words completely deserted her. She, the queen of polite small talk, who'd spent years making effortless conversation with everyone from cardinals to courtesans, could think of nothing to say to this man who'd come to mean far too much to her.

She stepped back, instantly regretting the cool distance that swept between them. "I . . . Excuse me. I need some air."

His dark bows lowered into a frown. "You can't leave the house. Don't even venture into the gardens. Not until we know where Petrov is."

She nodded and slipped away through the crowd, employing his tactic of pretending not to hear those who hailed her. She needed a moment of quiet to process the jumbled feelings churning in her chest.

The tiara was giving her a headache. She gave a half-hysterical laugh at the irony. Wasn't it one of Shakespeare's kings who'd bemoaned, "Uneasy lies the head that wears a crown"? The weight of her position was quite literally pressing down upon her.

She nodded to Mellors, who was guarding the corridor that led into the private wing of the house, and slipped into the unoccupied pink salon. The noise of the ball dulled as she closed the door behind her and sank into one of the pretty upholstered French armchairs.

She removed the tiara and placed it gently on a side table with a sigh. She'd drawn it from memory, so it wasn't exactly the same, but it was still remarkably similar to the one she'd crushed in Paris a year ago. Back then, she'd mourned the future Denisov brides who wouldn't be wearing it to wed, but Wolff had given her a chance to resurrect that family tradition.

Not that a wedding looked to be on the horizon for *her* any time soon.

Her stomach knotted in misery. Wolff's proposal, back at the Tricorn, had been utterly unexpected. Her instinctive refusal had been a rejection of the situation, rather than the man, although he hadn't seen it that way. She sighed. Despite what she'd told him, she did want to get married someday. And the thought of accepting any man other than him left a heavy ache in her heart.

He'd been right; he'd ruined her for anyone else—but not in the physical sense of having been the first in her bed. He'd ruined her because nobody else made her feel as wanted, as *seen* as he did—as if he understood the silly, stubborn woman she was beneath her royal robes, and preferred her to anyone else. She couldn't imagine another man touching her as intimately as he'd done. She wanted *him*. His kisses, his smiles. A lifetime of sparring and teasing and learning his secrets.

Anya stilled. Dear God, she'd fallen in love with him.

A rap on the door interrupted her stunned amazement, and Mellors slipped unobtrusively into the room. "There is a gentleman at the back door, my lady. He says he needs to speak with you in private. Most urgently."

Her heart lurched in alarm. "A Russian gentleman? Count Petrov?"

"No, madam. He says he is a barrister, one Oliver Reynolds. The fiancé of your friend Miss Ivanov?"

"Where is he?"

"At present, in the scullery. He did not want to interrupt the ball by using the main entrance. Shall I bring him here?"

Anya was already on her feet. "No, I'll go to him. Thank you, Mellors."

The majordomo nodded placidly.

Anya made her way to the back stairs and hurried down them. In the kitchen, she could hear raised voices— Lagrasse and Mrs. MacDougall were having a difference of opinion on how to make "proper" custard, but she was too worried to smile at their squabbling. She entered the scullery and one look at Oliver's face was enough to strike fear into her heart.

"Oliver! What is it? What's happened?"

The young man raked his hand through his sandy hair. "Thank God! It's Elizaveta. She's been taken."

"Taken? When? By whom?" Anya already suspected the answer.

"Less than an hour ago. We were returning from the theatre when a carriage pulled up alongside us. I barely paid any attention until two men jumped out. One struck

me down"—he rubbed the back of his head as if in painful memory—"and the other one caught Elizaveta around
the waist and bundled her into the carriage. They drove
off before I could do anything to save her." He looked as
if he was going to be sick.

Anya hugged her arms around her waist as equal parts
fury and terror coursed through her. "Those men were
working on the orders of a man named Vasili Petrov.
He's a monster."

Oliver's face went even greener, but he reached into
his jacket and pulled out a folded sheet of paper. The red
wax seal was Petrov's, segmented with a bow and arrow
and a full-masted ship to the lower half. "They threw
this at my feet. Said to deliver it to you." His Adam's
apple bobbed down as he swallowed. "They're going to
hurt Elizaveta, aren't they?"

Anya reached out and clasped his arm in a reassuring
grip. "Not if I can help it."

She tore open the seal and read the short note. It was
in Russian, presumably to limit the number of people
who could read it if opened.

*Princess, I have your friend. If you want her to
remain unharmed, you will bring the letters your
brother sent you to the stables of the dowager
duchess at midnight. My man will be waiting. Do
not think to have your English lapdog or his Bow
Street brothers accompany you. Come alone or
your maid will meet the same fate as your brother.*

Anya cursed soundly and glanced at the clock on the
scullery wall. It was already half past eleven. Oh, God,
what was she to do? She didn't have the real papers to
give him.

They'd expected Petrov to come to the ball tonight

and demand the "evidence" he thought she possessed.
Anya had chosen three of the letters she'd translated—
ones which might conceivably have contained something of import—and bundled them together with a
faded ribbon, just to have something to show him in
order to lure him somewhere private so that Sebastien
and his Bow Street cohorts could arrest him without
causing a scene. She should have known he wouldn't be
trapped so easily.

She dropped the letter to the side and gave Oliver a
weak smile. "Wait here. I'll be right back."

She raced back up the servants' stairs, slipped into the
dowager duchess's library, and found the packet of letters
in the desk. They were nothing but dull military reports,
but the Cyrillic text and official look of them might fool
Vasili's man.

Unfortunately, they wouldn't fool Vasili. As soon as
he opened them, he would realize they weren't the incriminating evidence he was after. Anya didn't want to
think what he would do to Elizaveta then. She needed
to find a way to get her friend released before Vasili discovered he was being duped.

She stuffed the letters into the pocket of her skirts and
returned to find Oliver still pacing below stairs.

"What does the letter say? Where are you going?" he
demanded.

She grabbed a paring knife from the side. "To meet
Petrov's man in the stables. Don't worry," she said with
far more confidence than she felt. "I'll get Elizaveta back
safely."

She would show the envoy the fake documents but
refuse to hand them over until Elizaveta was released
unharmed.

"Will you give me your jacket?"

Oliver frowned, but did as she asked, and she slipped

the oversize garment over her dress and tucked the knife into the sagging pocket.

"Surely you don't mean to go alone?"

"I must. Petrov was very specific."

Oliver swore even as she brushed past him. Lagrasse and Mrs. MacDougall were still quibbling over crème patissière, but Anya hurried past the kitchen and out into the mews yard. To her dismay, Jem Barnes, one of Wolff's Bow Street urchins, skulked out of the darkness as she entered the stables, silent as a cat.

"Oi, Princess, where d'ye think you're goin'? Wolff left orders you was to stay inside."

Anya cursed silently. How to get rid of him? Eclipse's inquisitive black nose appeared over the door of one of the stalls, and he gave a soft whicker of welcome. She sent the young man a confiding smile.

"I just came out here for a few minutes alone. It's so hot in the ballroom. I was going to talk to Eclipse."

Jem scrunched up his face. "Funny fing fer a princess to do." He sent a glance down at her glittering skirts beneath Oliver's outsize coat. "Ye'll get yer dress all dirty." He shrugged, as if the decisions of the upper classes were ever incomprehensible. "Well, I can't leave you alone, anyways. Wolff'd 'ave me guts fer garters."

Anya had to admire the lad's dedication, even if it was inconvenient. She'd just opened her mouth to tell him some story when a dark shape loomed out of the shadows behind him. Jem must have seen her horrified expression because he started to turn, but it was too late: Vasili Petrov dealt him a sickening blow to the side of the head with the handle of a pitchfork. Jem collapsed on the floor like a sack of grain.

Anya let out a shout of horror and sank to her knees next to the fallen boy. To her utter relief, he was still breathing, although he was definitely unconscious.

"You bastard!" she hissed, fury overriding her fright momentarily. "How could you? He's no more than a child!"

Vasili gave an unrepentant shrug. "I told you to come alone."

Anya's heart began to pound. She got to her feet, watching him warily.

"What? No greeting for your long-lost fiancé?" Vasili sneered. "You've led me a merry chase these past months, Princess. Fleeing from me in Paris, then hiding here in London. I have been most inconvenienced."

Anya set her chin. "I don't care. Where's Elizaveta?"

"Back at my ship. Do you have the letters from your brother?"

Anya tried to recall everything Sebastien had taught her about lying. "The ones that prove you're a traitor? Yes, I have them," *in a just and perfect world.*

His eyes gleamed with triumph. "I knew you were lying. Give them to me."

"They're somewhere you'll never find them."

Vasili's face hardened into a mask of fury. "You little bitch. This isn't a game." He took a threatening step toward her, and she shrank back in anticipation of a blow.

"You can have them when you release Elizaveta," she said quickly.

Vasili's lip curled. "Always giving orders, Princess. But in this case, I'm neither your servant, nor your subject. I'm your master."

"You are not."

"I soon will be."

He took another step, closing the distance between them. "Whatever you've done with them, you'll still not testify against me if you're my wife. I meant what I said in Paris. We shall be wed."

Anya fought a wave of nausea. Sebastien had shown

her how beautiful the act of making love could be. He was the kind of man she wanted to marry. Vasili was the complete opposite. If he attempted to consummate the marriage, it would be a grotesque violation fueled by violence and greed. She would not be subjected to such defilement. Even death would be preferable.

He made a sudden lunge forward, catching her off guard. He hoisted her off her feet. Anya struggled furiously, trying to incapacitate him, but her efforts were ineffective. He was almost twice her size and weight. He half-dragged, half-carried her to the back door of the stables. She tried to bite his forearm, but the thickness of his jacket prevented it.

"Oliver!" she shouted desperately. "Help!"

Vasili gave her a vicious shake. A carriage was waiting behind the stables, the door standing open, and with a savage jerk, he threw her up into it. She landed awkwardly across the single seat.

"Back to the ship!" he called to the waiting driver. "Go!"

He leaped into the carriage and closed the door with a slam. Anya tried to get up, but she was hampered by her skirts and Oliver's oversize jacket. Her heart pounded in terror as Vasili loomed over her. She fell back, kicking and punching wildly in the darkness, and experienced a fierce stab of pleasure when her heel connected with some soft part of his anatomy. He uttered a foul curse.

Then she saw his fist in her peripheral vision. And everything went black.

Chapter 34.

Seb glared at the door to the ballroom. Petrov still hadn't made an appearance, and where the hell was Anya? Why was she taking so long? An uneasy, prickling feeling assailed him, and he went in search of her, ignoring the beckoning smiles of the women as he passed and the jovial greetings of the men.

"Mellors, where is she?"

The servant needed no further clarification. "I believe the princess is meeting a gentleman in the scullery, sir."

Seb's eyebrows rose into his hairline. "She's *what*?"

"Not a Russian gentleman," Mellors said swiftly, as if that were any kind of reassurance. "I believe he is a friend."

Seb didn't wait to hear more. He pounded down the servant's stairs and past the open kitchen door. Mrs. MacDougall and Lagrasse were bickering about something. The scullery was empty, but a sheet of paper on the counter caught his eye. He snatched it up and cursed when he saw the indecipherable scribbles of the Russian alphabet.

Fear and fury thundered in his ears as he took the steps out to the mews two at a time. A shout from the stables caught his good ear, and he raced inside to find Jem Barnes on the floor with a thin, sandy-haired stranger crouched over him.

Seb hauled the man to his feet and slammed him hard against the wall.

"What the hell's going on here? Where's Anya? Who are you?"

"Oliver Reynolds," the man gasped, raising his palms in a gesture of surrender. "I'm a barrister. Don't hit me! I'm engaged to Elizaveta Ivanova. A friend of the princess." He gestured down at Jem. "I found him like that."

Jem exhaled a low groan and rolled over onto his side. He clutched the back of his head, and when he pulled his hand away, it was coated in blood.

Seb released the man and dropped to Jem's side. "Stay still, lad. You need a doctor." He glared up at Reynolds. "Where's the princess? I told her not to leave the bloody house."

The skinny man swallowed hard. "She came out here to meet a messenger from Count Petrov. He's taken my fiancée."

"He took her too," Jem muttered groggily. "The princess. Couldn't stop 'im."

A cold wash of terror froze Seb's blood. "Petrov has her? Where's he taking her?"

"I don't know," Reynolds groaned. "Maybe there's something in there?" He indicated the letter that was still crumpled in Seb's fist.

Seb gazed down at the meaningless squiggles and was filled with impotent fury. "Who speaks Russian?"

Jem and Reynolds sent him identical blank looks. He raced back inside, angrily aware that he couldn't just burst into the ballroom like a wild man.

"Mellors, bring me Prince Trubetskoi or the Russian ambassador, Lieven, to the pink salon," he ordered. "Immediately. And Lords Harland and Wylde too."

The majordomo nodded, his expression inscrutable, and Seb wondered what it would take to discompose the man. Nothing short of Armageddon, probably.

He caught sight of Anya's tiara lying abandoned on the side table and a shaft of terror pierced his heart. She should have kept it with her, to remind Petrov of her elevated position. To underline the wrath that would rain down upon his head if he hurt her.

Prince Trubetskoi stepped into the room. "You wished to see me, Lord Mowbray?"

Seb scrutinized the other man closely. Petrov was a friend of Trubetskoi. For all he knew, the prince could have been the one feeding Petrov sensitive information. They could be in league together, but it was a risk he had to take. He had to trust the man would translate the letter accurately.

"I need you to read this aloud. In English. Now."

Trubetskoi did so, his face a picture of shock when he comprehended the contents. "Who wrote this?

"Count Vasili Petrov. He believes the princess has evidence that he's been spying for the French since before Waterloo."

The prince shook his head in astonishment. "I can scarcely believe it. I've known him for years. I always knew he was ambitious, but I had no idea he was capable of such wickedness. This practically admits there *are* incriminating documents."

"It does. But I don't care about that. He's taken the princess. *My* princess." Seb turned to leave. "Thank you, Your Highness."

Alex and Benedict entered the library and sent him twin inquiring glances.

"I'm off to Bow Street," Seb said.

"Now? What's going on?"

"Petrov has the princess, but I don't know where he's taking her. The prisoner we're holding in the cells will know, though."

"The one who tried to snatch her from the Tricorn? He's refused to say anything for the past week," Alex cautioned.

Seb lowered his brows. "We clearly haven't been persuasive enough. I'll make him talk. Are you with me?"

Neither Alex nor Ben hesitated. "Of course."

"Then let's go."

"I have pistols in my carriage," Alex offered, hard on Seb's heels as they clattered down the kitchen steps.

"Me too," Benedict added.

"Good," Seb said grimly. "You're going to need them."

A murderous fury slid through his veins as he headed for the stables. He was going to find Petrov and put a bullet through the blackmailing bastard once and for all. His trusty Baker was back at the Tricorn, but he had a pistol in his saddlebag. It would have to do.

The ride from Grosvenor Square to Bow Street didn't take long, especially at a gallop, and soon Seb was greeting the night officer on watch at number three.

"Evening, George. We need another talk with our Russian guest."

The prisoner blinked in sleepy confusion when Seb, Alex, and Ben barged into his cell. Bypassing the usual preliminaries, Seb reached down, hauled him off the hard pallet, and smashed him hard against the wall.

"Where were you supposed to take the princess?"

The Russian sent him a cocky smirk. "Petrov has her, does he?"

Seb punched him in the stomach, and the man doubled over with a surprised "oof." The chains around his wrists prevented him from retaliating. Seb bent and whispered in his ear, ignoring the rancid smell of the man's unwashed body.

"I'll ask you one more time. Where. Is. The. Princess?"

The Russian shook his head stubbornly, and Seb let out a sigh of irritation. "I don't have time for this." He turned to Ben and Alex, who were flanking the door. "If he's not going to tell us anything, there's no need to keep him alive. Agreed?"

Alex merely shrugged, going along with Seb's bluff, and Ben did the same. Seb sent up a grateful prayer for having such intelligent friends. Both of them knew he'd never actually kill a man in custody, however great the provocation, but the Russian didn't know that.

The Cossack let out a surprised gasp. "What? You can't shoot me."

"Oh, I can," Seb growled. "Here in England, lords like us can do pretty much anything we like. If you die, I doubt we'll get more than a slap on the wrist. In fact, Sir Nathaniel will probably thank me for not burdening Newgate with another inmate."

Ben gave a dry chuckle. "He's doing you a favor, believe me. I've spent some time in Newgate. Death is better."

Alex gave an amused snort.

Seb withdrew his pistol, a lead ball, and a powder flask from his jacket pocket, and proceeded to load the weapon with brisk efficiency.

The Russian gave a strangled, disbelieving cry and retreated to the far corner of the cell, his hands raised in front of him in a paltry defense. "Wait!"

Seb poured an exact measure of powder into the pistol's pan and shook his head as if confused. "I just don't understand why you'd stay loyal to someone like Petrov. Do you think he cares about you? He's left you in here to rot for the last week, hasn't he?" He paused to let that sink in, then gave a nonchalant shrug. "If it's any consolation, it'll be quick. I'm an excellent shot."

"The best," Ben chimed in. "You should have seen him in Portugal. He could hit a target at two hundred yards with a wicked crosswind."

"Thank you." Seb sent him a dry nod of acknowledgment and turned back to the prisoner. "Now, would you prefer the head or the heart?" He lifted the pistol, pulled back the hammer, and levelled it smoothly. His arm didn't waver an inch.

"His ship!" the Russian shouted desperately.

Seb tilted his head. "I'm listening."

"Petrov wanted me to take her back to his ship," the Russian continued quickly. "The *Suvarov*. It's moored at Blackwall docks. That's all I know."

Seb lowered the pistol. The Russian slid down the wall in relief, and Seb took a savage satisfaction in the wet stain that spread across the front of the man's breeches as he pissed himself. He glanced at his friends. "Let's go."

Five minutes later, they were heading east along Piccadilly as quickly as the evening traffic would allow. Seb cursed every slow-moving carriage and late-night reveler who crossed his path.

A pounding need to hurt, to punish Petrov, coursed through him, along with a terrible spike of fear. His lack of control over this situation made him want to scream. He had to get to Anya. To protect her. God, she'd already braved and suffered so much in her life.

"Why a ship?" Alex asked as they slowed for a barrel-filled brewer's wagon. "Do you think he's planning to take her back to Russia?"

Seb growled at the mere thought. "Maybe. He wants to marry her. Not just for her money, but to guarantee her silence."

"That's it, then," Ben said. "Since they're not Church of England, he can't wed her here. I bet he needs a Russian Orthodox priest to make it legal."

"Maybe he's found one in London," Alex suggested. "Maybe he has one on board? That's what I'd do if I—"

Seb snapped, "Stop talking and ride."

The thought of Anya married to Petrov made him want to break things. Bones, mainly. She belonged with him, damn it. He'd rather die than see her with another man, let alone a blackmailing bastard like that. If anyone was going to marry her, it would bloody well be *him*.

A sense of calm acceptance slid over him as he registered the truth of that thought.

He wanted to marry her.

He wanted her in whatever guise she chose to adopt, whether it be princess, dowager's companion, or courtesan.

He would rescue her from Petrov, prove he was worthy of her, and ask for her hand again.

True, she'd refused him once, but his first proposal hadn't been the best, had it? In fact, now that he thought back on it, he hadn't actually proposed. He'd just told her they were expected to marry. No woman wanted to hear that. Especially not one as stubborn and determined to forge her own destiny as Anya. No wonder she'd turned him down.

He'd do a better job next time. He'd tell her all the reasons he *wanted* to marry her. Like the fact that he loved the way she challenged him. That he loved her strength and her arrogance, her humor and her wit. Not to mention that he'd never met anyone he desired more. One night with her had merely whetted his appetite. He wanted her in every way he could think of, and a hundred more besides.

"If that bastard hurts one hair on her head, he's a dead man," Seb growled to nobody in particular.

He kicked his heels to Eclipse's sides and remembered the first time he'd ridden into battle for her. He hadn't known it at the time, but he'd met his very own Waterloo on Hounslow Heath, in the shape of a lying, irresistible Russian blueblood.

Alex sat straighter in the saddle as they finally neared Blackwall docks. "Hoi. You remember that Russian who was killed? The other Orlov? The tavern where it happened is just over there. Ten to one Petrov had something to do with it."

Fear stabbed Seb's chest like shards of ice, and he breathed a plea to the frigid night air.

Hold on, Anya. I'm coming.

Chapter 35.

Anya was roused by a sharp slap on her cheek. She opened her eyes and peered groggily out of the coach window. They had come to a stop. She could see the blurry lights and the swinging sign of a tavern, hear the whores lounging in the shadows shouting obscene comments, the catcalls from the drunks who milled around. Her heart sank. This was *not* a good area.

Vasili caught her arm and pulled her out of the carriage, and she stumbled on the step, still dazed.

The huge, hulking shape of a ship loomed above her, and she frowned up in confusion. She must be at the docks. She squinted to read the painted nameplate on the side of the vessel: *Suvarov*.

Trust Vasili to have commandeered a ship named after a famous Russian military hero, she thought bitterly. Even in his choice of vessel, he craved reflected glory. She shook her head, trying to clear it. Her cheek hurt.

The dark shapes of two men were visible up on the deck, one at each end of the ship, and a huge figure in the distinctive fur-banded hat and long overcoat of a Cossack stood guard at the bottom of the gangplank. Anya immediately discounted him as a potential source of help. His expression was blank, with not a hint of interest in her plight.

Vasili hustled her forward. Her legs were shaking so badly, she could barely stagger up the inclined planks, but the weight of the paring knife in the pocket of her jacket gave her courage. At least Vasili hadn't searched her while she was unconscious. Small mercy.

They reached the deck. Anya slid her hand into her pocket and jerked away from Vasili's grip.

"Where's Elizaveta?"

She pulled the kitchen knife from the pocket and brandished it in front of her, painfully aware of how ridiculous a weapon it must appear.

Vasili laughed in genuine amusement. "Truly? You think to threaten me with that?" He reached behind him, pulled a pistol from beneath his jacket, and pointed it directly at her chest. "Drop it."

With a silent curse, she allowed the pathetic weapon to clatter onto the deck.

Vasili's gaze flicked to her skirts, at the silvery material visible beneath the oversize jacket. "Now remove that coat."

Anya shrugged out of Oliver's jacket. The cool night air raised goose bumps on her skin, but when Vasili's greedy gaze slithered over her exposed chest, she shuddered in revulsion.

He smirked. "I see you're dressed for the occasion. How fortunate." With the gun still trained on her, he used his left hand to open the door set into the space beneath the upper deck. "Into the cabin."

With no choice but to obey, Anya lifted her chin high and swept inside. She glanced around frantically. A table for maps filled the center of the room, with a padded bench built along one wall, but her attention went immediately to the doorway at the far end. Elizaveta, her hands bound in front of her, was seated on a small cot bed.

She stumbled to her feet with a choked cry of relief. "Anya! Oh, God."

Anya rushed forward. Elizaveta's hands were crushed awkwardly between them, but Anya caught her friend in her arms for a joyous hug.

"Oh no!" Elizaveta gave a shuddering sob. "I didn't mean for you to—"

Anya stroked her hair, noting her friend's reddened eyes and split lip with a wave of anger. Vasili, or one of his men, had struck her too.

"Shh. It's all right. I'm so glad to see you safe. Did he hurt you?"

"Vasili? He merely hit me a few times to say hello."

Anya glared over her shoulder at Vasili, who'd stationed himself by the door. She tugged at the leather cord that bound her friend's wrists. "Untie this at once."

He shook his head. "Not until after we're wed." He sent her a mocking glance. "I'm not having her hit me over the head with anything *this* time. She can be a witness."

Anya gazed around the cabin for something—anything—to use as a weapon. A spirit lamp hung from the rafters from a bent nail, but it was too high for her to reach. The map on the tabletop had been pinned at the four corners; perhaps she could stab him with one of those little tacks?

Completely at ease, Vasili shrugged out of his greatcoat. "I have a priest ready to marry us," he said with a chilling smile. "Father Barukov's come all the way from St. Petersburg."

Anya's stomach turned over in dismay. When she'd seen the ship, she'd assumed Vasili meant to take her back to Russia and perform the ceremony there. This was a disaster.

She clutched at her skirts—and felt the hard shape of a glass vial beneath her fingers. Her heart missed a beat. She'd forgotten Lagrasse's sleeping potion. If only there was some way to make Vasili drink the stuff.

She pasted a conciliatory smile on her face and took a step forward. Vasili eyed her warily.

"Very well," she said calmly. "I'm not such a fool that I can't see when I'm beaten."

Behind her, Elizaveta made a wordless sound of protest, but Anya shook her head.

"It's true. Nobody's coming to save us, Elizaveta, and I have no desire to be manhandled any more than I have been already. We might as well make the best of the situation."

Vasili's brows rose as he fought incredulity. "You'll marry me? Without protest?"

Anya gave a delicate shrug. "What good would protesting do? If all those years in the Russian court taught me anything, it's to be pragmatic. You wouldn't be my first choice of husband, Petrov, but we need never see one another once this is done. Get your priest. Let's get this over with."

Vasili still looked suspicious at her capitulation, but he turned and stepped out onto the deck.

As soon as Anya heard him turn the key in the lock, she rushed over to the bottle of vodka she'd spied on a side table. She tugged the cork out with her teeth, poured two large shots, and divided the meagre contents of the mandrake potion equally between the two glasses.

"What's that?" Elizaveta whispered.

"A sleeping draught. I can't be sure which one Vasili

will take. If necessary, I'll drink it too, to allay his suspicions."

A shudder of disquiet ran through her as she remembered what Sebastien had said. She had no idea of the proper dose; a few drops had been enough to render Stoke and Alvanley unconscious back at the Tricorn. But they'd both been near-insensible with drink anyway. Wolff had said it would take longer to work on someone who was sober, but how long was that? Ten minutes? Half an hour?

There were more than a few drops in each glass. What if it proved fatal?

Anya let out a steadying breath and faced that possibility. There was no hope of rescue; Sebastien had no idea where she was. Was death really preferable to marrying Vasili? Yes. She had no doubt that he intended to dispose of her soon enough anyway, through some tragic "accident" that would eliminate the threat of exposure once and for all. She could only be thankful that he'd decided to wed her first—to get his hands on her money—rather than just kill her immediately. Hopefully his greed would prove his downfall.

She picked up both glasses and went over to glance through the window of the cabin.

Vasili stood over an open hatchway where a set of steps led belowdeck. "Father Barukov, you may attend to us now," he called down.

Muffled footsteps came from below and a cloaked and hooded figure shuffled up from the opening. He wore the formal vestments of an Orthodox priest. From his stooped shoulders and slow gait, he appeared old and rather frail, weighted down by his clerical regalia: a dark, ankle-length robe with a white surcoat lavishly embroidered in gold. He carried a worn, leather-bound Bible in one hand and two thin circlets of laurel leaves tied with a white ribbon in the other.

Anya's heart began to pound. Those were the "crowns" he would hold above their heads during the traditional Russian marriage ceremony.

The key clicked in the lock, and Vasili entered with the priest. Anya tried to see the man's face, to see if there was even the slightest hint of compassion or hope of reprieve, but the hood of his robe obscured his features; she caught only a glimpse of dark beard.

Without even acknowledging her or Elizaveta, he placed the crowns on the chart table and started to flick through the pages of the Bible, searching for the correct place. His hands, Anya noticed, were not those of an old man, all liver-spotted and veined. They were those of someone younger, with long fingers and neatly cut nails. A wave of impotent fury scorched her. He was clearly another of Petrov's acolytes, either bribed or coerced into service. He would doubtless be selectively deaf, like Wolff. There would be no help from that quarter.

She offered one of the glasses of tainted vodka to Vasili. "Let's not completely ignore tradition, Petrov. We should make a toast to a long and happy marriage."

Vasili's lips curled at her dry tone, but he took the glass from her and raised it to his mouth. Anya watched him closely to see if he would drink, but when he hesitated, she lifted her own glass, tapped the rim against his own, and said, "*Za zdarovje.*"

To his health. And hers.

God help her.

She tipped back her head and swallowed the entire shot in one gulp, gasping at the icy fire that flooded down her throat.

At least if she died, she'd be with Dmitri. And her parents. That wouldn't be so bad.

Through watering eyes she saw Vasili swallow his own drink, and a spike of triumph warmed her as much

as the vodka had done. Now all she had to do was stall
long enough until they either fell asleep or died.

What a happy thought.

She turned toward the chart table under the guise of
needing somewhere to place her empty glass and put it
down next to the pin holding the map. Using her skirts
to conceal the movement, she tugged the pin free and
stepped closer to the priest. She might as well make
some attempt to sway him.

"I am Princess Anastasia Denisova," she said levelly.
"Cousin to the tsar. Whatever Petrov is paying you to do
this, I'll double it."

The click of the hammer on Vasili's pistol drew her
attention. "That's enough, Anya," he said pleasantly. He
pointed the pistol at Elizaveta, who'd taken a seat in the
corner of the cabin. "You'll say the vows, or I'll put a
bullet through your friend's head."

Elizaveta whimpered and ice slithered through Anya's
veins as hopelessness overwhelmed her. Damn Vasili. A
pin was no match for a bullet.

Why wasn't the sleeping potion working? Apart from
a pleasant glow in her stomach from the vodka, she
felt nothing out of the ordinary. And she was smaller
than Vasili. Since they'd taken roughly the same dose,
shouldn't she feel the effects of the drug before him?

He stepped forward to stand on the priest's other side.
"Let's get on with it, shall we?"

A strange calm settled over her. Would Sebastien care
if she married Vasili? Would he avenge her honor? He'd
said he'd never fight a duel for any woman. Petty squab-
bles, he'd called them. But perhaps—

She closed her eyes and prayed for a miracle.

Chapter 36.

"Petrov!"

The enraged bellow echoed from the dockside, and Anya's heart turned over in her chest. Twin arrows of joy and terror pierced her. "Sebastien," she breathed.

"I'm coming for you, you bastard!"

The crack of a pistol rent the night, followed by a series of shouts and a splash as someone ditched the Cossack guarding the gangway into the river.

"Anya!"

Heavy boots pounded up the gangplank. The two guards on deck shouted a warning and a barrage of masculine shouts and the crashing of wood ensued.

Vasili cursed, and Elizaveta let out a squeal of fright as something—or someone—forcibly struck the cabin door. The wood shrieked in protest, but the iron latch held. The sickening sound of fists connecting with bone, the crunch of something that might have been a nose breaking, and a bellow of pain followed. Twin flashes of light pierced the darkness beyond the cabin window and the crack of pistols followed almost instantaneously.

Vasili pushed the priest aside, caught Anya around the waist, and pulled her back against his body to act as a human shield.

"In here!" Anya shouted, then gasped as Vasili squeezed her ribs hard enough to crush the air from her lungs. She froze as the cold metal of his pistol kissed her temple.

"Be still," he commanded.

There was a deafening crash and the splintering of wood as the door to the cabin was kicked in. Wolff shouldered his way through, a pair of pistols aimed straight at Vasili. But he stilled when he saw Anya held captive in front of him.

"Hold!" Vasili shouted.

Anya's heart quailed. Wolff looked both savage and magnificent. Blood was smeared across his cheek—she couldn't tell if it was his own or not. His cravat was askew and the arm of his jacket had been ripped at the shoulder. It gaped open to reveal the stark white of his shirt. His chest rose and fell in a series of uneven gusts.

The expression on his face was one she'd never seen before. Two spots of red flushed his cheekbones, but his eyes were cold, almost entirely black as he glared at Vasili. He looked like an avenging angel searching for a soul to claim, and Anya's heart swelled with terror and love. Behind him stood Wylde and Harland, one on each side, both with pistols at the ready.

"Let her go," Sebastien said coldly.

Vasili's arm tightened around her waist. "Put your weapons down. I have the advantage. You're too much the gentleman to shoot a woman." He let that sink in for a moment then added, "Whereas we both know I'm a heartless bastard with nothing to lose. I'll have no difficulty at all in shooting my wife. She's served her purpose, after all."

Wolff's gaze flicked to hers for an agonized moment, then narrowed in renewed fury on Vasili's face. "Wife?" he whispered.

"That's right," Vasili crowed. "You're too late. We've already wed. She's mine."

Anya gasped. "No! That's not—oof!" Her denial was cut off by another cruel jerk of Vasili's arm.

A muscle ticked in Wolff's jaw, but he didn't lower his pistol. Anya opened her eyes very wide, silently pleading with him to take a shot. He was an excellent marksman. He'd shot that highwayman on Hounslow Heath in a similar situation, hadn't he? Surely there was some part of Vasili he could hit without endangering her. She suddenly remembered she was holding the map pin. Perhaps if she ducked and stabbed Vasili somewhere?

But the frustration on Wolff's face showed that Vasili had guessed the truth; Seb wouldn't fire while there was a gun to her head. No matter how good a shot he was, he wouldn't risk Vasili's finger tightening on the trigger in a reflex action.

Anya almost sobbed as he used his thumbs to uncock the pistols. He lowered them, but his eyes still burned with the promise of vengeance. "You might have married her, but she'll never be yours." His gaze flicked to her, and the emotion she saw there made her stomach swoop. "You'll be a widow soon enough."

"Step back," Vasili snarled. "You and your friends get off this ship or she dies."

Wolff's lips flattened into an angry line, but he did as Vasili commanded. Anya bit back a whimper as he backed through the shattered remains of the door and retreated across the deck.

Please. Don't leave me! I love you!

She pressed her lips closed to stop the traitorous words. A strange lassitude was stealing over her, a kind of tingling lethargy, and her stomach swooped as she realized its cause; the potion was starting to work. Please God that it would start to affect Vasili too.

The tense standoff was shattered by an eerie, inhuman groan that echoed from the depths of the ship.

Everyone froze as a hunched figure stumbled up the steps from below. When he straightened, Anya was confused to see an old man, wearing nothing but a cotton nightshirt. He seemed oblivious to the fact that he was intruding on a battlefield. He peered around the crowded deck, groaning piteously and clutching his forehead as though he'd received a recent blow.

Vasili frowned at the ancient figure. "Father Barukov?" His head whipped around to the priest in the cabin. "Then who—?"

Anya had completely forgotten about the clergyman. He turned from the table in a swirl of cloth and swept the cowl from his head.

The world dipped out of focus and Anya's knees almost gave out as she beheld a face she'd thought never to see again in this life.

No. It was the potion. Her brother was dead and—

"Surprised to see me, Petrov?" Dmitri said calmly, and Anya let out a croak of astonishment as the rumbling voice matched the beloved face. The impossible miracle of her brother—alive, *here*—engulfed her like a tidal wave.

Vasili let out an almost inhuman growl. "You're dead! I saw you myself at Waterloo."

Dmitri's blue eyes, so similar to her own, gleamed in fury. "Yes, you saw me, you bastard. You searched what you thought was my corpse."

Anya couldn't stop staring at Dmitri's face. He looked the same, and yet subtly different. Older, more careworn. His hair was longer, shaggier, and she'd never seen him with a beard, but it was indisputably him. Her entire body began to shake, and she wanted to laugh and cry at the same time. She sagged back against Vasili, heedless of the gun still pressed to her temple. The world started to spin.

Vasili hauled her back upright with an angry hiss. "Stand up."

Dmitri reached slowly into his clerical robes and withdrew a folded piece of paper. "This is what you're after, Petrov. Your letter to General Ney. You tell him the Tsar's army's too far away to help the British if he attacks immediately."

Vasili's chest rose and fell in deep gusts against her back. The pistol's muzzle shook by her ear. He was clearly as shocked as she was to see her brother alive.

"Give it to me," he panted.

Dmitri held the paper out toward them. "Take it."

Anya immediately saw his intent; Vasili would either have to release her or take the pistol from her head if he wanted the letter.

He seemed to realize it at the same moment. "You take it," he ordered her with another painful squeeze to her ribs.

With a trembling hand, she reached forward and took the folded note.

Vasili grunted his pleasure and angled his chin at Dmitri. "Now get out. Don't make me shoot your sister."

Dmitri's gaze flicked to hers as he edged sideways toward the exit, his hands up near his ears in a gesture of surrender. He sent her a sweet, heartbreaking smile, almost an apology.

"You can have the letter, Petrov," he said softly. "I've already shown it to the Tsar. He's proclaimed you a traitor to Russia. There's a warrant out for your arrest."

Anya gasped as Vasili jolted against her back. Dmitri

was completely exposed in the doorway. He wasn't even covered by the men outside; his body was blocking any shot they could take. Her chest felt as though it were being crushed, and not simply from Vasili's iron grip. Her brave, foolish brother was trying to goad Vasili into shooting *him*, instead of her.

Oh, God. She couldn't lose him. Not when she'd just found him again.

"Devil!" Vasili roared. In a single movement, he shoved Anya away from him and aimed his gun at Dmitri's chest.

"No!" With all her strength, Anya stabbed the map pin she was holding into Vasili's shoulder. He roared in fury as his gun went off, a deafening report in the enclosed space. From the corner of her eye, she saw Dmitri stagger back against the map table in a flurry of black-and-gold cloth.

Vasili swung on her with a shout of fury. He backhanded her, catching her with the muzzle of the pistol, and pain exploded in her skull. She fell back, dazed, and heard Elizaveta scream a warning. She lifted her arms to shield her head, anticipating another blow, but it never came.

Another shot rang out, the sound like the crack of a tree limb breaking. In the stunned silence that followed, she lowered her hands to see Vasili frozen in front of her, his eyes wide in shock. His mouth opened as if he was about to ask her a question, but then he glanced down at his chest, coughed once, and simply collapsed at her feet.

Anya stared down at him in confusion, expecting him to get up, to grab for her, but he remained utterly motionless. A neat hole the size of a sovereign had appeared on his chest. A bright ring of red began to seep outward, discoloring the pale blue fabric above his medals, and she let out a gasp of horror as she realized it was blood.

Her vision swirled. "Oh, God. Is he dead?"

"Extremely."

Sebastien came striding across the cabin, pistols still in his hands, and the next thing she knew, she was caught in his fierce embrace. He pulled her tight against his chest and angled his body to obscure her view of Vasili's corpse.

"Don't look," he ordered harshly.

His words vibrated against her, and Anya melted into the welcome comfort of his arms. Eyes closed, she clutched the front of his shirt in her fists and pressed her nose into his chest, sucking the scent of him into her lungs on a shuddering intake of breath. Her chin throbbed where Vasili had hit her, but she concentrated on Seb's fingers threading through her hair and the hard press of his lips on the top of her head. A tremor ran through his muscles, like that of a racehorse after a fast run.

She shuddered too. "I stabbed him with a map pin."

"Good girl."

"It's not true. We weren't married."

With a sudden gasp, she recalled Dmitri. She pulled out of Seb's arms and surged toward the corner where he'd fallen, expecting to find him dead on the floor. But with a low groan, he pushed himself to his feet. Anya hurled herself into his arms.

"Anya!" Dmitri hugged her back as tightly as a bear.

Words came pouring out of her mouth in gasping, halting jerks as she tried to understand the incomprehensible. "It *is* you! You're not dead? How is this possible? Oh, thank God, you're here! You're here."

Dmitri buried his face against her shoulder then pulled back, smoothing her hair away from her damp face with shaking hands. He gazed at her, his eyes roving over her features as if greedy for the sight of her, then he pressed a hard kiss to her forehead.

"I always knew I'd find you! They said you were dead, in Paris, but I knew you were too stubborn for that." His voice was a hoarse croak. "Do you know how long I've been looking for you? Months and months! Why didn't you come back to St. Petersburg? Where have you been all this time?"

Both of them were talking at once, each one staring at the other as if afraid they might disappear again, each one cataloguing the changes a year of separation had wrought.

Anya felt light-headed, unreal, as if she were in some fantastical dream from which she never wanted to wake. She could scarcely draw a breath around the ball of incredulous joy welling in her chest. "What happened to you? I thought you'd been killed at Waterloo."

He gave a watery laugh. "Almost. Bonaparte gave it a bloody good try. As did Petrov."

He lifted his left arm so the wide sleeve of the priest's robes slid down to his elbow and casually inspected his wrist. A bloom of red stained his shirtsleeve. Anya's heart almost stopped.

"You're bleeding! He hit you!"

Dmitri shrugged and squeezed her with his free arm. "He grazed me when he fired wide, that's all. It would have been my head if you hadn't distracted him, clever girl."

Anya felt faint at how easily her impulsive move could have backfired, but a noise from behind them interrupted her self-recrimination. Elizaveta stood in the doorway, her eyes brimming with tears and her smile wide, despite her split lip. Wolff, Harland, and Wylde all wore identical expressions of fascinated curiosity.

Well, Anya amended silently, Harland and Wylde looked curious. Wolff looked like he wanted to tear Dmitri limb from limb. He glared at her brother's arm, which was still around her waist, and lifted his brows in haughty inquiry.

"And who on God's green earth are *you*, sir?"

Chapter 37.

It took everything Seb had not to stride across the cabin, pry Anya from the handsome stranger's arms, and carry her off into the night. He wanted to take her back to the Tricorn, strip her naked, and inspect every inch of her to convince himself that she'd come to no serious harm.

God, the sight of Petrov's gun to her head had almost stopped his heart. And when the fake priest—whoever he was—had stepped between himself and Petrov, blocking any chance of a clear shot, he'd almost pulled the trigger anyway and risked going through some nonvital part of the man on the off chance the bullet would have enough velocity to hit Petrov too.

If the Russian hadn't been holding Anya so closely, he would have done it. Thank God she'd created a diversion and given him a clean shot straight to Petrov's heart.

Anya wiped her eyes and stepped toward him. She looked dazed, but so happy she was almost glowing.

"Oh, my goodness. I never thought I'd get to make this particular introduction, but Sebastien, I mean,

Lord Mowbray, this is my brother. Prince Dmitri Alexei Denisov."

Seb's temper ratcheted down a notch. Brother. Of course. He hadn't caught the connection amid all that frenetic Russian.

He couldn't throw the bastard overboard after all.

Bollocks.

The man held out his hand, and Seb reached out and grasped it, noting the subtle similarities between the two of them. Same blue eyes, the same wide cheekbones. There was a definite family resemblance.

A whole raft of conflicting emotions battered at his chest. Relief that Anya was safe mingled with pleasure on her behalf because the beloved brother she'd thought was dead had, by some miracle, been restored to her.

Hot on the heels of those sensations, however, came a crushing wave of defeat. With her brother alive, she was no longer unprotected. Why would she need *him*?

Seb wanted to hit something again. He glanced down at the lifeless body of Vasili Petrov and could summon not an ounce of remorse for the fact that he'd just killed the man. He would have been tried and hung as a traitor, anyway. He'd just done the Tsar a favor and saved him the embarrassment of a publicly damaging court case. No doubt Sir Nathaniel at Bow Street and Lord Castlereagh at the Foreign Office would approve of such an expedient outcome to their investigation.

The real priest, a doddery old fellow with a wispy, greying beard, shuffled forward and knelt by Petrov's side, presumably in the hope of administering last rites, but there was no chance of that. Petrov had been dead before he'd hit the ground.

A shot to the heart had been too quick, considering the torment he'd inflicted on Anya, Seb thought savagely. If he'd had the chance, he would have made sure the bastard suffered long and painfully for his actions. It was a shame he couldn't kill him all over again. Still, the threat to Anya had been eliminated, which was what he'd set out to achieve.

God, this was the second time she'd seen him kill. First, those kidnappers back at Hounslow, and now Petrov. She must be utterly repulsed by him. He opened his mouth to say something, anything, but Alex beat him to it.

"Delighted to meet you, Prince Denisov. I'm sure you have a great deal to discuss with your sister. May I suggest we all adjourn to somewhere more comfortable?"

Anya pulled out of her brother's embrace but kept hold of his hand, as if she couldn't bear to let go of him. Seb suppressed a growl.

"That is an excellent idea." She turned to her brother. "But I'm afraid I might have to wait a little while for an explanation."

Seb frowned. Anya's words were slurred, her movements slow and uncoordinated. Had the blow to her jaw given her a concussion? He took a concerned step toward her. "Why?" Fear made his tone harsher than he intended. "What's the matter?"

Anya sent him an apologetic smile. Her pupils were huge, her face rather flushed. "Because I've had a dose of Lagrasse's potion. And I think it's finally—"

She didn't finish the sentence. Her eyes fluttered closed. Seb caught her reflexively as she collapsed in his arms.

He sent a panicked look over at the woman in the corner, who was presumably her kidnapped friend, Elizaveta. "What did she do?" he demanded.

"She tricked Petrov into drinking some kind of sleeping potion. In the vodka."

"Christ," Seb breathed, appalled. "How much did she have?"

"Half the little bottle. Petrov drank the other half."

"Bloody hell." Panic seared his insides. He lifted Anya's slim body and cradled her against his chest. She weighed next to nothing. "I'm taking her back to the Tricorn."

Her brother made no objection. He tugged the clerical robe over his head to reveal a plain shirt and black breeches and sent the elderly priest an apologetic look. "Reverend Father, I do apologize for stealing your robes and knocking you down. But it was for a worthy cause."

The priest grumbled something at him in Russian, but then he made the sign of the cross in front of his face, so Seb assumed all was forgiven. He hoped the blessing extended to Anya too. He carried her through the shattered remnants of the door.

Alex and Ben stood aside to make room, and he caught Benedict's eye. "Someone should stay here and deal with that." He gestured at Petrov's body on the floor.

"Well, *I'm* not doing it. I left Georgie back at the ball with no explanation at all. She thinks I'm getting a drink. She'll throttle me if I don't get back soon."

"Same," Alex muttered. "Emmy hates it when I go on adventures without her."

Seb let out an irritated exhale. "Fine. You two go back to the ball and claim your wives. Tell Dorothea that Anya is safe, but needs to recover at the Tricorn."

He turned to address the ancient priest, who'd draped a handkerchief over Petrov's lifeless face. "Father, I'll leave you to deal with your countryman. You may take him back to Russia or arrange for a burial here, at your discretion. Count Petrov is no longer of interest to His Majesty's government."

He had no idea how much the old man understood, but at that moment, he didn't particularly care. He needed to get Anya back to the Tricorn as quickly as possible. He strode out of the cabin and down the gangplank, taking care not to jostle her any more than necessary. Her shallow breathing and flushed cheeks worried him more than he cared to admit, and his stomach churned in panic. She was so small. What if she'd taken a fatal dose?

Realizing he'd have to surrender his precious burden in order to mount Eclipse, he gently transferred her into her brother's arms and vaulted into the saddle, then beckoned for Denisov to pass her back up to him. He settled her across his lap, her head tucked in the crook of his arm, and tightened his hold protectively.

Ben, Alex, and the friend all descended the gangplank.

"Perhaps you should transport the princess back to the Tricorn in the carriage?" Alex suggested, pointing to the nondescript hack still waiting outside the dockside tavern. "That way, Prince Denisov can ride with you." His eyes sparkled with devilry; he'd correctly guessed Seb's unwillingness to share Anya, even with her own brother.

Seb scowled down at him. "It'll take too long. She needs to be in bed. The prince can take your horse."

Alex lifted his brows. "And what about me?"

"You take the carriage." Seb tipped his chin toward Anya's friend. "Miss Ivanova needs to be escorted back to Grosvenor Square. We left her fiancé at the ball."

Alex sighed in reluctant assent, and Benedict nodded. "I'll ride behind you, Alex."

Alex surrendered his horse, a handsome bay named Cadiz, to the prince, who mounted with all the ease of a man accustomed to the saddle. Seb's stomach clenched as he recalled Anya, in her stable boy's clothes, mounting in just such an effortless way. He waited with barely concealed impatience as Denisov tied a handkerchief around his forearm to staunch the flow of blood from his bullet wound.

"Come on," Seb said. "Let's go."

The ride back to the Tricorn seemed endless. Seb spurred Eclipse as fast as he dared through the darkened streets, willing Anya to wake, but she remained distressingly still in his arms. He swallowed a rare feeling of helplessness.

He found himself remembering the first time she'd shared a horse with him, back on Hounslow Heath. He'd tensed in exquisite agony when her small hands had grasped his waist, dangerously close to the betraying bulge in his breeches. She'd been so prickly then, so full of life.

He glanced down at her now. The contrast was worrying. He pressed his lips to her hair, inhaling the familiar scent of her perfume. It made his stomach twist. He let out a shaky breath and grasped the reins tightly, holding her steady in the crook of his arm. If only she were some fairy princess, like in her book of Russian tales, to be woken from her slumber with a kiss.

As soon as they reached the Tricorn, he shouted for Mickey.

"She drank Lagrasse's sleeping draught," he explained, striding down the hall. "Go and see if he has something to help. Quickly. I don't know how much she's taken."

Mickey gave an unhappy grunt and lumbered off.

Seb mounted the stairs and kicked open the door his own rooms with his foot. Denisov was close behind him, but Seb didn't give a damn about the propriety of it. He wanted her in his bed. He laid Anya down and started to unlace the ribbons that secured her dress, and sent Denisov a challenging glare. "Her corset will restrict her breathing. It needs to be loosened."

Denisov nodded in agreement, and Seb uttered a prayer of thanks that the man was going to be sensible.

The last thing he needed was some sputtering older brother getting all starchy about her reputation when she was in grave danger of succumbing to poison.

He wanted nothing more than to rip the damn dress off, get into bed next to her, and hold her in his arms until she woke, but he forced himself to remove the garment gently without damaging it. He removed her corset, leaving her covered by a modest cotton chemise, then tugged the sheets up to her chin and pulled a chair close to the bedside. He placed two fingers on the side of her neck and felt for her pulse. It was racing. Denisov perched on the other side of the bed and the two of them stared down at her face.

"What should we do? Try to wake her? Make her sick?" Denisov asked anxiously. Lines of strain bracketed his mouth, and Seb felt a sudden stab of kinship with the man. The thought of losing Anya was equally unbearable for both of them.

"I don't know. I've never seen the effects of it on a woman," he said. "And she may have taken too large a dose." He frowned. "Her heart rate's very rapid."

He stroked her hair back from her forehead. She felt hot to the touch. Her cheeks were pink and her breathing unnaturally fast.

Seb ground his teeth. He hated not knowing what to do. He'd seen hundreds of battlefield injuries; give him a dislocated shoulder, a gunshot wound, or a broken limb, and he'd know precisely the treatment to give. But he was infuriatingly inexperienced when it came to potential poisoning.

What the hell had she been thinking? When she woke up, he was going to strangle her for taking such a foolish risk. *If* she woke up—

His brooding thoughts were interrupted by Mickey, carrying a tray, and a bustling Lagrasse, who had fastened a voluminous red banyan robe over his portly form. A jaunty nightcap was perched on his head, and Seb realized with a start that he'd never actually seen the chef without a hat of some sort.

"She drink my sleeping potion, eh?" Lagrasse said briskly. He inspected Anya, much as Seb had done, measuring her pulse and taking a peek at her eyes beneath her lids.

"What can we do?" Seb demanded.

"I have a remedy," Lagrasse said. "She must drink zis." He gestured to a tiny bottle on Mickey's tray. "It is made from the calabar bean." He poured two drops of the yellow-brown liquid into a glass of water on the tray and swirled it around to mix. "Try to make 'er drink."

Seb slid his arm beneath Anya's shoulders and eased her slightly off the pillows. Her head lolled, and he had to support it with his shoulder and jaw. Lagrasse handed him the glass. Her eyelids fluttered open when Seb held it to her lips, but there was no recognition in her faraway gaze when she looked at him.

"Drink," Seb murmured. "Anya, you have to drink."

He tilted the glass, but she turned her head and weakly tried to push him away.

"Please." His voice was coaxing, rough with emotion. It betrayed the true depths of his feelings to every man in the room, but he was past caring. What did his pride matter if she died? He tried again. "Anya, it's Wolff. *Seb.* Drink for me."

He wasn't sure she could even hear him, but he managed to get her to swallow a small amount of the liquid, and laid her back down with a sigh of relief. He glanced up at Lagrasse. "Now what?"

Lagrasse gave a Gallic grunt and indicated the other two glasses on the tray, both of which were filled with amber liquid.

"Ze brandy is for you," he added grimly. "Zis will be a long night, monsieurs."

He crossed to the washstand, claimed the porcelain basin, and handed it to Seb. "There is a chance she may be sick, you understand." He glanced down at Anya's face and concern pinched his features. "But maybe not. 'Ave faith. Ze lady is a fighter, but we must let her rest. All we can do now is wait."

Chapter 38.

Anya drifted in a strange fog of sensation. Her thoughts were racing, scenes jumbled and fell over one another like some nauseating kaleidoscope. She kept seeing Vasili's fist lashing out toward her, the astonished look on his face, the ring of blood on his jacket.

Her body felt weightless, as insubstantial as dandelion fluff, as if the slightest breeze might blow her away. Only the memory of Sebastien's arms anchored her to the earth. She burrowed deeper into the delightful sensation, recalling the pleasure of being held, the warmth of his breath against the top of her head, the reassuring feel of his heartbeat beneath her shoulder.

An involuntary shudder ran through her. God, how easily that strong heart could have stopped if Vasili's aim had been true. The terror she'd felt when first Seb, and then Dmitri, had been in his sights rushed over her anew. The two men she loved most in the world. She couldn't imagine life without either of them.

Soft sounds began to intrude upon her consciousness.

The click of a door. The crackle of a fire. The tick of a clock. She let them flow over her like water.

Her thoughts eventually became more definite. Petrov really was dead. Which meant the threat that had haunted her for so long had finally been eliminated. Anya knew she ought to feel some emotion other than relief at Vasili's demise, but she couldn't seem to dredge up much sympathy. Better men than him had died because of his treasonous deeds. Justice had been served, even if it had taken a slightly circuitous route.

A noise somewhere beyond her snagged her attention. The deep, comforting rumble of male voices trying to speak quietly. Anya listened, not quite ready to open her eyes.

"Why isn't she waking up?"

That was Dmitri's voice, so dear and unexpectedly sweet that her heart contracted with fierce joy.

"She will."

That was Sebastien, his tone slightly less confident than usual. Anya suppressed a smile. He sounded worried about her. How wonderful.

"She might not wake for another few hours," Seb said. "You might as well give me an account of your adventures, Denisov, to pass the time. What happened to you? The princess thought you were dead."

Anya realized that she was in a bed. But where? Was she back at the dowager duchess's house? Her own tiny Covent Garden apartment? She opened her eyes just a crack and recognized the deep burgundy hangings of Sebastien's bedchamber. So, she was back at the Tricorn. A wash of inexplicable pleasure warmed her.

"Not dead," Dmitri said from her left side. "Merely insensible. The last thing I remember from the battle itself was a giant of a Frenchman coming at me with a saber—and then nothing, until I woke up to find some-one tugging on my legs. The battle was long over. It was the following day, and some cheeky sod was trying to steal the boots right off my feet! I sat up and must have given him a dreadful shock because he took one look at me, all covered in gore, and screamed as if he'd seen the devil himself. I shouted right back at him. He dropped my feet and took off running."

Dmitri let out a wry chuckle at the macabre image, and the sound was echoed by a deep rumble from her right. Sebastien was sitting next to the bed; the familiar scent of him teased her nostrils.

"I must have lost consciousness again," Dmitri continued, "because when I next awoke, I was in a cart, being dragged to a hospital in Antwerp. My skull had been cracked like the shell of an egg. My recovery took months, and I quickly discovered that there were huge gaps in my memory. I could recall some things with amazing clarity—like the time Anya got stuck in the tree in the orchard when she was eight and threw plums at me when I tried to help her down."

Anya smiled inwardly at the memory, but didn't open her eyes. She heard Seb exhale lightly.

"That sounds like the kind of thing she would do."

Her heart gave a little somersault. Was she just imagining the dry fondness in his tone?

Dmitri snorted. "Unfortunately, I'd forgotten the few months prior to the battle. I didn't recall being in Vienna, or General di Borgo, or the fact that Anya was waiting for me in Paris. I thought she was safely back in St. Petersburg. As soon as I was well enough to travel, I set off home. I was almost in Moscow when I finally remembered everything.

"I'd been looking into rumors that someone was passing

information to the French, and I'd intercepted a letter that proved it was Petrov. I was going to give it to the Tsar at the Duchess of Richmond's ball, but the orders came to march to Waterloo—at three in the morning. I stashed the letter at the inn, intending to return for it later."

Anya felt a rush of air beside her as Seb stood. His footfalls retreated across the room, she heard the tinkle of glass and the splash of liquid, and deduced he was pouring a drink. Her suspicions were confirmed when she caught a pleasant whiff of brandy and heard Dmitri's low murmur of thanks.

"The duchess's ball was held in a barn where the carriages were usually stored, since it was the only place large enough to accommodate so many guests. I hid the letter high up on one of the rafters, behind a bird's nest. It was still there when I returned, months later. I went to Paris to find Anya, but everyone I spoke to said she'd disappeared."

Anya almost made a murmur of distress.

"I knew she was far too stubborn to drown herself, as everyone seemed to think."

Dmitri's voice held a note of pride that warmed her heart.

"And when I heard Petrov had been found unconscious in her apartment, I knew there was more to the tale. I followed him here to London, hoping I'd find her. I've been spying on him for weeks, trying to get on board that ship of his in case she was being held prisoner, but when I finally managed it, all I found was that doddering old priest."

Anya opened her eyes. She tried to speak, but it came out as more of a croak, and she realized her throat was parched. The two men hovering at her bedside came into focus and Dmitri's face broke into a wide smile of relief.

"Anya, you're awake! Thank God!" He smoothed

his hand over her forehead. "You feel much cooler now. Have a drink."

Anya returned his smile then risked a glance over at Sebastien, but his expression was harder to read. He looked grim. Dark stubble shadowed the angles of his jaw, and his eyes searched hers as if seeking confirmation of some question he hadn't asked.

Anya pushed herself up on the pillows and accepted the glass of water he offered with a nod of thanks. She turned to Dmitri.

"Vasili thought you'd sent me that evidence. He wanted to ensure my silence by marrying me. I fled to London, but he had his men try to kidnap me."

Dmitri let out an angry oath, but she put a soothing hand on his arm and shot a grateful glance over at Seb. "Lord Mowbray rescued me. And took it upon himself to protect me, despite his initial reservations."

Anya gazed at him across the distance of the bed, and her heart pounded as she struggled to find the right words to convey the immense gratitude she felt.

The love.

"In fact," she croaked, "he has saved my life on several occasions, and I owe him a debt I can never repay."

Wolff's face might have been made of granite, it was so stern. He shifted his weight as if uncomfortable with her praise, but his eyes never left hers.

"It was my duty," he said gruffly. "Any one of my colleagues at Bow Street would have done the same."

Anya's spirits sank at his brusque dismissal of his heroism. As if she were simply another onerous case with which he'd been burdened.

"Thank you, my lord," Dmitri said formally. "You cannot imagine the torment I have suffered, believing my beloved sister in the hands of that monster."

Sebastien lifted his brows. "You think I cannot?"

Dmitri frowned at that enigmatic statement, and Anya's heart clenched in sudden hope. What did he mean? That he was capable of imagining torment because of his wartime experiences? Or that he, too, had been plagued by fear because he cared for her?

The stubborn man refused to elaborate. He straightened and placed his empty brandy glass on the polished side table.

"You have a lot of catching up to do. I'll leave you."

He gave them a curt bow and disappeared through to the adjoining sitting room.

Anya let out a small sigh.

Dmitri's eyes twinkled with speculative interest. "Little sister," he said, switching to the Russian they were both more comfortable with. "You *have* been having adventures, haven't you?" He lifted his brows and tilted his chin at the outer room, and Anya felt her cheeks heat.

"I don't know what you mean." She reached for the glass of water on the side table.

"Do you love him?"

Anya almost choked on her water. "Dmitri! What kind of question is that?"

"An honest one." A serious look passed over his face. "My months in the hospital gave me ample time to think; it's amazing how being so close to death helps clarify the mind." His fingers closed over hers. "I came to realize that nothing really matters except people. Not things. Not possessions. *People.* Life is worth living because of relationships. With family. With friends. With lovers." His gaze caught hers. "What really matters is love."

Anya felt tears prick her eyes at his fervent honesty. He was right. How simple it was.

A sudden urgency seized her. "Yes. I love him," she said fiercely in Russian, knowing Sebastien wouldn't understand, even if he was listening outside the door. "I don't know when it happened, but it's true."

Dmitri's smile lit up his whole face. "I can't say I'm surprised. Not after seeing the way he's been with you. He's been like a man possessed."

Anya frowned and glanced at the window. "I can't have been asleep for that long. It's still dark."

Dmitri shook his head. "You've slept for a whole day and a night. And Lord Mowbray has never left your side. He's been here watching over you, forcing you to drink water and milk for hours."

Anya gaped at him.

"I think he loves you too," Dmitri said with a smile. "He's sent away every caller—and there have been many—Elizaveta, some dowager duchess, a woman named Charlotte—and tended you himself."

"I would marry him," Anya confessed. "But I don't think he wants to marry me. He asked me once, but it was only to protect my reputation. I told him it wasn't necessary."

She frowned down at the sheets at her waist, pleating them absently with her fingers. "I think he thinks I should marry someone better than him. Someone with a loftier title or a fatter purse. But Dmitri, there *is* no one better than him. Not for me. He's everything I ever wanted in a husband. He's loyal and fierce, protective and kind. He makes me laugh," she added with a sigh. "Even when he doesn't mean to."

Dmitri gave her hand another squeeze. "That sounds like an excellent start. You have my full support. If there's anything I can do to help, I shall do it."

Anya's heart expanded with love. She was so grateful that he was back in her life.

He stood. "Now, if you don't mind, I think I shall go

and eat some of Monsieur Lagrasse's excellent blini and get some sleep. I'll leave you in Lord Mowbray's excellent hands."

He waggled his eyebrows, and Anya laughed at the roguish twinkle in his eye. Honestly, he was as bad as the dowager duchess when it came to unsubtle matchmaking. "Good night."

Chapter 39.

Seb stood staring out of the window, one forearm braced against the wooden frame as he tried to make sense of the host of emotions swirling in his chest.

Relief was easy to identify, the relief of having Anya finally wake up and smile at him again. Frustration was there too, and restlessness, and a low-level anger that should have been extinguished along with Petrov's life, but still seemed to persist with no particular target.

He let out a huff of air. God, Anya had probably shaved ten years off his life. His hair would doubtless turn prematurely grey from the combination of worry and shock of almost losing her. Despite all his experience of battle, he couldn't think of a time when he'd ever felt so desperate or so frightened as when he'd discovered her being held hostage, with Petrov's gun to her head. Or when he'd thought she might not recover from the sleeping draught.

He scowled at the view in front of him, not really seeing it. It was because he'd never felt for anyone else what he felt for her. True, he'd worried for his friends during the war, but Alex and Ben had been highly skilled and as capable as himself of getting out of trouble. Anya had been defenseless.

Seb let out another huff. Well, *almost* defenseless. She'd stabbed Petrov in the arm with a map pin. And drugged him too. Brave girl.

The mews yard beyond his window was dark, the cobbles and rooftops of St. James's silvered with moonlight. The stars looked as if some slapdash baker had flung a handful of flour across the night sky. Seb glared upward. Those stars were an illusion. From this distance, they looked cold and insubstantial, but up close, each was its own fiery sun.

Anya was like that—cool and unattainable from afar, blindingly attractive when you got close.

Not that he'd have the chance to get close to her ever again. Now that her brother was back in her life, she'd doubtless be going back to Russia to reclaim all her bloody palaces and vodka distilleries and the like.

He could hear the two of them in the bedroom, chattering away in Russian, presumably catching up and making plans that most surely didn't include him. Why would she even consider marrying an English gaming club owner when the world was once again at her feet?

Infuriated with himself, and life in general, Seb tugged open the cuffs of his shirt. He'd already discarded his ruined coat and boots during the agonizing hours he'd spent at Anya's side, willing her to wake up. Both jacket and boots were beyond repair. Much like his heart.

He ran his hand over his jaw and winced at the prickles. He hadn't shaved for two days. God, he must look a wreck.

Denisov stepped out of the bedroom and closed the door quietly behind him.

"Now that Anya appears to be out of any danger, I'm going to retire. Will you ensure that someone's on hand all night, in case she has need of anything?"

"Of course." Seb nodded and saw him out, then glanced at the bedroom door, listening for any sounds from within. Was Anya asleep again? Should he go in and check on her?

Resisting the temptation to see her again, he returned to his place at the window.

Bringing her to his rooms had been a mistake. Seeing her lying in his bed was both a pleasure and a torture. He wanted her to wake there every day, for his to be the first face she saw each morning.

Impossible.

The click of the bedroom door made him turn. Anya hovered in the doorway dressed in one of his dark red Banyan robes. She must have filched it from his dressing chest. Little thief. He tightened his grip on the window frame.

Did she have anything on *under* the robe? The two sides were crossed high at the neck, and it was so long it puddled on the floor around her feet.

He managed an unwelcoming scowl. "What are you doing out of bed? You need to rest."

She didn't look deterred by his gruff voice and fearsome glower, nor did she appear any the worse for her near-death experience. She sent him an easy smile that nevertheless heated his blood.

"I'm not sleepy. I've done nothing but sleep for the past twenty-four hours."

Seb prayed for strength. Her hair was loose around her face, a honey-colored river he wanted to fist. Did the bloody woman have no idea how attractive she looked, all rumpled and pink-cheeked? He stifled a groan.

She wandered into the room and leaned casually against the front edge of his desk.

"You promised Dmitri someone would be on hand all night. In case I had need of something."

Seb frowned, instantly solicitous. "Do you? Have need of something?"

She bit one corner of her lip. "Oh, yes."

Her tone was a mixture of innocence and wickedness. His pulse pounded against his ribs. "What do you need?"

She clasped her hands together in front of her and met his gaze. "I need to say thank you. For coming after me. For shooting Petrov. For everything."

He shrugged, a quick lift and drop of his shoulders. "You're welcome."

"I was worried about you. I thought Vasili was going to shoot you."

"I thought the same about you," he said. He crossed the room without thought and scowled as he located the bruise where Petrov had hit her with the pistol. "Christ, Anya, your cheek." She flinched as he reached out and touched the spot lightly with his knuckles. "You have a bruise." Fury filled him. "Bastard. I'm glad I shot him."

"So am I. You saved me."

He was so close, he could see the individual lashes framing her eyes, smell the warm perfume of her skin. His entire body urged him to close the distance and put his mouth on hers. But if he touched her, he'd never be able to stop.

"I need something else," she whispered.

"What?"

"I need you."

Seb stilled. She blinked up at him, and he struggled not to drown in the blue of her eyes.

"We can't do this," he groaned, half protest, half plea.

She went up on tiptoe, caught the front of his shirt, and tugged him close. "Yes, Sebastien, we really can."

Anya was tired of playing games. She pressed her lips to Seb's, urging him to respond, and for one dreadful moment, he froze.

Then he broke. With a wordless sound of need, he pulled her to him, tilted her head to the perfect angle, and kissed her back.

Anya almost swooned. This was no practiced, tentative exploration. It was exactly what she wanted: darkness and heat and total abandon. His lips shaping hers, his tongue swirling inside her mouth to tangle with her own. She closed her eyes in delight, pushing closer, melting into his wonderful warmth. They fit together so perfectly, concave to convex. His heart was pumping fast under her palm, and she wished his clothes gone—wanted to feel him, all of him. Body to body, skin against skin.

Her knees were so wobbly, she was fairly certain it was only the desk holding her up. She was playing with fire, but she needed this tonight. Her near-catastrophe had brought everything into sharp focus. She wanted him. Not just as a lover, but as a life partner, a husband. She had to tell him she'd been wrong to refuse his proposal. Had to show him how perfect they were for each other.

With a sound like anguish, he pulled back, panting. He swept his hands through his already disordered hair. "Anya, this is madness."

Tension throbbed between them. Anya stared at his jaw, his face, absorbing the full force of his masculine beauty. With a deep breath for courage, never taking her eyes from his, she peeled apart the front of the dressing robe, dislodging the sash from around her waist. She let it slither from her shoulders. The material dropped to the desk behind her with a faint hiss.

She was naked underneath. The single lamp that burned on the sideboard sent a warm glow over her body. Her stomach clenched as his dark gaze roved over her skin, drinking in the sight she was so shamelessly offering. She lifted her chin and pushed her hair back over her shoulders.

This was the final hand; she was betting everything on the chance of success. She might not have marked cards or weighted dice, but she would use whatever tricks she had in her arsenal to win this game. If that meant making herself vulnerable, stripping herself bare—both physically and emotionally—then that was what she would do.

"I want *you*, Sebastien. Here. Now."

Always.

He shook his head. Her spirits plummeted at what she thought was rejection, but then he lifted his hands and cradled her cheeks.

"I can't deny you anything," he said with a groan.

He rested his forehead against hers and then bent and pressed a featherlight kiss to the bruise on her cheekbone. His tongue followed, skimming across the abrasion as if he could banish the hurt with his touch. A shiver ran through her, from her breasts to her belly.

Anya turned her head, trying to capture his mouth, but he avoided her seeking lips. Instead, he placed his hands on her shoulders and slid them down her bare arms until he could interlace their fingers. His chest skimmed hers, and she let out a ragged gasp of pleasure as his shirt brushed her naked skin.

With gentle pressure, he guided their joined hands behind her back, momentarily holding her captive against the hard edge of the desk, and Anya felt a breathless thrill of desire at the subtle hint of dominance. If any other man had held her imprisoned like this, she would have been fighting tooth and nail to get free, but she trusted him completely. He would release her the moment she asked him to.

She wouldn't ask.

She strained closer. She could feel the hard length of his arousal through his breeches. It pressed insistently against her belly and she writhed against him, urging him to abandon whatever shred of control he still possessed.

"Anya."

He said her name on a low growl of hunger, and his chest expanded as he took in a lungful of air. In a flurry of movement, he released her hands, lifted her up onto the desk, and stepped between her thighs. His hands pushed deep into her unbound hair. He tightened his fingers, gripping a fistful of the strands with a quick twist that sent pleasure and pain spiraling through her limbs. Her heart somersaulted as he fastened his lips to hers.

This kiss was wild, an admission of defeat and a glorious declaration of victory. Anya answered it fiercely, kissing him back with all the love in her heart.

He slid his hand down her throat and captured her breast, and she arched her back, offering more. He bent and caught her nipple in his mouth. His lips fastened over the taut peak, and she writhed in delight as he feasted, lavishing the sensitive flesh with tiny licks and tugs.

Anya wrapped her legs around his breeches-clad hips, and he made a rumbling sound of approval in his chest. His hand shaped the indent of her waist, the curve of her hip, then smoothed over the sensitive skin of her thigh. He recaptured her mouth an instant before his hand dipped between her legs; he drank in her gasp of pleasure, swirling his tongue at the same time as his fingers slipped between her folds.

Anya lifted her hips, urging him on. She was slick,

ready for him, and his finger entered her in a slow, delicious invasion. Hot delight shimmered over her skin. A second finger joined the first, stretching her in the most pleasurable way, but after only a few blissful movements, he withdrew. She opened her mouth to protest until she felt him fumbling between them to undo the buttons of his falls.

He freed himself, tugged her to the very edge of the desk, and positioned himself at the entrance to her body. Panting, his dark hair in glorious disarray, he braced one palm on the leather desktop beside her hip and caught the nape of her neck with the other.

"This? You want this?" His cock slid against her, a teasing threat, and Anya tilted her hips in joyous invitation. Their eyes met and held.

"Yes," she panted. "Yes."

He entered her in a slow, steady glide, his eyes never leaving hers. They both groaned in unison. Anya felt as if she were sharing her very soul; the connection between them felt sacred, almost magical.

"More," she demanded.

He bared his teeth in a smile that was as feral as it was wicked. He withdrew almost to the point of leaving her. "More? I'll give you more, *princess*."

Anya almost laughed. Yes! *That* was how she wanted him to say it. As a teasing endearment instead of a title. The muscles of her stomach contracted as he pressed forward again, and he let out a heartfelt groan.

"God, you have *no idea*."

"Everything," she breathed. "Give it to me."

She curled up toward him, seeking the sensations he'd shown her before, and the change in angle rubbed a spot inside her that sent the promise of pleasure shimmering through her veins. She clutched at his shoulders as he repeated the move, and every wicked, dragging slide sent her closer to the peak. Her thoughts splintered. Her inner muscles contracted, gripping him tightly, and with a sharp cry, she plunged over the edge of a glorious, mind-numbing climax.

She'd barely returned to earth when he pulled her off the desk, turned her around, and bent her over the hard wood. The banyan robe had long since fallen to the floor and the cool slide of the leather desktop was a shock against her sensitive breasts and hot cheek. Seb stroked the length of her spine, squeezed her bottom, and slid back inside of her with a groan of pleasure.

The momentum of his body rocked her forward, and Anya bit her lip at this delightful new sensation. She'd thought she couldn't experience any more pleasure, but feeling Seb within her, hearing his impassioned pants as he strove for completion, made her heart sing with a fierce, glad possessiveness. She wanted to satisfy his every craving, to give him the same explosion of spiraling darkness he'd given her. She wanted to give him everything. Her heart, her soul, her love.

Instinctively, she pushed back against him, urging him deeper still, and smiled as he growled in approval. He bent over her, enveloping her, his chest against her back, and buried his face in the crook of her neck. His left ear—his *deaf* ear—was right next to her lips, and some perverse impulse compelled her to whisper, "I love you."

He tensed, and for a moment she thought he'd heard her, but then his climax claimed him. His every muscle stiffened as he pulsed inside her like a heartbeat, on and on. His full weight eventually pressed down on her as he relaxed, utterly spent, and she savored the masculine weight of him despite the slight discomfort.

She bit her lip and quelled the urge to laugh. Never had she felt so thoroughly ravished. If she'd known *this* was the pleasure awaiting her when he'd propositioned her back at Haye's, she would have accepted his scandalous offer without a moment's hesitation. In fact, she'd probably have been the one to offer *him* five hundred pounds.

After a long moment, he straightened and stepped back. She felt a rush of cool air on her bare bottom and an unaccustomed wetness between her legs.

Anya's levity fled. He'd spent himself inside her. Considering the timing of her monthly courses, there was a slim chance she could fall pregnant. The thought of carrying his child didn't fill her with dismay. On the contrary, she'd like nothing better than to bear his child, but she was damned if she'd do it outside of wedlock. Unconventional she might be, but she refused to become notorious throughout Europe as the "unmarried, pregnant princess."

It was time to bring him up to scratch.

Chapter 40.

Seb stepped back from Anya's naked body, cursing himself in every language he knew. The explosion that had robbed him of his hearing had clearly addled his brain too.

No, that wasn't true. It was *Anya* who addled his brain. He had no control, no finesse when it came to her. The scent of her made him fevered. The touch of her skin sent him over the edge into full-blown insanity. He was putty in her hands.

Shame and regret poured through him like acid. God, she was a *princess*, practically a virgin, and he'd just tupped her over his desk as if she were a common dock-side whore. Christ, they hadn't even made it to his bed. He was still wearing his shirt and breeches. He was an animal, unfit to call himself a gentleman.

His gut clenched. For the first time in his life, he'd been so carried away by passion that he'd forgotten to use protection and spilled himself inside a woman.

Shit. Shit. Shit.

He closed the front of his breeches with shaking

hands as she straightened and retrieved the robe from where it had fallen to the floor. She shrugged it on, keeping her eyes downcast, and he regarded her warily, trying to gauge her reaction. Was she angry? Insulted? Ashamed? He gestured awkwardly toward his bedroom door. "There's water and linens through there. If you want to, ah, freshen up."

His voice was a husky croak, and he cleared his throat. God, he sounded like some callow youth who'd never spoken to a woman in his life.

She inclined her head. "Thank you."

She sailed past him, head held high. The overlong robe trailed after her like a royal train, and it occurred to him that he'd never seen her look more regal. Or more out of his reach. The door to his bedroom clicked closed, and he stood there in sudden bemusement. He'd imagined her in his bedchamber a thousand times, but never when *he* was banished to the sitting room.

He heard the faint splash of water as she poured the ewer into the basin, then various rustling sounds. His anxiety grew with every moment. God, he was such an idiot. He'd messed everything up right royally. The unintentional pun made him flinch.

He loved her. He needed her in his life. He wanted her with a desperation that would have been funny if it weren't so painful.

He raked one hand through his hair as despair and blind panic churned in his gut. He wanted to marry her, more than anything in the world, but if he proposed now, she'd think it was only because he was trying to be noble, trying to protect her reputation if she should fall pregnant.

He didn't want her to accept him because she feared the consequences of being an unwed mother. His own mother had married his father for precisely that reason—to legitimize him and avoid a scandal—and while he was very grateful for his position as a duke's son, theirs had not been a successful union. Ben and Alex had been right—marrying for anything other than love was a surefire recipe for disaster.

He wanted Anya to marry him because she loved him too. Was that too far beyond the realms of possibility? He paced over to the fireplace then back to the desk.

Sod it. He couldn't let her leave without at least trying to win her. He wasn't a coward. If she refused him, so be it, but he couldn't let her return to Russia without asking, couldn't go the rest of his life wondering *what if*.

Yes, he was a selfish idiot to even ask. She was far above his touch, not just socially but morally too. She was a thoroughly decent human being. She taught harlots to read, for God's sake, whereas he ran a gaming hell catering to despots and gamesters.

But he'd never met anyone with whom he was more compatible. She wasn't a woman who needed constant coddling. She was utterly competent in her own right, a quality he found desperately appealing. And she kept her head in a crisis—an excellent skill both in battle and for dealing with the *ton*. She would be an unshakeable ally and a stalwart friend.

The door to the bedroom opened, and his heart pounded against his ribs exactly as it had when the order to advance had come at Waterloo. He could almost hear the tinny thud of the drums.

She'd commandeered one of his shirts—he could see the white linen peeking out from the edges of his robe—and brushed her hair. Her cheeks were flushed a delicate shade of pink, except for the purple bruise on her cheekbone where Petrov had walloped her.

Seb crossed the room until he stood in front of her.

He dropped to one knee.

He took both her hands in his, and cleared his throat.

"Anya. Anastasia. Miss Denisova."

God, he wished he'd taken a tumblerful of brandy from the decanter from the sideboard. He forced his tongue to work.

"I love you. With everything I have and everything I am. I don't deserve even the smallest piece of you, but—" He took a steadying breath. "Will you do me the very great honor of—"

Her fingers tightened on his. "No," she said firmly.

He stiffened and lifted his head to look at her face. Her expression was almost pitying.

"I am a Russian princess," she said. "You're an English earl. This is not—"

He flinched as if absorbing a blow and felt his shoulders slump in defeat.

"I'm sorry," she said briskly. "It's protocol. I outrank you. There are *rules*."

He almost laughed. *Rules.* He was sick of bloody rules. But she was still speaking, and he forced himself to listen, even if he only had one working ear. Oddly, she sounded far more composed than him. Perhaps she was so used to receiving and dismissing propositions that this was nothing new.

"You can't propose to me," she was saying. "A person of lower rank is not permitted to propose to a royal princess."

"Yes. I understand. I should never have—"

She tugged at his hands to make him look up again. She was smiling, but there was a suspicious sheen in her eyes, as if she were on the verge of tears.

"No, you don't understand." There was a breathless laugh in her voice. "It is *I* who must do the asking."

His heart definitely stopped. "What?"

Her voice quavered in a most un-royal way as she lowered herself until she was kneeling too. "Lord Mowbray. Sebastien. I love *you*. Will you do me the very great honor of—"

Seb pulled her toward him with a sound that was half laugh, half growl. "Yes! God, yes. I will."

She threw her arms around his neck and plastered herself against his chest, almost knocking him to the floor. He tightened his arms around her, then cupped her face and fused their mouths together for a kiss that made his blood pound and his head spin.

After several heated moments, he pulled back and rested his forehead against hers. Her breath fanned against his lips as he let out a deep, relieved exhale mingled with a shaky incredulous laugh.

"Bloody hell, woman, you nearly stopped my heart with your refusal."

She gave a soft chuckle. "One must observe the formalities."

"Of course," he said, mock-stern. "Never let it be said that we failed to observe the formalities." He cocked a brow, his assurance returning in a rush. "So, does this mean I get to be a prince?"

"I'm afraid not."

"Will you have to give up the title of Princess if you marry me? You'll still be the Countess of Mowbray, of course, but compared to Princess of Russia, I know it's not—"

She pressed her fingers over his lips to silence him. "No. I'll still be a princess. But being your countess will mean a great deal more." She lowered her head until her lips hovered teasingly over his. "Being called your wife will be the very best title of all."

He kissed her again to reward this excellent sentiment,

and she groaned as his tongue slipped inside to tangle and taste. Then he pulled her upright, caught her behind the knees, and lifted her high against his chest.

"Come here, Princess mine. I'm sweeping you off your feet. Like they do in all the best fairy tales."

He shouldered his way through to the bedroom and deposited her gently on the bed. As he looked down at her, he was filled with a whole jumble of emotions, foremost of which was a sense of disbelief. It mingled with pride and a relief so sharp, he caught his breath. Not only had he survived the war, but now—by some miracle—this gorgeous, vexing woman was his, to love and to cherish forever.

"I want to wake up next to you," he said gruffly. "Not just tomorrow. But every morning. For the rest of my life."

The smile she sent him melted his heart. He could swear he felt it dissolving in his chest like in one of her snow-filled fairy tales. Ridiculous.

"That sounds perfectly acceptable." She held out her arms in invitation, and he crawled onto the bed next to her.

"Do you want to live here?" he asked. "Or would you prefer to go back to Russia? I don't care where we go, as long as I'm with you."

She stroked her fingers through his hair, playing with the strands, petting him as if he were a tame wolf, and Seb allowed himself an inward smile. He didn't mind that comparison in the slightest. Especially if he got to gobble her up on a regular basis. Or whisk her away into the deep, dark woods and ravish her.

"I wouldn't want you to leave your friends or Bow Street," she said. "And it would be a shame to abandon the Tricorn, since it's so popular. I'd like to visit Russia, of course, but we can live here in England."

"In that case, I'll buy us a proper town house. Maybe

somewhere near Alex and Ben, in Mayfair. And a country house too, if you'd like one. You can choose it. Or we can build our own, if you can't find one you like. Maybe not as big as a Russian palace, but still, I have plenty of money. You can have whatever you like."

Anya chuckled at his steady stream of plans. She slid her palm over his chest, and he felt his blood heat in response. "I wouldn't be averse to living here."

He lifted his brows. "Here? At the Tricorn? In a gaming club? Scandalous Princess."

"No more scandalous than marrying you," she teased. "Besides, I like it here. The rooms hold fond memories."

"Whatever you wish." Seb gathered her into his arms then let out a groan as a dreadful thought occurred to him. "Oh, God, I bet there are all *kinds* of ridiculous Russian superstitions surrounding weddings, aren't there?"

Anya's laugh was a puff of warmth against his chest. "One or two. But don't worry, I'll teach you the most important ones."

Chapter 41.

Sebastien Wolff, Earl of Mowbray, stood at the bottom of the steps leading up to his great-aunt's front door and tried to quell an overwhelming sense of excitement and trepidation. He couldn't remember ever being this nervous, not even on the eve of battle.

It was—*finally*—his wedding day. He'd waited, if not with perfect grace, then at least with reluctant impatience, for the three weeks necessary for the banns to be called.

He'd barely seen his intended over the past few weeks, stolen moments and sly kisses snatched at the various social events he'd had to endure just to catch a glimpse of her. Propriety had been observed, much to his disgust and increasing frustration.

The morning after he'd proposed—no, after *she'd* proposed—he'd kissed her a sleepy goodbye and sent her back to her own chambers. Then he'd asked her brother for her hand.

He would have married her with or without her brother's

permission, of course, but Dmitri had laughingly pro-
fessed his delight that someone was finally taking his
wayward sister in hand, and had offered his most sincere
congratulations.

The ceremony would be performed in the dowager
duchess's drawing room at precisely eleven o'clock. Seb
couldn't wait. But first, he had to comply with Russian
tradition and complete a series of ridiculous challenges
set by his friends and relations.

"Would you please explain to me what's going on?"

Dmitri, his soon-to-be brother-in-law, patted him on
the shoulder. "You, the groom, have to prove yourself
worthy of Anya's hand. You must perform certain tasks
or answer certain questions. Each correct answer will
take you a step closer to your bride."

Seb sighed. Loudly. "I've already rescued her from
kidnappers. Twice, if you count that man in my stables.
And I saved her from Petrov."

"That doesn't count. That was before you got engaged."

Seb rolled his eyes. "This is positively medieval. You
know that?"

Dmitri shrugged. "You must make a concerted effort
to rescue her. You can't simply waltz into her house and
take her out."

"Of course not," Seb groused. "That would be *far* too
sensible."

At Dmitri's insistence, he mounted the steps and
knocked on the front door. A stony-faced Mellors
opened it.

"Good morning, my lord." The corner of his mouth
curved upward in a most uncharacteristic smirk. "I hope
you're ready."

He stepped back to reveal Dorothea stationed in
the hallway seated on a straight-backed chair in front

of the staircase, her skirts spread around her like some mythical Greek gatekeeper. His brother, Geoffrey, stood guard next to her, a broad smile on his face.

"Sebastien!" she beamed. "About time! We're all ready for you."

Seb glanced up the stairs. Elizaveta was waiting for him halfway up the first flight, and he spotted a grinning Benedict and Georgie on the first landing. Alex was leaning over the second-floor balcony railings.

"You must ascend the stairwell," Dmitri said. "And pass all the tests. Anya's on the very top floor."

"Of course she bloody is," Seb muttered.

"I'm the first obstacle," Dorothea crowed. "As head of the family, I demand that you offer something of value, to show you prize her."

Seb pulled a flat leather box from inside his jacket. "Well, that's easy. Look. I bought her a wedding gift."

He opened the catch and Dorothea sucked in a breath at the sight of the necklace, bracelet, and earrings he'd bought.

"Sapphire and diamond, to match her tiara!" she said in a congratulatory tone. "Clever boy." She glanced at the gilt name stamped on the interior silk. "Bridge and Rundell, eh? I hear their waiting list is months' long for new commissions."

Seb felt a flush rise on his cheeks. The answer revealed that his love for Anya had existed even before he'd admitted it to himself. But what was the point in denying it? He'd probably been in love with her from the moment he'd rescued her in the rain. Maybe even before that.

"I ordered them at the same time I ordered the tiara."

Dorothea sent him a pleased, knowing smile. "A lovely choice. You may pass."

Seb kissed her hand, returned the box to his jacket

pocket, and ascended the first few steps to Elizaveta. The pretty Russian smiled and bobbed a curtsey.

"My lord."

"Mrs. Reynolds," Seb said with a smile. Anya's friend had recently married the sandy-haired barrister, Oliver Reynolds, the one Seb had threatened on the night of the ball. Both he and Anya had attended the small service in St. Martin-in-the-Fields only a fortnight ago.

Seb had managed to sit next to Anya in the church, despite the strict seating protocol. He'd enjoyed the feel of her shoulder pressing into his as they sat squashed in the uncomfortable wooden pews, and his heart had pounded with anticipation of repeating those same solemn marriage vows to her. The fact that he was so desperate for even the slightest touch from her was something he accepted with dry resignation. He doubted he'd ever get enough of her.

"As Anya's oldest friend, I have a series of questions to see how well you know your intended." Elizaveta said. "Firstly, what's her favorite color?"

Seb frowned, trying to recall the dresses Anya had worn since she'd been staying with his aunt. She'd ordered a whole new wardrobe, as befitting her newly elevated status, but there was no one color she favored. In truth, he'd rarely noticed her dresses, except to note the number of buttons and hooks to estimate how long it would take him to remove them once they were alone.

Then he remembered her favorite cape, the one she'd brought from Paris, and the sapphires and diamonds in his pocket.

"Blue and silver-white," he said confidently. "Ice colors."

Elizaveta beamed. "Yes! Next question, where did you meet your fiancée?"

Seb was beginning to enjoy himself. "Well, if you must know, in a brothel."

Her eyebrows shot up, and Seb distinctly heard Dorothea gasp and Benedict snort. He chuckled. "It's a long story. I'll tell you all some other time."

"You will indeed," Dmitri growled from his shoulder. "Next question."

"All right. What's her favorite book?"

Seb's mind went blank. He and Anya had discussed many things, but her preference for literature hadn't been one of them. He cast around and recalled the illustrated volume in his study. "I know she's very fond of Russian fairy tales," he hedged. "Especially ones that involve wolves and princesses."

He couldn't wait to recreate some of *those* in the privacy of their bridal bedchamber tonight.

Elizaveta narrowed her eyes, but seemed satisfied. "Close enough. Last question. When did you kiss for the first time?"

"Also the brothel. Haye's in Covent Garden." Seb ignored Dorothea's grumble of disapproval and tilted his head up toward Benedict. "I think it's only fair to point out that you, Benedict Wylde, once assured me that I'd never find a good woman to marry in a Covent Garden brothel. Take it back."

"I stand corrected," Ben shouted down. "I'm delighted to have been proved wrong."

Seb nodded. "Any more questions?"

Elizaveta shook her head and stepped aside. "You may proceed."

Seb arrived at the first landing to discover Georgie standing next to her husband.

"Did you know," she said by way of opening, "that it's about seventeen hundred miles from London to St. Petersburg?"

Seb blinked. "Is that my question?"

"No, it's not your question, I just wondered if you knew. Benedict says you're planning to take Anya there on your wedding trip. So if you sail at an average of five knots, it will take you around two weeks to get there by sea."

Seb sent Benedict a confused glance, but his friend simply shrugged. He was, apparently, used to receiving this kind of unwanted nautical information from his better half.

"That's, um, good to know," Seb said. "I'll bear it in mind. But if that's not my question, what is?"

Georgie sent him a no-nonsense look. "My test is a mental one. A riddle. We need to make sure you're clever enough to keep up with your wife. She's very intelligent."

"I know that."

"Apart from the inexplicable lack of common sense she's exhibited in choosing *you* as a life partner," Alex heckled from the landing above.

Seb sent him a poisonous glance. "Go on, then," he prompted Georgie. "Let's hear it."

"What flies when it's born, lies when it's alive, and runs when it's dead?"

Seb frowned. What flew? Birds? Musket balls? What lied? Men did, all the time. At least in his experience. And what ran when it was dead? Impossible. He scowled at a grinning Benedict.

"I'll give you a hint," Georgie whispered. "It's cold. And there's plenty of it in Russia."

Seb's brow cleared as the answer came to him. "Snow!"

"Yes! Well done."

Benedict stepped forward. "Right. My turn. My test is one of strength. To make sure you're strong enough to protect your future wife." He braced his legs apart and crossed his arms over his chest. "You have to lift me out of the way."

Seb groaned. Benedict weighed at least the same as himself. He was all muscle. Still, it could have been worse; they could have made him wrestle Mickey.

He stepped forward, bent his knees, and wrapped his arms around Benedict's waist. The fabric of his jacket stretched alarmingly across his back, and he heard an ominous ripping sound as the seams strained beneath his arms.

Bloody hell. He wasn't *dressed* for picking up grown men. He was dressed to marry the woman he loved. But what was a new jacket compared to a lifetime spent with Anya? Nothing at all. He'd burn every item in his wardrobe if necessary.

Still, it was a damn fine coat.

"Wait."

He let go of Benedict, stripped off his jacket, and folded it over the banister. Then he turned back, caught Benedict's wrist in one hand, ducked, and shouldered him in the stomach so he folded forward over his shoulder. He braced his thighs and picked him up with a low grunt of exertion.

"Damn it, Wylde," he wheezed. "You never weighed this much when I dragged your scrawny arse out of that ditch near Badajoz."

A flash of recollection hit him, and for a moment, Seb wasn't on the dowager's landing in Mayfair, but chocking on the hot, swirling dust of a Spanish plain. He'd carried his friend in exactly this way when Ben had been wounded during the storming of the citadel. Seb had pulled him out from under a shattered cart and carried him back to the safety of the British lines, with French musket fire shredding the air all around them.

Thank God they'd both survived.

"Don't break anything!" Dorothea's panicked voice echoed up the stairs, interrupting his reverie. "Mind the china!"

Seb staggered a few paces to the side, narrowly avoiding a side table perilously cluttered with Meissen figurines, and deposited Benedict back on his feet with a grateful gasp.

He hoped he hadn't strained anything. He intended to be in full working order for his wedding night. The thought brought an invigorating rush of blood to his head. And lower down.

He straightened and used the wall mirror to smooth his hair back into some semblance of order, then shrugged back into his jacket. "Right, what next?"

"Up here," Alex called, and Seb mounted the stairs to the second floor. Emmy, Alex's wife, was waiting for him with a mischievous smile on her elfin face.

"Stand and deliver," she said, with mock fierceness. "You must pay a ransom for your bride. A contribution to my favorite charity."

"The one she set up with her brother," Alex added helpfully. "The Danvers Benevolent Fund. It helps wounded veterans find meaningful employment instead of being reduced to begging in the streets."

"A worthy cause," Seb murmured. "So what do you want, my lady?"

Emmy's twinkling gaze dropped to the stick pin adorning his cravat. "Well, I do *love* diamonds." She smiled. "And that is a particularly fine solitaire, Lord Mowbray. I will accept it as payment for your passage."

With an inward groan, Seb lifted his hand to surrender the pin, but Emmy stopped him.

"Oh, you can give it to me after the ceremony. I wouldn't dream of ruining your cravat."

"Decent of you," Seb growled sarcastically.

"All right. Last challenge," Alex said. "Everything ready, Mellors?"

"Indeed it is, sir," Mellors replied calmly.

The butler ascended the staircase, as stately as ever, and offered forward a porcelain bowl. Seb peered inside. It held what appeared to be a fist-sized lump of ice. A dark shape, like a tiny fish, was suspended in the center.

"What's that?"

"The key to my sister's rooms." Dmitri chuckled, indicating the closed door behind them. "You have to open the door and claim your bride."

Seb scowled, wondering if it was supposed to be symbolic, a chipping away of the ice to reach the vital heart. He knew what it was like to shield himself by cloaking his heart in a protective layer. His mother had died of smallpox when he was a child, and he'd lost numerous friends and colleagues during the war. He'd found it easier to keep an emotional distance to lessen the potential hurt. He'd given a little less of himself away each time.

Until Anya.

"Maybe you can lick it?" Alex's cheerful suggestion cut through his introspection. "You've got to melt it somehow."

"Or bash it with a hammer," Benedict added.

"That's Anya's preferred method," Elizaveta said slyly.

Seb picked up the slippery, icy lump. Pain shot along his fingers and throbbed in his palm as his skin reacted to the cold. He held his hands out in front of him so the water didn't ruin his boots as it began to drip.

"Hurry up!" Alex chuckled. "You're making a puddle on the carpet!"

"Why not take off your shirt and put it under your armpit?" Ben suggested.

Seb scowled at him. "Do you know how long it took

me to perfect this cravat? Six tries. I'm not undoing it for anyone. Unless it's my wife," he added with a grin.

Mellors offered forward the bowl and held it while Seb cupped the ice and moved it around in his hands like a bar of soap. Then he breathed on it, using the warmth of his exhale to melt the ice chunk even faster. His fingers throbbed, but he persevered, and when it got small enough, he put the whole thing in his mouth. Cheeks bulging, he sucked it like a throat lozenge until he tasted a metallic tang.

He withdrew the key with a shout of triumph and elbowed Alex out of the way of the door.

"Anya?" he called through the wooden panel. "I'm coming in."

The key turned in the lock with a satisfying click and he pushed it inward. He stepped inside, caught a brief glimpse of Anya standing across the room, and turned to face the crowd in the hallway. They were all assembled: Dorothea and Geoffrey, Benedict and Georgie, Alex and Emmy, Dmitri, Elizaveta, and Mellors. His family, by blood or by friendship. He loved them all dearly.

Seb sent them a wide smile—and slammed the door.

Chapter 42.

Seb turned to face Anya and his breath caught in his throat. She was a vision in pale blue and white. Her hair was pinned in elaborate curls and her eyes sparkled almost as much as the diamonds in her tiara.

"You passed all the tests!" She laughed. "I knew you could do it!"

"You look stunning," he croaked.

She crossed the room and fell into his arms. "You don't look too bad yourself." She lifted her face for a kiss, and he took her lips greedily.

"God, I've missed you so much," he breathed. "I can't wait to marry you." He pulled back and reached into his jacket. "Here, I got you a gift."

"Another one?" She sent him an amused, quizzical smile. "You've given me hundreds of gifts already. Gloves, scent bottles, fans. You know I don't need things like this, Sebastien. I only want *you*."

"I know. But I like giving them to you, so you're just going to have to get used to it."

She sent him a chiding smile and opened the box, then muttered something in Russian. Seb didn't know exactly what she said, but it sounded gratifyingly breathless. He was going to have to learn her language at the earliest opportunity.

"I thought we could start a new tradition," he said. "Denisov brides might wear that tiara when they wed, but you'll be a Wolff by the end of the day. These are for you, to pass down to future generations."

He fastened the necklace around her throat and pressed a kiss to her exposed shoulder. He enjoyed the way she sucked in a little breath at the contact.

"Thank you."

"I think you'd better start teaching me Russian. What's the word for wife?"

"It's pronounced zhena. Or you could call me lyu-bee-ma-ya. It means 'beloved one.'"

He enjoyed the movement of her lips as she shaped the words.

"Or maybe daragaya," she said. "That means 'darling.'"

"Da-ra-ga-ya," he echoed obediently.

"Very good. Or you could simply say, 'moya.'"

"And what does that mean?"

"Mine."

"I like that." He dropped a soft kiss on her lips. "Very much." He glanced at the clock on the mantel. "Are you ready to go downstairs? It's almost eleven."

She nodded and squeezed his hand. "Yes."

Anya felt as light as a snowflake as she descended the stairs on Seb's arm.

The feeling of buoyant happiness had surrounded her ever since he'd accepted her proposal. It was so un-usual, so different from the state of anxiety she'd had for months, that she'd hardly dared to believe it at first. But the longer it remained, the more she believed it could become a permanent state.

Sebastien loved her. He'd shown her with his body when they'd made love, and with words and actions in the weeks since. Even though they hadn't managed to do more than steal a few heated kisses, he'd been a most attentive fiancé. He'd danced every permissible dance, flirted outrageously with her at every function they'd attended, and made love to her with honeyed words so effectively that she'd been on the verge of throwing herself into his arms and doing something decidedly scandalous on any number of occasions.

Now, at last, the torture was over, and she was thoroughly impatient to give herself to him. And to claim him in return.

They entered the drawing room and she smiled in delight to see so many of her loved ones there. The dowager had stoutly declared that all of Anya's friends, irrespective of their profession, were welcome in her house. Which was why Charlotte, looking utterly ravishing in seafoam silk, was seated next to Dmitri, and a shameless Jenny was flirting outrageously with Prince Trubetskoi.

"I can't believe you managed to persuade Father Barukov to perform the service," Anya whispered to Seb.

He chuckled. "I've paid for his passage home to Moscow. It's the least he could do. And besides, I thought it only sensible to have our wedding sanctioned by both the Church of England *and* the Russian Orthodox church. I want to know you're my wife on every single continent."

Anya accepted a bouquet of white roses from a beaming Jenny. The priest began the service, and her heart swelled with happiness as she and Seb exchanged rings and made their vows. She almost burst with pride when

Tess stepped forward and in a wavering but clear voice read aloud a passage from the Song of Songs.

She slid a glance over at Elizaveta, who sent her a supportive smile even as she swiped at her tears of happiness with Oliver's oversized handkerchief.

The dowager duchess, seated on Elizaveta's other side, sent Anya a conspiratorial smile. Her satisfied, cat-who-got-the-cream expression suggested she considered herself fully responsible for orchestrating this particular happy ending.

Dmitri, Anya noted with a secret smile, was barely paying any attention to the service; he seemed completely enraptured by Charlotte. He'd barely taken his eyes from her, and the two of them were deep in hushed conversation.

Anya mentally crossed her fingers for them. That would be a sweet match. Both of them deserved to find happiness after everything they'd experienced. Dmitri would care nothing for Charlotte's less than spotless past, being no angel himself. And Charlotte, for her part, would be the very best wife, loving, caring, and worldly wise. She would be just the person to help Dmitri heal.

The priest cleared his throat and Anya returned her attention to the final part of the ceremony. Father Barukov placed a twisted crown of laurel leaves on her head, then gestured for Sebastien to bend down so he could do the same to him.

Then Sebastien took her hand and extended it in front of them. His fingers clasped hers tightly as the priest wrapped the material of his stole around their joined hands, symbolically binding them together. With one last benediction, they were officially proclaimed husband and wife.

A rowdy cheer broke out from the assembled guests,

and Anya laughed up at Seb, glowing with happiness to see him looking so proud. His eyes caught hers and her stomach fluttered at the promise she read in them. She hoped he would bend down and kiss her, but everyone stood and crowded around to offer their congratulations. Mellors directed several footmen to distribute bubbling glasses of champagne.

Dmitri came forward, holding a fresh loaf of bread in his hands, and Seb glanced at him in confusion.

"Russian tradition." Dmitri grinned. "Before we begin the toasts."

Anya let out a chuckle of delight.

"This bread," Dmitri declared loudly, "provided by the excellent Chef Lagrasse, will settle the delicate matter of who will give the orders at home."

A chorus of amused cheers and dry comments erupted from the crowd. Dmitri held the round loaf out at head height between Anya and Seb, forcing them to step apart.

"Our newlyweds must bite off a section without using their hands. The one who takes the biggest bite will be the one who wears the breeches in the household."

Sebastien lifted his brows at Anya in distinct challenge. "I rather like you in breeches," he murmured.

Anya sent him a saucy smile. Keeping her hands by her side, she leaned in and bit into the loaf, taking the biggest mouthful she could manage. Seb did the same, and she could barely stop herself from laughing as their eyes met over the domed crust. He twisted his head to tear off a giant piece and she did the same, her cheeks bulging comically as she started to chew.

She couldn't possibly consume such a huge chunk. She caught it in her hands, recalling the way she'd swallowed her diamonds, back in Paris. How long ago that seemed. And what an unforeseen end to her journey.

Dmitri inspected the bread to give his verdict.

"It's a close-run thing," he said solemnly.

Anya leaned forward. "Nonsense. My bite is clearly bigger."

"It is *not*," Seb countered.

Dmitri slanted them a teasing smile. "Oh dear, the first argument." Everyone laughed. "But I'm afraid he's right, sister dear. His bite is definitely bigger." He shot Seb a laughing glance and thumped him on the shoulder. "I wish you luck, my friend."

All three of them took a glass of champagne from Mellors's proffered tray. "And now," Dmitri declared. "The toasts."

Seb caught her eye and they shared a secret smile that brought heat to her cheeks and a flush to her entire body. "Oh, I know how important toasts are to you Russians," he drawled.

"This should really be done with vodka," Dmitri said. "But we can start with champagne, I suppose. The first toast is made to the newlyweds." He raised his glass and everyone else followed suit.

"The newlyweds!"

Seb lifted his glass and Anya obediently took a sip of the tart liquid, enjoying the fizz on her tongue.

"Now, we all know that alcohol leaves a bitter taste in the mouth," Dmitri stated. "And a remedy to bitterness is sweetness. So for the next toast, the married couple must sweeten the drink with a kiss, because kisses are sweet, are they not?"

"Here, here!" Alex cheered.

Dmitri turned to the rest of the group. "And you must all shout *Gorko!* which means 'bitter' in Russian, to remind them of their duty."

Seb handed his glass to Benedict, and Anya handed hers to Elizaveta. He stepped closer, slipped his arms around her waist, and drew her forward. Anya held her breath as he bent and pressed his lips to hers in a kiss that stole her breath. It was a kiss full of promise and love, and it made her heart turn over in her chest. Cheers of "*Gorko! Gorko!*" echoed all around them, and they pulled apart with great reluctance.

"Is that sweet enough for you, Mrs. Wolff?" her husband murmured against her lips.

Anya smiled. "Perfect, Mr. Wolff. Just perfect."

Catch up on the Bow Street
Bachelors series by
Kate Bateman

This Earl of Mine
To Catch an Earl

Available now from
St. Martin's Paperbacks